"You are going to disrobe in front of me?" Shiloh squawked, her voice two octaves higher than normal.

Logan rose to his feet with the graceful ease of a mountain cat, then shrugged casually. "I planned to undress behind your back, but that's really up to you. If you want to watch—"

"I certainly do not want to watch!" she loudly objected.

Shiloh glared at her taunting captor when he jerked the soggy-fringed shirt over his head. The sight of his rippling muscles and washboard belly had her struggling to breathe normally.

Blast it, she couldn't figure out this man. One moment he seemed a dangerous threat, and the next instant he was playfully teasing her. His unpredictability made it impossible to guess what he planned to do next.

* * *

The Ranger
Harlequin® Historical #805—June 2006

CAROL FINCH
The RANGER

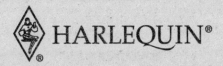

HARLEQUIN®

TORONTO • NEW YORK • LONDON
AMSTERDAM • PARIS • SYDNEY • HAMBURG
STOCKHOLM • ATHENS • TOKYO • MILAN • MADRID
PRAGUE • WARSAW • BUDAPEST • AUCKLAND

ISBN 0-373-29405-0

THE RANGER

This edition published by arrangement with Harlequin Books S.A.

® and TM are trademarks of the publisher. Trademarks indicated with
® are registered in the United States Patent and Trademark Office, the
Canadian Trade Marks Office and in other countries.

www.eHarlequin.com

Printed in U.S.A.

Please address questions and book requests to:
Harlequin Reader Service
U.S.: 3010 Walden Ave., P.O. Box 1325, Buffalo, NY 14269
Canadian: P.O. Box 609, Fort Erie, Ont. L2A 5X3

This book is dedicated to my husband Ed and our children, Christie, Jill, Kurt, Jeff, Jon, and Shawnna. And to our grandchildren, Brooklynn, Kennedy, Blake, and Livia, With much love.

Chapter One

⁓⤳⤳⤳⤳⤳⤳⤳⤳⁓

West Central Texas, 1870s

Logan Hawk glanced this way and that, calculating his chances of stealing the stolen money and making a fast getaway. Five bandits were sprawled beside him on their bedrolls, and if they woke up, they'd blast him out of the saddle. As dawn filtered across the rugged landscape, Hawk eased to his side then came silently to his feet.

Although he'd infiltrated this outlaw gang three months earlier to gather information for the Texas Rangers, he decided to get out while the getting was still good. He had posed as an Apache renegade, who scouted for the bandits, in exchange for a share of the loot. But he had yet to figure out who was mysteriously orchestrating the operations of this band of brigands— as well as the other three outlaw factions that were wreaking havoc in West Central Texas. Someone had taken meticulous care to make sure the bandit gangs were working in tandem like a well-oiled machine.

In addition, Hawk hadn't picked up any leads

about who had killed his mentor and friend eight months ago.

Casting another cautious glance at the sleeping men, Hawk noted the bank of roiling clouds that forewarned of a spring thunderstorm. If he didn't get moving, the crackle of lightning and the rumble of thunder would rouse these hombres.

Hawk hadn't unsaddled his black mustang pony before last night's raucous celebration so he could make a quick exit this morning. Neither had he bothered to undress. He hoped to be to hell and gone before the gang members roused from their drunken stupor and noticed he was missing.

Hawk skulked toward the stash of stolen money. Kneeling behind the scrub bush, he scooped up the saddlebags. He spared the scraggly-looking thieves one last glance as he circled the stand of cottonwood trees to retrieve his horse.

With the saddlebags tied in place, Hawk swung onto his mount. He breathed a long-suffering sigh of relief as he walked his horse through the grove of trees. Rubbing shoulders with these outlaws and pretending to be one of them left a sour taste in his mouth. He was more than ready to associate with someone who had more respect for humanity than these cutthroats. Like the other scoundrels he'd encountered during his seven-year stint with the Texas Rangers, these men had no consciences whatsoever. Their souls were as black as the devil's.

Of course, he hadn't needed to spend three months with this particular pack of ruffians to figure that out. One day had been plenty....

His thoughts scattered when thunder boomed overhead. A shout of alarm and a call to arms rose behind him. Hawk cursed sourly. Well, so much for his uneventful departure from the bandit camp with the confiscated loot in hand. He glanced back to see banditos staggering clumsily to their feet to mount up and give chase. Although he'd released the other horses, they hadn't wandered far so it didn't take long to regather them. Damn the luck! The desperadoes were hot on his trail in nothing flat. Hawk nudged his pony into a faster pace to take a shortcut that would provide him with a better head start.

And he was going to need one because the furious hombres were bellowing threats about which of his body parts they were going to chop off for stealing their stolen money.

Shiloh Drummond backstroked across the river, enjoying her early-morning swim. The nearby cove, flanked by a thirty-foot limestone cliff, provided protection, seclusion and a sense of peace. And what she really needed right now was a sense of peace so she could get a firm grip on her composure. The events of the past week had shattered her emotions and crushed her feminine pride in one fell swoop.

She needed this time alone before rejoining her older brothers at their family ranch. She needed time to gather her poise and bolster her bruised pride before she had to explain why she'd returned from New Orleans unexpectedly. She'd been humiliated beyond words, but she refused to let her brothers see her fall to pieces while confiding the events that had sent her running home prematurely.

She inhaled a fortifying breath and conjured up the image of the dashing Southern gentleman who had charmed her—and then had broken her heart. She muttered under her breath when tears filled her eyes, as they had so often this past week.

How was it possible to think you loved someone so completely…and suddenly despise him so thoroughly? Shiloh didn't know, but she had learned a hard lesson about the illusion of love. She wasn't going to risk her heart again—ever. The pain and humiliation weren't worth the trouble.

Shiloh Drummond had officially sworn off men forevermore. And her brothers had better not plan any future matchmaking, either, or she would make them dreadfully sorry for trying to arrange her life! If they hadn't ganged up on her and sent her to Louisiana to experience so-called "proper society" none of this would have happened.

Shiloh's bitter thoughts trailed off when she heard a rumbling sound overhead. She glanced toward the bank of dark clouds that piled on the western horizon like dozens of angry fists raised in threat.

Angry. She could certainly identify with that. After her hellish week she wanted to strike out at something or someone—namely Antoine Troudeau—to relieve the fury and hurt boiling inside her.

Shiloh frowned, bemused, when the rumbling sound intensified. Alarm shot through her when she heard unidentified shouts in the distance. Gunshots rang out, destroying what little serenity she had salvaged from her early-morning swim. Her survival instincts kicked in, sending her surging away from the base of the stony ridge to paddle across the river. She needed to retrieve the clothing she'd recently washed so she could conceal herself in the boyish garments and hat that served as her disguise.

More gunshots filled the air and Shiloh realized the

pounding of horses' hooves, not the distant growl of thunder, caused the rumbling noise. Afraid of being spotted, while she thrashed around in nothing but her wet chemise, Shiloh swam toward her horse. She flinched when the gunfire seemed to come from directly above her.

When she glanced over her shoulder a gasp of astonishment exploded from her lips. It looked as if a renegade Indian, riding a coal-black, wild-eyed mustang, was falling from the sky—and was about to land right smack-dab on top of her!

"Oh, God!" Shiloh sucked in a quick breath and swam sideways to get clear before the mustang's flailing hooves collided with her head.

"What in the hell?" came a surprised male voice that was much too close for Shiloh's comfort.

Horse and rider splashed down, swamping Shiloh and causing her to choke on a wave of water while trying to grab a quick breath. Her hair hung over her face like a mop, making it impossible to see where she was going. Worse, the renegade commenced muttering in an Indian dialect and she couldn't translate. When he grabbed her arm and yanked her toward him, she didn't have time to cough and draw air into her lungs before he dragged her beneath the surface.

Panic set in when she realized her deprived lungs were about to burst. Shiloh instinctively clamped herself around the renegade, desperate to climb up his body to inhale a precious breath. His arm came around her, pushing her upward so she could replenish her starved lungs. Her relief was short-lived because he dragged her beneath the surface again.

Anxious though she was to escape and to plant her feet on solid ground, the pop and splatter of gunshots incited another jolt of panic. She surfaced long enough to glance up at the rocky ridge where five bearded, heavily armed riders were firing at *her* because she had the misfortune of crossing paths with the renegade that had his arm clamped around her.

Talk about being in the wrong place at the wrong time! Shiloh thought as the renegade shoved her underwater again.

Although she tried to wrest free, the brawny warrior held firm. He tugged her alongside him as he swam downstream—away from the hail of gunfire pounding down on them. Desperate for another breath, Shiloh floundered upward to drag in much-needed air. To her everlasting relief the Indian didn't try to yank her beneath the surface again, forcing her to swallow another gallon of water. He did, however, jerk her toward the clump of reeds that lined the river.

"Keep your head down," he demanded gruffly. "I'll fetch your horse."

Shiloh didn't trust him not to take her horse and make a fast getaway. *His horse,* she noted had come ashore upstream—too far away for her to latch on to it without risking being shot full of bullets.

"Oh, no you don't!" She snaked out her hand to anchor herself to the leather holster that hung low on his hips. "That's *my* horse and you aren't going to…!"

Her voice transformed into a howl of pain. Fire shot through her left arm. Bewilderedly, she glanced down to see blood seeping from the gash on her arm.

"Damn it, if you'd stayed put that wouldn't have happened," he scolded as he hooked his arm around her waist, clamped her body against his and rolled across the creek bank toward her horse.

Offended though Shiloh was at having her barely

clad body molded to the hombre's muscled torso she didn't object. There were more serious problems with which to contend—like bullets thudding in the sand and splattering in the reeds. And vile curses raining down that promised the tortures of hell.

For a fleeting moment Shiloh thought the renegade had rolled on top of her to shield her from another gunshot wound. But then he gathered himself so quickly to bound to his feet so he could catch her horse that she decided she was probably giving him credit for chivalry where credit wasn't due.

"Sneaky damn Injun!" one of the men on the cliff bellowed hatefully. "You'll pay dearly for this! And you sure as hell haven't seen the last of us, you red-skinned bastard!"

That said, the scraggly-haired hooligan and his co-horts opened fire again. Bullets pinged off the rocks and trees while Shiloh and her captor headed for cover.

Once on solid footing, Shiloh tried to lurch away from the dark-eyed hombre who was dressed from head to toe in wet buckskin. Her escape attempt failed miserably. Her captor did, however, snatch up the tattered boys' clothes she had been using as a protective disguise. He thrust them at her as he half carried, half dragged her to her horse.

"What the hell are you doing out here in the middle of nowhere all by yourself?" he demanded as he shoved the heel of his hand against her rump to hoist her onto the horse.

"What the hell are *you* doing dropping from the sky with a bunch of unkempt ruffians breathing down your neck? I was managing just fine until you interrupted my swim and ruined everything!" she snapped right back at him, fear and anger combining to make her voice razor sharp.

Despite the distant gunfire, he cocked his head to appraise her momentarily before he bounded up behind her. Shiloh wasn't sure what to make of the expression on his bronzed face or the twinkle in his ebony eyes.

He actually seemed amused by her snippy retort. Well, she was *not* amused. Maybe she had been too reckless by striking off from town alone. But she'd had her pride trampled for the first time in her life, had her feelings shredded to bits and her heart broken. She had desperately needed time alone. She was familiar with this area, knew how to ride and shoot expertly and felt reasonably safe and secure…until this renegade showed up and brought hell with him!

Now her arm was oozing blood and pulsing with pain. Plus, being shot at repeatedly rattled her. Fear and indignation had her quivering uncontrollably. She'd had a nightmarish week and it didn't show any signs of improvement. In addition, she had sworn off men less than a week ago because they were nothing but trouble. And poof, this wild renegade dropped from the sky, accompanied by five trigger-happy demons, to remind her why men were the curse of a woman's life.

Shiloh's thoughts were still reeling when her captor burst out with a loud whistle that threatened to blow holes in her eardrums. She recoiled reflexively, then glanced sideways to see the black mustang, laden down with several saddlebags, perk up its ears. Like a well-trained dog coming to heel, the muscular pony trotted after his master who dug his heels into her horse and took off hell-bent-for-leather.

Shiloh became uncomfortably aware of the man's powerful body plastered against her. His chin dug into her shoulder and his arm was like a vice around her waist while they zigzagged through the willows and pecan trees that lined the river. Her damp chemise— that clung to her breasts and rode immodestly high on her thighs—left her feeling vulnerable and exposed. She squirmed self-consciously as they raced through the underbrush to put a greater distance between them and the ruffians that had been shooting at them.

"Don't even think what you're thinking," the renegade growled in her ear.

Shiloh stiffened, amazed the man had all but read her mind. She was indeed contemplating the possibility of vaulting off the horse and taking her chances alone.

"Be patient," he added as he glanced over his shoulder. "When we're in the clear I'll climb on my own horse and leave you to yours…. Well, damn."

Shiloh glanced back to see what had annoyed him. To her dismay, she saw the five burly hombres picking their way down the narrow trail to give chase.

"Sit tight," the renegade instructed as he loosened his grasp on her waist.

He crouched on the rump of her horse like a trick rider then sprang onto the mustang that now loped alongside them. Shiloh saw her chance to veer away— and she took it. She nudged her mount in the flanks, urging it into a swifter pace as they emerged from the gnarl of trees and underbrush. She took off across the open meadow, relying on equestrian skills she had mastered as a child.

"Come back here, damn it!" the renegade yelled at her. "If those outlaws catch up with you then you're as good as dead…or worse!"

The way Shiloh had it figured she was as good as

dead...or worse...if she *didn't* elude her captor right now. She had heard the horrifying tales of what Indians did to women and she wouldn't put anything past the rugged-looking renegade that glowered at her and raced after her in fast pursuit.

Hawk wasn't surprised by the woman's hostility or her desperate attempt to escape when they reached the clearing. After all, he and his horse had come dangerously close to landing on top of her when they swandived off the cliff to elude the outlaws. Plus, she didn't have the slightest idea who he was and what was going on.

But what befuddled Hawk to no end was why this dainty-looking female, dressed in skimpy wet undergarments, was swimming in an area that was ten miles from the nearest town and seven miles from the string of ranches that lined the north fork of Echo River.

When Hawk thrust out his hand to grab the woman by the arm, his eyes nearly popped from their sockets. To his disbelief *she* slid to the opposite side of the horse like a trick rider in a Wild West show. Worse, he became completely distracted when her breasts nearly spilled from the scooped neckline and one leg—bare all the way to her hip—lay draped over the saddle.

Hawk already knew how this woman's supple body felt while meshed intimately against him because they had rolled through the grass to dodge bullets. But this was even worse. The sight of her alluring feminine assets were burning into his brain like a searing brand.

He did not need to become sidetracked while trying to overtake this woman before she got hurt again. He had enough trouble dodging the pack of vengeful outlaws that were out for his blood because he'd stolen their loot. One look at the stream of blood trailing down the woman's arm was another reminder that she'd been frightened and injured because of her ill-timed association with him. She'd suddenly become his responsibility. Inconvenient or not, he had to protect her.

Hawk cast off his rambling thoughts and lunged for the reins to the woman's horse. He might not be able to get hold of her, but he sure as hell could take control of her mount!

He bit back a grin when the woman cursed him up one side and down the other for leading her mount in the direction she didn't want to go. This female might look like a bewitching young lady, but she was a spitfire through and through.

And he wasn't going to make the mistake of taking her for granted again.

"Let me go!" she snapped as she pulled herself back into the saddle, while they galloped toward the rocky canyon that had once been Hawk's stomping ground.

"You stick with me, sister, and you'll be fine." He hitched his thumb toward the riders that burst from the clump of trees to fire off their pistols ineffectively. "If they catch up with you things will be a lot worse."

"Being kidnapped by you doesn't seem much better," she sniped as she tried to wrest the reins from his hands.

When a rifle shot rang out, Hawk reached over to shove the woman forward on her horse, then plastered himself against his mount. The bullet whizzed past them, too close for comfort. Hawk spared a quick backward glance as he veered left abruptly, headed for the old Apache trail that zigzagged between the boulders and scrub trees on the steep incline.

Thunder boomed overhead. Hawk sent a prayer to
both Indian and white deities for rain—an abundance
of it. To his amazement the sky opened up, allowing
him to make his way up the winding trail, washing
away the prints as he went. He glanced around the
scraggly juniper that was presently concealing him
from view and watched the outlaws split up in an attempt to locate their prey in the sudden downpour.

He noticed that the woman gave him the strangest
look as he led her horse to higher elevations.

"Are you some sort of Indian wizard?" She glanced
skyward, then peered curiously at him.

"Grandson of an Apache medicine man," he said,
laying it on thick. "Heap big magic. I know all the
tricks of the trade. If you cross me, paleface, I'll place
a curse on you."

He was surprised that she clamped her mouth shut
and didn't say another word while he followed the
steep trail. When pea-size hail pattered around them,
Hawk hunched his shoulders and ducked his head.
They should be at the cave in less than a quarter of an
hour so he could tend the bloody wound the woman had
sustained—because of her unfortunate association with
him.

The unpleasant thought pricked his conscience
again.

Hawk glanced sideways—and got lost in the green-
est eyes he'd ever seen. She was staring straight at him
with wary curiosity, resentment and a fair amount of
fear. Her face was pale, he noticed. She'd lost a con-
siderable amount of blood during the strenuous ride
and she definitely needed medical attention.

Her dazed expression worried him. As a precau-
tion, Hawk urged her horse closer, just in case she

fainted. The last thing he wanted was for this displaced female to tumble off her horse and crack open her head on a sharp boulder.

"It won't be much farther." He gestured toward the overhanging ledge twenty yards above them. "We'll... oh, hell."

Hawk's arm shot out the instant he saw the woman's eyes roll back in her head and her body slump sideways on the saddle. He caught her the split second before she tumbled to the ground. Scooping her off her horse, he situated her limp body into a jackknifed position across his lap so he could keep a firm grip on her.

Hawk shook his head and sighed heavily. When he awakened this morning, planning to elude the outlaws and rejoin his company of Rangers, he never expected to be dodging bullets and dragging an auburn-haired, emerald-eyed female, dressed in flimsy, revealing unmentionables, along with him.

Despite his noble attempt not to look down, his traitorous gaze settled on the damp fabric that clung to her shapely derriere like a coat of paint. His attention shifted to her bare legs and a jolt of pure lust bombarded him.

"Enough of that," he admonished himself as he set his sights on the cave tucked into the rocky ledge above him.

Just because the most beguiling female he'd ever encountered had landed in his lap—literally—he wasn't going to be distracted from his personal and professional crusade. He damn well intended to avenge his mentor's death and see justice served...just as soon as he patched up this misplaced female, eluded the vicious hombres breathing down his neck and reported to his Ranger battalion.

Chapter Two

Shiloh regained consciousness, grimacing at the fiery pain shooting down her left arm. "Ouch!" Dazed, she tried to free her arm from whatever was holding it down.

"Sorry about that," came the deep baritone voice that belonged to the rough-edged renegade. "I was hoping I'd have your wound cleaned and packed before you came to. Guess you weren't that lucky."

"Bad luck seems to be the only kind I've had lately," she mumbled as she pried her eyes open to appraise her captor.

The first thing that registered in her foggy senses was the firelight that flickered across his rugged bronzed features. A beaded headband encircled his raven hair. Thick braids brushed across his noticeably broad shoulders. He looked as wild and tough and untamed as the mustang pony he had been riding earlier.

Frowning, Shiloh surveyed her surroundings. They were tucked inside a cave, protected from the pursuing gunmen and inclement weather. She was *stuck* with this man, she realized uneasily. She was unsure of his intentions toward her, but she had the unshakable feeling that they weren't honorable. She had every reason to be wary of him.

"Brace up, sister," he said as he hovered over her. "I'm going to cleanse the wound again before I bandage it."

Shiloh bit back a shriek and panted for breath when he dribbled whiskey on her upper arm. She instinctively tried to snatch her arm away from him again, but he held it fast.

"Looks worse than it is," he assured her. "Your arm will be stiff and sore for a few days, but we'll keep a close eye on it so it doesn't get infected."

Shiloh blinked, bemused. It suddenly hit her like a rockslide that this man, who looked every bit the renegade in full regalia and spoke an Indian dialect, also had an impressive command of English. Earlier, she'd been too busy fighting for her life to register that fact. Getting shot had demanded most of her attention.

She frowned warily as he pulled a tin of ointment from one of the saddlebags. "Who *are* you?"

"Logan Hawk." He smoothed the salve on her pulsing arm.

Shiloh sighed as a cool, numbing sensation overrode the fiery pain. "What is that stuff? It works incredibly well."

"Old Indian remedy." He fished out several strips of fabric to wrap around her arm. "So, what's your name, sister?"

Shiloh refused to trust this man, even if he was tending her wound. Furthermore, she was never going to trust *any* man, with the exception of her brothers—unless they tried to marry her off again. But if her captor thought that being civil and helpful would gain her confidence then he thought wrong. She wasn't about to give her real name so he could hold her for ransom, after he ravished her repeatedly, while keeping her hostage in this isolated cavern.

"Bernice Colbert," she lied, borrowing her cousin's name.

She averted her gaze to watch him bandage her arm. For a man who looked rough and tough she was astonished by his gentleness. He was an intriguing contradiction….

No, he isn't! When she felt herself softening toward the ruggedly handsome stranger, she redoubled her defenses. She had recently discovered that she was a lousy judge of men. She had a broken heart to show for it. Plus, she had been carrying around this heaping load of demoralizing shame. This unexpected encounter with this puzzling renegade wasn't going to deter her from holding all men everywhere in low regard.

Logan Hawk eyed her for a long pensive moment, nodded approvingly then said, "Smart lady. Never divulge your real name to a stranger. You aren't Bernice, are you?"

The man seemed to be a mental step ahead of her. That wasn't good because she was in a vulnerable situation. She suspected Logan Hawk was a wily con artist who had perfected the tricks of his trade. He made all the right noises in his attempt to gain her trust so she'd lower her guard.

But she wasn't falling into that trap again—ever.

"Look, Mr. Hawk—"

"Just *Hawk* will be fine," he inserted.

"If that's who *you* really are," she said suspiciously. And if she was quick to assume an alias then he might be doing the same thing. "Why don't you save us both the trouble and tell me exactly what expectations you have here."

He frowned, befuddled. "Expectations?"

She stared pointedly at her carpetbag that lay atop several leather saddlebags. "By now you have rummaged through my belongings to see that I'm not carrying much cash and no identification and a single-shot derringer, which I'm sure you confiscated." She watched a wry smile purse his full lips—and she resented the way his amused expression affected her. "So you aren't sure how much profit you can make from our unexpected encounter. Until you figure it out you're putting on your party manners to try to earn my trust. But you might as well know right off that it won't work."

He sank down cross-legged beside her. A hint of a smile still quirked his lips. "So my limited amount of charm isn't going to win you over, is that what you're saying?"

She nodded her wet head. "That's precisely what I'm saying, Mr. Hawk."

"I see." He stroked his stubbled chin pensively. "So you think I should save myself the trouble and just dispose of you so you won't slow me down while I'm making my fast getaway from the desperadoes."

"That's not exactly what I had in mind," she grumbled, and then fidgeted apprehensively.

"I didn't think so." He hitched his thumb toward the mouth of the cave where rain poured down in torrents, forming a curtain of water that sealed them off from the outside world. She noticed his dark eyes dancing with devilry as he stared down at her. "But if I *do* decide to give you a shove off the ledge because you're more trouble than you're worth no one will be the wiser. Whoever happens onto your battered body will think this nasty weather caused your fall."

Shiloh swallowed uneasily as she followed his gaze to the opening of the cavern. Maybe putting ideas in his head wasn't the best approach. But simpering, whining and begging weren't her forte. Raised by two older brothers, she had taught herself to be mentally tough and to stand up to them. She never kowtowed to men and she wasn't about to start now.

She suddenly became aware that Hawk had seen to her comfort by placing her on the padded bedroll. He'd covered her up with the quilt that had been strapped to her horse.

Damn it, why was it taking so long for thoughts and observations to register in her mind? Obviously the incident that had thrust them together—and had left her in uncertain danger—rattled her.

He thrust a piece of pemmican at her. "You're probably hungry. This is all I have to offer, *Bernice,*" he said with a knowing grin. "If you'll do me the courtesy of turning sideways I'd like to shed these wet buckskins."

Her eyes flew wide open in alarm. "You are going to disrobe in front of me?" she squawked, her voice two octaves higher than normal.

He rose to his feet with the graceful ease of a mountain cat then shrugged casually. "I planned to undress behind your back, but that's really up to you. If you want to watch—"

"I certainly do *not* want to watch!" she loudly objected.

Shiloh glared at her taunting captor when he jerked the soggy fringed shirt over his head. The sight of his rippling muscles and his washboard belly had her struggling to breathe normally. Damn the man, he knew exactly how physically appealing he was. She cursed her feminine curiosity for conspiring against her, making her appraise every masculine inch of exposed skin.

Scowling at the ornery devil, Shiloh rolled onto her side and presented her back. She definitely disliked Logan Hawk. No matter what his secret agenda, he was comfortable with his masculinity. He also seemed to delight in ruffling her feathers for sport.

Blast it, she couldn't figure out this man. One moment he seemed a dangerous threat and the next instant he was playfully teasing her. His unpredictability made it impossible to guess what he planned to do next.

"You can look now," Hawk prompted a few minutes later.

She twisted around and blinked in surprise as she surveyed his dark breeches, shirt and vest. He had unbraided his long hair and tied it at the nape of his neck. But this more civilized veneer didn't fool Shiloh one bit. She had witnessed Hawk's daredevil escape from the desperadoes. She presumed he was at least *part* Indian, judging by his bronzed skin, high cheekbones, onyx eyes and raven-black hair. He was also an exceptionally skilled rider and capable frontiersman—as well as being about as far from a refined gentleman as he could get. Oddly enough, that was a point in Hawk's favor—after her disappointing dealings with Antoine Troudeau.

He was responsible for her loss of humor, her faith in men and her self-confidence. She also questioned her desirability and appeal as a woman now. Shiloh had his duplicity and deceit to thank for that, damn him!

"Not that I mind you parading around in your skimpy garb," he remarked, "but I recommend that you get dressed, too. This cave is cool and damp. You don't need to catch a chill while nursing a bullet wound. By the way, I'm sorry you got in the way of a shot that was meant for me."

He smiled apologetically and she hated that she was enormously affected by the expression that crinkled his eyes and cut dimples in his stubbled cheeks. She needed to remain on constant alert because men were untrustworthy scoundrels—especially one who took her captive. Yet, there was something about his matter-of-fact manner and sometimes impersonal demeanor that put her at ease. He was nothing like the pretentious aristocrats she'd met in New Orleans.

When he presented his back so she could dress, she reached into her carpetbag for the one and only set of dry clothes she had with her. She darted a wary glance at Hawk at irregular intervals while she shed her chemise then fastened herself into her blouse and riding breeches.

The fact that he made no attempt to pounce while she was dressing was another point in his favor. But Shiloh reminded herself that, given their unconventional introduction and this potentially dangerous situation, the jury was still out on Logan Hawk.

Friend or foe, she didn't know. She wasn't going to let her guard down for a single moment until she knew for certain.

Her thoughts scattered and suspicion settled solidly in her mind when she accidentally knocked one of the saddlebags sideways. It toppled from the pile and several banded stacks of bank notes tumbled onto the stone floor.

Her eyes rounded, realizing he was a *thief!* One who was obviously very good with disguises and impersonations. He was a shyster and scoundrel and she was a fool if she lowered her guard around him.

"You stole this stolen money from your cohorts," she accused harshly. "Is that why they were shooting at you?" She cursed sourly as she gestured toward her left arm. "It is unfortunate that *I* was wounded when *your* vindictive friends were trying to fill you full of lead."

Self-preservation demanded that she bolt to her feet and dart to safety. But the abrupt movement caused her head to spin and she swayed on her feet. When he tried to steady her, she hatchet-chopped his wrist until he let loose.

"If you plan to dispose of me eventually, then I'm not leaving the how and when up to you," she snapped as she stamped forward. "If you're going to shoot me then you might as well do it now."

"Hold up, Bernice," he called after her. "You've got the wrong idea here." When she continued toward the mouth of the cave he scowled then came after her. "I know this looks bad—"

"I'll say it does." Again, she jerked her arm from his restraining grasp. "You're a bandit and you're no better than those men who were shooting at us."

Hawk hooked his arm around her waist before she could burst through the curtain of rain. He gestured toward the pallet. "Go sit down and I'll make us some coffee before I explain what's going on."

She tilted her chin rebelliously and squirmed for release. "I'm not thirsty. You can explain here and now."

He bit back a grin when she flashed him one of those this-better-be-good glares. He set her to her feet, and—keeping a firm hold on her so she didn't do something rash—he heeled-and-toed out of his left boot.

When he showed her the badge concealed inside the hollow heel, she gaped at him. He extended the silver star for closer inspection.

Her luminous green eyes popped, then narrowed doubtfully. "A Texas Ranger?" She scoffed caustically. "Of course, you are. That's why your friends are after you for stealing their loot. I'd hate to venture a guess as to what happened to the unfortunate lawman that you stole this badge from."

When she tried to dart past him again on her way into the downpour, Hawk jerked her back beside him. "You aren't going anywhere until I know for certain that the bandits aren't out there, waiting to pick us off. If you want to get yourself killed—and obviously you do because you were paddling around alone in the river, miles from the protection of civilization—then that's your business, lady. But I'm on assignment." He tapped his chest. "I'm not about to jeopardize my mission because you don't believe I'm who and what I say I am."

He made a stabbing gesture toward the pallet. "Now…sit…down…damn it," he said slowly and succinctly. "I'm going to make coffee." He turned her toward the interior of the cave. "You won't accomplish a damn thing by going outside, except getting wet again and maybe exposing our whereabouts to those cutthroats."

Although she stamped over and sat down, her expression indicated she was none too happy about being ordered around. Well, too bad, he thought. He'd put forward his best manners for her benefit, but she was still being contrary and hostile. Nevertheless, she was going to do as he said and that was that.

"Are you still sticking with the name Bernice?" he

asked as he scooped up the pot to brew coffee over the small campfire he had positioned near the cave entrance.

"Are you still sticking with the name Logan Hawk?"

"Yep, it's my name. I'm half Apache," he confided. "My father, John Fletcher Logan, was a white trapper and trader who came and went from our clan's camp. My mother was the daughter of Gray Hawk, a medicine man, who decided that marrying his daughter to a white man, so that he could learn English and understand the way the white man thought, was good magic. My grandfather chose his totem as my totem because the hawk is known to be swift and fierce."

He spread his arms wide. "Logan Hawk. Half white man's name. Half Apache."

He glanced over his shoulder, noting that she was still regarding him skeptically. He didn't know what caused her to be so mistrusting, but he supposed he really couldn't blame her. He had always been one to err on the side of caution, too.

"Now, would you mind telling me what the devil you were doing in the wilds without a bodyguard or chaperone?" he asked while the coffee boiled on the fire.

She crossed her arms over her chest and thrust out her chin. "Yes, I do mind. It's none of your business."

His lips twitched as he cast his feisty companion another glance. She might look alluring and feminine, but she was definitely a hellion at heart. He liked that about her—in an exasperated kind of way. He also liked the way she looked and felt when she was pressed familiarly against him….

Hawk squelched the titillating thought immediately. He expected better of himself. This wasn't the time or the place. He avoided emotional attachments to females. His tumbleweed lifestyle and his lack of acceptance in white society taught him to expect little of nothing from anyone.

The less complications the better was his motto.

When the coffee was hot, he poured two cups. As he handed a cup to her, he noticed she still regarded him warily. She also refused to take a sip until he did. She was so mistrusting that she suspected he might drug or poison her.

Cautious didn't begin to describe this woman. He drank his coffee and wondered who had made her so suspicious.

"Last year a Texas Ranger showed up in this neck of the woods," she said between sips of steaming coffee. "He claimed that he had been sent to evict the Mexican sheepherders who were nesting on property that belonged to a local rancher named Frank Mills. Two men died and their wives headed for the hills, overcome with grief and fear.

"Although there wasn't enough evidence to convict Frank of hiring that bloodthirsty gunslinger to impersonate a Ranger, we suspected he was responsible." She stared him squarely in the eye. "So don't expect me to take your word as gospel, Hawk. I only believe half of what I see and even less of what a man tells me."

Hawk was aware of the incident she mentioned because he had been sent to apprehend the murdering imposter. His Apache upbringing always put him at the top of the list for tracking elusive, high-profile outlaws.

"Just so you know, the imposter paid the consequences," he assured her solemnly.

Her delicately arched brows shot up. "Did he? You know that for a fact?"

He nodded grimly. "I saw to it that he never hurt another living soul, but he didn't confess. There was no evidence to convict Frank Mills of conspiracy. A damn shame that."

She looked as if she wanted to believe him, but he could see her withdrawing emotionally. He wondered if his mixed heritage and unconventional appearance contributed to her distrust. It did where most folks were concerned.

Whites had a tendency to judge him by his bronzed skin, dark eyes and jet-black hair. Not to mention the damage done by the white man's one-sided bad publicity against Indian tribes. Most white folks didn't care who he was on the inside. He was an Indian; therefore, he must be the enemy.

The Rangers battalion was one of the few exceptions. His band of brothers judged him on merit, not skin color.

Hawk discarded the unproductive thought and reminded himself that he was also guilty of holding a grudge against whites because of their unfair treatment of his people.

And his people were the Apache. Just because he was *half*-white didn't change that fact.

"So…what do you intend to do with me?" she questioned.

"Take you home when the rain lets up," he replied. "Just where is home, hmm?"

She scoffed at his subtle attempt to gain information. "Nice try, Hawk. Now tell me again why you have several bags of money and five unhappy banditos dogging your heels? Oh, yes, I'm supposed to believe that you're one of the good guys and I'm supposed to place unfaltering faith and trust in your willingness to see me home safely. Right?" She glared at him. "Well, you're wrong about that. I'm going to need more than your word that you aren't a threat."

Hawk scowled, nearly at the end of his patience with this prickly female. "Are you always this contrary, Bernice?"

"No, this is one of my good days." A mischievous smile surfaced before she could bite it back. "I'm usually worse."

"I'm starting to believe it," he mumbled.

Chapter Three

Hawk stood watch at the mouth of the cave, relieved to note that the rain had let up—temporarily at least. He wanted to be on his way. Being confined to this small space with this maddening but alluring female tempted him to do something foolish and reckless—like yielding to the outrageous urge of kissing her to see if she tasted even half as good as she looked. Staring at her lush, Cupid's bow mouth for more than a moment at a time was sensual torment.

Forcing himself to get his mind back to the business at hand, he poked his head outside. "Well, damn," he grumbled.

When she walked up behind him, he cautiously glanced back at her. He half expected her to approach him, toting a log for the campfire as her makeshift weapon. He braced himself, in case she decided to pound him on the head.

Fortunately she wasn't armed, just curious.

He pointed in the direction of the men who were riding through the valley. "They aren't giving up the search," he grumbled. "But then, I did confiscate a lot of stolen money." He waited a beat then said, "I'm sorry you ended up in the middle of this. The outlaw gang I infiltrated three months ago won't want you to walk away, either. Not when you can identify them. This gang doesn't leave eyewitnesses behind."

Shiloh gulped uneasily as she watched the five men weave around the boulders and trees at lower elevations. "Where are our horses? What if the outlaws spot them?"

"They won't," he assured her. "I stashed them in another cave. One of the advantages of these rocky hillsides that my people always favored, when this land was part of the Apacheria, is that you can come and go like a fleeting specter. If you know your way around this valley you can be visible one minute and vanish into thin air the next."

He called her attention to the battered stone precipice looming above them. "When the wind blows in from the southwest, swirling and dipping around that peak, you can almost swear there are whispering voices on Ghost Ridge. Which is why this is sacred ground to the Apache. According to the legend, the spirits congregate here, ready to guide us if we are wise enough to listen."

He sounded convincing and believable, Shiloh mused as she scanned the towering peak. But it would be a cold day in hell before she took a man at his word again. She had no way of knowing for certain that he wasn't making up the legend to prey on her gullibility and gain her allegiance. Furthermore, she couldn't swear that he *wasn't* trying to double-cross his cohorts who were out for his blood—and hers—because she could identify the group of ruffians.

Shiloh glanced down at the rain-drenched riders in

the valley below then shifted her attention to the man beside her. "Nothing like having to settle for the lesser of two evils," she grumbled, exasperated. "You or them. Tough call."

Her comment inspired his rumbling chuckle. "At least there's only *one* of me compared to *five* of them. And one of these days you'll apologize for mistrusting me, just because I'm half Apache."

Shiloh tipped her head back to compensate for the difference in their height. He had to be at least six feet three, and an impressive male specimen—much as she was reluctant to admit it. "I don't hold your heritage against you," she corrected. "It's being a man that I object to. Your gender has so many flaws and so few saving graces."

He continued to monitor the search party in the distance. "A man-hater, are you? Is anyone in particular responsible for souring you on the rest of the male gender?"

"That's none of your business, either." She lurched around to pace the shadowy confines of the cavern. Thinking of Antoine's deceit always caused her emotions to roil in frustration.

"At least tell me the scoundrel's name," Hawk requested. "I might decide to look him up and shoot him down for you after I finish this assignment."

Shiloh glanced over at him, jolted again by his arresting profile and the hint of amusement in that deep baritone voice. This man couldn't be all bad...could he? He had offered to avenge the hurt and humiliation she had suffered recently. He had patched her injured arm and found refuge from the rain and from the gunmen who were chasing them.

The moment she felt herself weakening, wanting to

believe he was on the side of law, order and honor, he ruined it all by saying, "Unless of course you deserved what you got. You didn't have it coming, did you?"

Well, so much for actually starting to like Hawk, she thought in annoyance. Shiloh stiffened her spine, elevated her chin and rapped out, "No, I most certainly did not have it coming! I was manipulated and misled and entirely too naive and trusting. But that won't happen again. I guarantee it!"

He shrugged those impossibly broad shoulders as he stared over the valley. "I guess we all have to learn a few lessons the hard way, Bernie," he said, adopting a shortened version of her alias. "It's my job to ask the hard, and sometimes offensive questions. Since we're stuck here together, at least until nightfall, I thought this might be our chance to get to know a little more about each other."

"We already know each other better than I prefer," she muttered resentfully.

Shiloh well remembered the feel of their bodies meshed together, while rolling across the ground to avoid gunfire. Also, they had been pressed tightly together while galloping off on her horse, while she'd been garbed in nothing but her wet chemise. Yet, despite her vulnerability he hadn't made even one attempt to…

The thought caused Shiloh to halt in her tracks. "Well, no wonder."

Hawk glanced sideways and frowned. "No wonder *what?*"

She dismissed him with a flick of her wrist then went back to pacing. Maybe it was her fault that she had been jilted. Maybe there was something unlovable and undesirable about her. Obviously she didn't inspire many lusty or romantic ideas in men.

Which was why this supposed Texas Ranger—who'd had ample opportunity to take advantage of her during their isolation—hadn't touched her in a sexual way. He hadn't made even one improper advance, despite the situation that had left her nearly naked in his arms several times. Why was that?

Because he was completely honorable and trustworthy? Doubtful, thought she. It was because she lacked feminine appeal, personality and charm. Which was why Antoine had disregarded her feelings for him and broken her heart by turning his attention and affection to someone else.

It was demoralizing to have to accept the fact that she possessed very little sex appeal and no alluring charm. The deflating realization caused her shoulders to slump. If she couldn't attract or intrigue this rough-edged frontiersman, she couldn't beguile a man she'd fallen in love with, either.

"Well, hell," Hawk muttered, his deep voice echoing through the dimly lit chamber.

When she noticed his profound concentration on the goings-on outside the cave Shiloh went to join him. She scowled sourly, too, when she noted that two men had dismounted near the mouth of the box canyon and looked to be setting up camp to outwait them. Three men rode back in the direction they had come.

"Morton DeVol and Everett Stiles are guarding the escape route while the other outlaws gather the provisions from their hideout," Hawk speculated. "I was hoping they'd give up so we don't have to rely on the treacherous trail that leads over Ghost Ridge to the canyon beyond."

Shiloh stared anxiously at the towering summit of jagged rock. "We have to climb over *that?*" She had the unmistakable feeling that her aversion to height was going to make the trek an unnerving challenge.

"That's right, Bernie," he confirmed. "In the rain… in the dark. Lucky for you that I've used that winding path several times before."

"Well, that makes me feel so much better. Can't wait to get started," she said unenthusiastically.

At twilight, in the drizzling rain, Hawk grasped Shiloh's hand and led her outside. Waddling like ducks, they made their way beneath and around the protruding rock barriers. They were careful not to expose their whereabouts to the relentless outlaws who had pitched a tent in the valley below.

Shiloh made the mistake of looking over the ledge—and felt her stomach drop a quick twenty feet. She must have squeezed Hawk's hand apprehensively because he halted on the narrow path to glance curiously at her.

"What's the problem?" he whispered.

Shiloh gulped down her apprehension and struggled for hard-won composure. "This might be a good time to let you know that heights make me a little dizzy and uneasy."

"How dizzy? How uneasy?" His dark-eyed gaze sharpened and he stared grimly at her. "You aren't going to go hysterical on me while we're scrabbling up the peak with our horses, which are going to have their own problems with footing, are you?"

Shiloh glanced over the cliff, drew a shaky breath and smiled with bravado. "I'll try to remain calm…."

Her voice dried up when he cupped her chin in his hand, demanding her undivided attention. "There will be no trying to pull yourself together when the time comes," he insisted harshly. "You'll do what you have to do, understand?"

Annoyed with his insensitive attitude, she slapped his hand away then squared her shoulders. "Understood. Now lead the way, Chief Tough-As-Nails. Heaven forbid that I should freeze up or fall to my death on Ghost Ridge. Never mind about me," she said with a dismissive flick of her wrist. "After all, I'm just the inconvenience you nearly landed on in midstream this morning and then decided to drag along with you. I don't know why you didn't leave me behind. It's obvious that I'm only slowing you down."

Hawk couldn't help but smile at her spunk and sass. He didn't like learning that heights rattled her, knowing she would be testing herself to the limit of her abilities when they scaled the lofty peak. But the sparkle of determination he saw in her cedar-tree green eyes assured him that she wasn't a fainthearted shrinking violet. She would do her best to scratch and claw her way up and over the ridge—or die trying. He would be right beside her every step of the way to make sure it didn't come to that.

Hawk led the way to the larger cave where he had sheltered the horses. Shiloh waited outside. Her attention fixated on the craggy peak that posed an intimidating personal challenge. She couldn't imagine how she and the horses were going to make the nearly impossible trek, especially at night, especially during a misty rain.

Her anxious thoughts trailed off when Hawk reappeared to hand her the reins to her horse. "I'll let you lead your mount until we get to the most difficult part of the trail, then I'll take control of it."

"I'll manage that, too," Shiloh insisted, holding her head high as she surged off.

"Wrong way," Hawk called out, a smile in his voice.

Shiloh sighed heavily as Hawk walked off in the direction they had come, then veered around an oversize boulder to follow an inconspicuous trail that led up the steep incline. Obviously he knew this canyon like the back of his hand. She envied his knowledge and skill. But at least she wasn't floundering around in unfamiliar territory with some greenhorn that could get them lost or injured as fast as she could.

"This is one of those places where it's not a good idea to look down," Hawk cautioned.

Shiloh braced herself when the trail narrowed to such extremes that Hawk's mustang, which was directly in front of her, didn't have enough space to walk without scraping its side on the jagged stone wall. There was nothing but a fifty-foot gorge on the other side. Shiloh grabbed a quick breath and prayed that her horse didn't stumble and jerk her over the edge before she could release the reins.

To make the difficult trek worse, thunder rumbled overhead, the earth shook and the sky opened up again. Shiloh found herself soaked to the bone in less than five minutes. To compound the problem, there was barely enough light for her to see where she was going. Fear pounded in rhythm with her accelerated pulse. The voice inside her head kept chanting that her next step might be her last.

"This escape route has disaster written all over it," she said fatalistically.

"It's a damn sight better than trying to shoot our way past the crack-shot gunmen that are blocking the canyon exit," Hawk countered.

"I'm not sure one route is better or worse than the other…. Dear God…"

The eerie sounds that Hawk had mentioned this morning suddenly demanded her attention. It did indeed sound as if haunting voices from beyond the grave were howling in the wind. A chill—and not from the soaking rain—slithered down her spine. Shiloh didn't consider herself superstitious, but this treacherous trek after sunset, with a stiff breeze and stinging raindrops constantly slapping her in the face, was working on her jumpy nerves.

She did not need disembodied voices and tormented wails undermining her composure and preying on her fear of height.

She nearly jumped out of her own skin when Hawk's hand folded unexpectedly around her ice-cold fingers. She'd been so distracted by the otherworldly sounds that she hadn't heard him ease up beside her.

"This is where the path becomes slick and hazardous."

"Well, shoot, and it's been such a piece of cake thus far," she quipped.

His white teeth flashed in the gathering darkness. "Sarcasm must be your way of dealing with difficulty," he noted. "A woman after my own heart."

She stared at the nearly impossible path ahead of them then spared him a glance. "I'm not after your heart, Hawk. I've sworn off men with good reason. I just want to get out of here alive so my two bro—" She slammed her mouth shut so fast that she nearly clipped off her tongue. "Well, damn it all."

"So you have two brothers. So what?" he said, seemingly disinterested. "It's not the end of the world if I'm privy to that information. I already told you that I'm not holding you for ransom. My objective is to rejoin my company and report my findings. Then I'll have one of my compatriots take you home."

"Right. You're honorable, noble and heroic. Don't know why I ever doubted your intentions." She stared pointedly at the saddlebags of money strapped to his horse. With an audible sigh she turned her attention to the winding trail above them. "I really wish you did have wings, like your namesake, Hawk. Flying looks to be the only safe way to scale this embankment to reach that rain-slick peak."

"Change of plans," Hawk suddenly declared as he pulled the reins from her hand. "I'll take you up first, then come back for the horses."

"That's not necessa—"

Her voice evaporated when she stepped forward to reclaim the reins—and slipped in the mud and loose rock. Hawk snaked out an arm and hooked it around her waist before she fell on her face. He kept a firm grasp on her as he propelled her between the jutting boulders.

"Footing here is tricky on a good day. In pouring rain it's downright perilous. Take shorter steps and widen your stance," he instructed.

They went about twenty-five yards before he halted beside the eroded crevice that gaped in front of them. Leaving her braced against the boulder, Hawk backed up a step then launched himself through the air to avoid the space where the trail had given way to forty feet of nothingness.

He held out his hand to her. "Now it's your turn."

There was just enough daylight left for him to note the color had seeped from her face. But to her credit she gritted her teeth and marshaled her resolve. His respect for her elevated another notch as she crouched in preparation for leaping toward him. He had seen this woman during several telling moments today and he admired her gumption and determination.

Whoever Bernice Colbert really was, she was one spirited, independent and courageous woman.

Hawk braced himself when she hurtled toward him. Since she wasn't as long-legged as he was, she didn't quite make it over to solid ground. When she shrieked and lost her balance, his hand shot out to grab her wrist. Thankfully, she was only airborne for a few moments before he hauled her against him.

To his surprise she threw her arms around his neck and practically hugged the stuffing out of him. Hawk was sorry to say that his male body responded instantaneously to having her supple curves and swells pressed familiarly against him. He reminded himself repeatedly that this was *definitely* the wrong time and wrong place for a lust attack.

Damn it, what was there about this defensive, elusive, hostile woman that kept getting to him? He'd dealt with several female victims during his years with the Rangers, but not one had affected him the way this one did.

"You can let go of me now," he murmured as he accidentally brushed his lips against the side of her neck.

And it was an accident, he tried to convince himself. He was only nuzzling against her because she needed comfort and reassurance after her near brush with calamity.

Shiloh tried to loosen her fierce grasp on his neck, tried not to burrow her head against his sturdy shoulder. But for those few unnerving seconds, when it felt as if the earth had dropped out from under her, panic had overwhelmed her. She had grabbed hold of Hawk and clung to him for dear life. She savored his solid strength, enjoyed the feel of his warm breath against her cold skin.

Arousing sensations flooded through her, thoroughly baffling her. How could she possibly be attracted to this man? She still wasn't sure if she trusted or even liked him. But he sparked the same kind of sensations that she had experienced when Antoine had taken her in his arms while they danced at parties in the palatial ballrooms of New Orleans.

She shouldn't have felt those vulnerable feelings then and she shouldn't be feeling them *now*. With *him*.

What the blazes was the matter with her?

Aggravated with herself for experiencing pleasurable tingles she swore never to feel or trust again—and at the worst of all possible moments, and with a stranger, no less—Shiloh lurched back to brace herself against the crumbling stone wall.

"Sorry," she said unevenly. "My survival instincts must have caused me to get a little carried away."

"You have both feet beneath you now. You'll be okay."

His crackling voice drew her bemused frown. "Are you all right, Hawk? Did I injure you when I threw myself at you?"

"No." He cleared his throat and looked away. "I'm fine."

He lied. He was not fine. He wasn't even remotely close to fine. He did not want to be attracted and distracted by this prickly woman. He didn't want the slightest emotional ties to her or any other woman. Period. He didn't have a personal life because his professional life with the Rangers was a demanding challenge. He didn't have the time or inclination for tender feelings that conflicted with duty.

Unfortunately, today's sequence of unfortunate events was conspiring against him. For one reason or another he'd had his hands all over this woman. Necessity had also demanded that he plaster his body against hers more times than he cared to count. Now he was so aware of her scent, her appearance and the feel of her that he couldn't look at her or touch her without reacting fiercely.

And, damn it, this had to stop! He had to concentrate on the serious task of getting them up and over Ghost Ridge to reach Sundance Canyon—a haven that held bittersweet memories that he didn't want to deal with unless absolutely necessary.

Which it was right now.

Annoyed with his uncharacteristic preoccupation with this female, he clamped hold of her good arm and half dragged her uphill. He was anxious to reach the peak before total darkness descended. He gave her a boost onto the rain-slick boulder that led to the next leg of the treacherous journey.

"This is where the horses will have the most difficulty," he said as he gestured for her to continue on without him.

"Dear God…"

He heard her voice wobble, saw her drop to her knees. She clutched her stomach when she made the critical mistake of glancing at the wild tumble of boulders that filled the V-shaped arroyo beside them.

"Look at me!" he barked sharply. "This is not the time to lose your nerve. If you can't proceed without me, then you'll have to wait here until I return with the horses. Find something to anchor yourself to until I get back."

She bowed her neck then surged from her knees to her feet. "I'll be fine," she called over her shoulder. "I'll—"

"Watch out for that—" Hawk cursed mightily when she banged her head on the jutting rock.

Her groan died beneath the report of long-range rifles. Bullets whistled over their heads and zinged off the rocks. Hawk cursed the fact that the bandits had spotted them and were trying to pin them down so they could catch up.

Cursing inventively, Hawk scrambled over the slick boulder, trying to reach Bernie before she took another bullet or staggered so far sideways that she keeled over the ledge and bounced off every sharp-edged rock until she landed in a broken heap at the bottom of the ravine. Unfortunately, the volley of bullets startled her and she lost her footing. Hawk made a wild grab for her, but only connected with air.

Serenaded by gunfire and the ringing in her ears caused by the blow to her forehead, Shiloh cartwheeled over a boulder. The world spun before her eyes and nausea churned in her stomach. One moment she was glancing back at Hawk and the next instant she smacked her head—hard—into the jagged overhang. And then bullets started flying.

She shrieked in terror when she couldn't gain her balance. But there was nothing beneath her right foot. The wind was howling like a chorus of banshees, it was spitting rain again and now the crack-shot bandits were after them.

Wild eyed, she tried to pivot on her left foot and throw herself down on the narrow trail. But momentum and a fierce wind pushed her over the edge. She could see nothing but the ghastly shadows of boulders that reminded her of prehistoric monsters waiting to gobble her alive.

She cried out when her left foot slipped and she banged her hip against the rocks. Panting for breath, she dug in her nails as she slid downward, hoping to find a handhold before the pull of gravity dragged her to her death.

"Hawk!" she howled, even though she knew there was nothing he could do to help her.

Despite her best attempts, she slid downward, bumping over the angular stones and eroded pebbles that left her feet dangling over the ten-foot drop—and then the rest of her body went over the ledge before she could anchor herself.

She crash-landed on another jagged boulder, twisting her ankle—and knocking the air clean out of her.

The wind wailed like the eternal damned, drowning out her hoarse cry for help. Her panicky gaze leaped to Hawk. She was amazed by his ability to bound from one boulder to the next like a graceful cougar, in his attempt to reach her. There was just enough daylight left for her to see the grim expression on his face. She heard his pithy curses above her as she clutched her throbbing ankle and struggled to draw breath.

Shiloh couldn't decide if the pain in her head, the fiery sensations in her injured arm or the throb in her aching ankle hurt the worst. It was too close to call.

"Bernie? Are you all right?" Hawk called down to her when the bandits ceased fire to reload.

"My name is Shiloh," she confided with a seesaw breath.

The way she had it figured, she was going to be stuck in this crevice of this rocky ravine until buzzards came along to pick her clean. There was no way she could climb back to the ledge and no way for Hawk to reach her without endangering his own life. Plus, the bandits were hot on their trail and they would execute her when they found her.

"You need to know the right name to engrave on my headstone," she added defeatedly, then shooed him on his way. "Might as well go on without me."

Grimacing she shifted onto the hip she hadn't bruised during her fall, then tried to stretch her swollen ankle out in front of her. She glanced up to see Hawk's head appear from the shelf of rock above her.

"You aren't dead yet, *Shiloh*," he growled down at her. "You have too much spirit and resilience to adopt that defeated attitude."

She tried to bolster her flagging spirits, she really did. But when she glanced down, hopelessness engulfed her like a suffocating fog.

"Just sit tight."

She smirked. "I have a choice?" She gestured to the narrow cavity that held her like stone jaws, then winced when more gunfire erupted.

"I'm going after the horses and my lariat," he told her. "I'll be back for you."

Her last ray of hope died when darkness swallowed her up and the sky opened. The wind kicked up and the echoing sounds, reminiscent of howling phantom voices, swirled around her. She slumped against the unyielding boulder as rain pounded down.

She knew Hawk wouldn't come back for her because she was slowing him down. He could be up and over Ghost Ridge, hiding in the valley beyond, with his stolen loot, before the desperadoes could catch up with him.

Shiloh sighed heavily, battling the numerous aches and pains that pummeled her weary body. She resigned herself to the fact that she was stuck here, listening to the phantom voices wailing in the wind, waiting for the outlaws to arrive to put her out of her misery.

Chapter Four

Hawk scurried along the rain-slick path to retrieve his lariat and the horses. He cursed himself, harshly and repeatedly, for not taking better care of Shiloh. And he'd be damned, he was *not* engraving her name on a headstone, no matter how grim her future looked right now.

Hawk clutched the reins of his sure-footed mustang then tied a lead rope to Shiloh's mount. Her steed was reluctant, but the mustang forced it to follow—or be dragged.

Hawk patted the mustang's muscular neck. "Sorry, Dorado. We've been to hell and back together many times. This is just another tough day on a tough job."

The coal-black gelding nickered, as if in agreement, and methodically towed the skittish mare along behind him.

By the time Hawk reached the place where Shiloh had slipped and fallen, lightning was flickering from one low-hanging cloud to another. Hawk was able to make out the silhouettes of DeVol and Stiles as they picked their way around the boulders. Although they hadn't located the path, they were making headway and they posed a threat.

Feeling a sense of urgency Hawk turned his attention back to Shiloh who was wedged in the ravine below. *Your fault,* the voice of conscience scolded him as he secured the lariat to the saddle horn. This morning he had stumbled onto Shiloh, unintentionally forcing her to suffer through all sorts of perilous situations, the worst of which was a nasty fall down the rugged embankment. But she was wrong if she thought he was going to turn his back on her to save his own hide.

Thunder grumbled overhead, causing the mare to bolt sideways then slam into the stone wall. "Easy, girl," he soothed, then anchored the lead rope to a scrub bush.

Hawk clamped his hands around the dangling lariat then eased over the rough ledge. He cast a wary glance at the two outlaws that were trying to overtake him then worked his way down to the next shelf of rock. When lightning flickered on Shiloh's slumped form, he scrabbled north toward the crevice. His feet shot out from under him when he hit the slick mud at the base of a boulder. He grimaced when his shoulder slammed into the slab of stone.

Hawk steadied himself with the rope and gathered his feet beneath him. He inched along the narrow ledge until he was an arm's length from Shiloh. He nudged her shoulder, but she didn't respond.

Hawk sighed heavily. "Why can't just one thing be easy?"

His hard, unadorned life in the Apache camp in Sundance Canyon was a constant exercise in survival training. His experiences with the Rangers consisted of one dangerous foray following closely on the heels of another.

Maybe this is all there is to life, he mused as he reached out to hook his arm around Shiloh's limp body. With a heave-ho he scooped her from the V-shaped wedge between boulders. Maybe it was simply a man's lot in life to face one challenge after another and try to bury the unpleasant memories he encountered along the way.

His pessimistic thoughts scattered like buckshot the moment he levered Shiloh over his shoulder and felt her luscious feminine curves against his masculine contours. For some reason her weight seemed more of a comfort than a burden to him. Damn if he could figure out why.

When she moaned groggily and clung to him, as if he were a pillow she was trying to snuggle up against, his trying day—hell, who was he kidding?—his trying life—didn't seem so bad. Shiloh was warm and soft and cuddly…and he better not get sidetracked with these ridiculous whimsical thoughts. He still had a rugged hillside to scale and this was just a part of his job— rescuing folks from disastrous situations. Just because Shiloh's sassy disposition and feminine allure sparked an ill-fated fascination inside him didn't change a thing. He'd be every kind of fool if he let himself forget that.

Hawk clamped his arm across the back of Shiloh's thighs then shifted her on his shoulder so she wouldn't fall. Grabbing the rope anchored to the mustang that waited above him, he walked south along the narrow ledge, using the same route going up the hillside that he'd taken coming down.

He was one third of the way up the steep embankment when Shiloh regained consciousness. When she reared up, trying to get her bearings, Hawk clamped his arm tighter around her hips.

"It's just me," he reassured her hurriedly. "It will be a lot easier for me to negotiate this slope if you'll stay where you are and hang on to me."

"You came back for me." Her voice held a hint of wonder. "I expected you to be long gone by now," she said as she locked her arms around his waist.

"Just goes to show you how badly you misjudged me." He grunted as he pulled himself hand over hand to another stone slab. "Right now I'm the best friend you could have because I'm familiar with this area. I grew up here with my clan. I'll get you to a place that's dry and safe and then patch you up."

"Nice of you, since I wouldn't be in this shape if I hadn't run into you in the first place. Now here you are, dragging me all over creation."

Despite the jibe, Hawk detected the hint of wry humor and gratitude in her voice. She wanted him to think she was a foul-tempered shrew, but he had come to realize that beneath that prickly facade was a woman of character and personality. True, she didn't trust him—but he couldn't blame her for that. Also true, someone had hurt her deeply and she held every male on the planet responsible.

But who was he to criticize? For several years he had held all palefaces everywhere accountable for the tragic loss of his family and the only way of life he had ever known. Which was why taking refuge in Sundance Canyon was going to be as much of a blessing as it was a curse. He was familiar with the area that would always feel like home to him—but the place triggered too damn many haunting memories.

"Thank you for coming back for me," Shiloh murmured a moment later, then gave his ribs an appreciative squeeze.

A jolt of pleasure zapped him, but he valiantly tried to ignore it. "You're welcome. It's part of my job."

No matter how many hair-raising predicaments he and Shiloh encountered he wasn't going to become emotionally attached to her, he promised himself sensibly.

"Just hang on a little longer. We're almost to the ledge." He waited a beat then said, "I'm going to twist you around and plant my hands on your fanny so I can lift you over my head. Don't go getting indignant on me again. I don't want either of us to take a spill and give DeVol and Stiles a chance to do their worst."

"Is this an excuse to put your hands all over me again?" she asked suspiciously. "I already have as many of your handprints on me as I have bruises."

"Are you asking if I'm going to enjoy it?" He chuckled. "Probably. But it's the most practical method of getting you to safety. That's my first consideration."

"Right. All noble intent. How can I keep forgetting that," she mumbled against the taut tendons of his back.

"When I say go, you're going to twist and lunge in the same motion," he instructed. "You'll probably land hard, but I won't be in a position to be gentle with you while I'm dangling over the cliff and hanging on to this lifeline…. Ready?"

"As I'll ever be," she murmured.

He felt her tense in anticipation of being shoved onto the shelf of jagged stone. But to her credit she didn't wail in pain and give away their position to the pursuing bandits. He did hear her muffled gasp and moan and figured she had landed on her swollen ankle or bruised hip. But you had to admire a woman who was being put through hell and hadn't dissolved into whimpers and tears. Shiloh was the bravest, most adaptable women he'd ever encountered.

"Scoot back, Shiloh," he cautioned as he pulled himself upward. "I don't want to accidentally kick you when I come up and over this ledge in a hurry."

"I'm clear," she called out.

Gathering himself, Hawk surged upward, slinging his leg sideways so he could roll across the stone slab. He came to a stop, flat on his back. Shiloh hovered beside him. To his astonishment, she bent over and kissed him right smack-dab on the mouth. But her alluring taste, feel and scent was gone as quickly as a lightning strike, leaving him oddly disappointed.

And yet…he was relieved that the moment hadn't lasted very long. The very worst thing that could happen was for him to become addicted to the taste of a man-hating firebrand who was only going to be another footnote in his life, and in his career as a Texas Ranger.

"Thank you for saving my life," she murmured. "Maybe I can return the favor someday."

"Let's hope not." Hawk rolled over then stood up in one swift motion. "That would suggest I'd dragged you into another dangerous scrape. You've had too many of those, thanks to me."

"Well, it's better than being jilted and betrayed by a man who claimed to have tender feelings for you."

Shiloh clamped her mouth shut so fast she nearly bit off her runaway tongue. She hadn't meant to reveal that information, but she wasn't thinking straight. Which explained the impulsive kiss she'd bestowed on Hawk. She didn't know what possessed her, other than the fact that she was rattled, relieved to be back on solid footing and grateful to be alive.

It wasn't because she'd succumbed to the forbidden attraction she felt for him, she assured herself. Falling for this brawny tumbleweed of a man would never do. She had to remember not to depend or rely too heavily on Hawk. He was a man, capable of hurting her.

But maybe she could use him as a sounding board and confide what happened in Louisiana. She could test her ability to control her emotions during the telling of the humiliating incident to Hawk. She could rehearse now so she would be better prepared when she told her brothers what had sent her dashing home from New Orleans unannounced.

Given the emotional distress of this fiasco, and her multiple injuries, even Hawk might not think her weak and foolish if she broke down in tears.

Shiloh didn't protest when Hawk hoisted her to her feet, then sat her atop his mustang. She smiled in amusement when the horse slung its head sideways to pick up her scent. She was relieved the animal didn't take a bite out of her leg to show its disapproval.

"So you got jilted by a fool that didn't appreciate you," Hawk remarked as he grabbed the reins and started up the rain-drenched path, keeping his eyes peeled for the ever-present desperadoes. "Worse things have happened."

"Like this misadventure?" She smirked as she stared down at the waterlogged bandits that were sprawled on a boulder, struggling to regain their footing. "Like nearly drowning when a wild man and his horse practically landed on me in midstream while I was out of my protective disguise? Or are you referring to being shot in the arm because bloodthirsty outlaws are furious with *you?* Not to mention scraping the hide off my knees and hips and twisting my ankle when forced to go mountain climbing at night…in a rainstorm."

"Exactly. And I said I was sorry about all that."

"I'll have you know that getting your pride trampled, being lied to then carelessly discarded feels ten times worse than suffering a few strains, sprains and bruises," she contended. "When a man claims he has eyes only for you, while he's dallying with someone else, you learn your lesson well, believe me. Men want only two things from a woman."

"Two?" Hawk asked, amusement coloring his voice. "Where was I when these rules and regulations were passed out? I thought there was only one reason for needing a woman. I must've missed that part of my education while living in the Apache village."

His tone turned hard and clipped, startling her. "But in my defense, I was too busy trying to keep my clan from starving and dying because the army boxed us in the canyon for the winter and then killed as many of us as possible so we wouldn't cause an uprising when we were forcefully removed to reservations in New Mexico and Indian Territory."

Shiloh inwardly cringed at his comment. She felt petty and self-pitying in comparison to the trials and tribulations he'd faced. She was bitter about losing her heart to a man who found her unappealing and uninteresting, but Hawk had to deal with the extermination of his Apache family and way of life.

"I'm so sorry," she murmured. "In comparison, I have no reason to complain. But it still hurts to discover there is very little about yourself to like or admire. My brothers led me to believe otherwise. I should have realized they were too partial to exercise sound judgment.

"I went naively out into the world and discovered that Antoine Troudeau only *pretended* to like me… until someone with better social connections and a larger inheritance came along. Hearing that Antoine and Aimee Garland had been found together in her bedroom shortly after Antoine asked to contact *my* brothers so he could ask for *my* hand, was a devastating emotional blow. It also sent me running home with a lot more speed than dignity and common sense."

"Which is why you were paddling around in the river without a chaperone," he presumed as he weaved around the gigantic stone slabs that formed the peak of Ghost Ridge. "Understandable, even if it was a risk to your personal safety. But I guess I can't blame you for striking out alone. I also needed time alone to conquer my bitter thoughts after the army took my clan prisoner and herded us off like cattle."

"Were you allowed to go your own way when the soldiers learned that you were half-white?"

Hawk snorted derisively. "*Allowed?* Hardly. My brother and I escaped captivity with several other braves. Two of them were shot down the first day. Another friend died the third day from the wound he suffered. My brother, Fletcher, and I eventually took refuge with an old friend who advised us to change our appearance and split up so the army couldn't track us down easily. Fletch headed north and I went southwest."

"And you haven't seen your brother since? I can't imagine not seeing my brothers regularly, especially after we lost our parents in the fire that destroyed our original homestead. We needed mutual compassion and support to deal with our loss."

"Fletch and I made a pact to rendezvous two years later at Jackson Hole, where the trappers and traders camp."

She held her breath. "Did he show up?"

"Yes. He had taken a job scouting and riding shotgun for a stage line in Montana while I found the same kind of work in Arizona. Since then he has relocated in Colorado as a cattle detective and bounty hunter and I came back to Texas."

Shiloh was relieved that Hawk had *one* family connection left. No one deserved to be alone and isolated. Except maybe those ruthless cutthroats that were out for her and Hawk's blood.

"I presume the army is unfamiliar with your white name and that's why they've had difficulty tracking you down."

"That and the fact that our style of clothing and appearance has changed drastically the past decade." Hawk drew the horses to a halt. "This is where the trail becomes even more difficult. You'll have to dismount."

Shiloh eased from the saddle, grateful that Hawk was there to steady her on her good leg. The other one was throbbing in rhythm with her heartbeat.

The wind had picked up again, howling and whistling around the jagged precipice. Shiloh shivered uncontrollably in her damp clothes. These were the same unnerving sounds that echoed in her ears the instant before she stumbled off balance and fell into the ravine.

Hawk must have sensed her unease because he cuddled her closer rather than prop her against a boulder for support. She was beginning to realize that he wasn't a soulless outlaw. He might very well be an outlaw that seized every opportunity to make money, but he obviously had a smidgen of compassion and integrity.

"I'm going to take the horses over the ridge." Hawk stepped away, leaving her feeling cold and alone again. "Don't go wandering off while I'm gone and alert the bandits."

"Wouldn't dream of it." Shiloh glanced sideways, grateful that the darkness concealed the plunging depths of the canyon and granted her relief from her fear of height. "Please be careful. I promised to return the favor of saving your life, but I'm going to need time to recuperate. One bad leg and arm will seriously hamper my rescue skills."

He chuckled lightly. Then, to her complete surprise, he leaned down to kiss her cold lips. As before, when *she* had impulsively kissed *him,* she got just a quick sampling. But she dared not ask for more—for fear she'd like it too much.

That was definitely taboo for a woman who had recently sworn off men and vowed to form no emotional attachments.

"Why'd you do that?" she whispered curiously.

"That's in case the Great Spirit decides it's my time to follow the Ghost Path to rejoin my clan." He handed her one of his saddlebags. "If I don't make it back, there's enough pemmican and hoecakes to last you until your ankle heals and you can cross over to Sundance Canyon. The Ranger battalion is headquartered at an abandoned outpost eight miles from here."

When he turned away, Shiloh clutched the collar of his shirt and pulled him back. "I know I didn't put my best foot forward, but if we never see each other again, I'd like to die knowing that I'm not the worst possible match for a man." She peered earnestly at him, wishing her feminine pride wasn't pressing so hard when staying alive should be the only thought on her mind. "Even if I'm the last person you'd be interested in, Hawk, would I at least be worth consideration as a wife?"

He could hear the need for reassurance and acceptance in her voice and he wanted to strangle that French bastard that had shattered her self-esteem. "I'm not the marrying kind, but you'd be at the top of my list," he insisted. "You've got courage, spunk and spirit. Any man who doesn't appreciate those qualities in a woman can't be much of a man."

"Do you really think so?" she asked, her gaze searching his hopefully.

"I really think so...."

He cursed his lack of self-restraint when he impulsively angled his head to kiss her again, as if it were his right and his privilege—which it wasn't and it never would be.

Damn it, once he got started kissing her he couldn't seem to stop. What the devil was the matter with him? It was out of character for him to respond so recklessly to a woman, especially when faced with the arduous task of keeping them both alive. Willfully, he dragged his mouth away from hers before he did something insanely stupid—like help himself to a long, deep taste of those dewy-soft lips and crush her luscious body against his.

"Sit tight, Shiloh," he said, his voice raspy and disturbed—much to his dismay. "DeVol and Stiles won't find you here. I'll be back as soon as I can."

Hawk led the horses along the winding trail, chastising himself for taking another quick taste of Shiloh. Damn it, he kept breaking every hard-and-fast rule about remaining distant and detached during assignments. This had to stop right now! A moment earlier would have been even better.

Hawk forcefully tamped down the warm tingles of lusty pleasure pulsating through him. He concentrated on scaling the difficult section of the trail. Even his mustang turned skittish when the footing became difficult. The mustang balked and nearly jerked Hawk's arm from its socket in protest.

"This isn't the first time I've asked you to stick your neck out, Dorado," Hawk told the mustang. "I don't know what I'm going to do if you become as contrary as Shiloh."

The second time he tried to coax the mustang into bounding uphill, the wailing wind picked up. The jittery mare reared up then slammed into the mustang. Both animals shifted nervously beside him.

"Enough!" Hawk growled impatiently. He slapped Dorado on the rump, forcing him to bolt forward. The mare whinnied in fear when she was forced to follow the mustang. The horses collided with each other and struggled to regain their footing on the ledge above him.

Hawk muttered several salty oaths when the sky opened up and rain pounded down on him. He wondered what else could possibly go wrong with this escape from the vicious outlaws. But he wasn't sure he wanted to know. It might destroy what little enthusiasm he had mustered for the occasion.

In grim determination, Hawk climbed over the slabs of rock to regather the horses' reins. Together they scaled one angular stone slab after another.

A half hour later, Hawk stood on the summit that had felt like the top of the world when he was a child. From here, he had stared into the past and into the future, wishing for a better life. But no amount of Apache training had prepared him for the near extermination of his clan. No amount of consoling platitudes could make him forget how he had hated the whites for their butchery and treachery.

Hated that part of himself that was born white.

Furthermore, he had never forgiven his father for siring two sons and then riding off with a fortune in furs to buy himself a proper wife and a place in society, much like Antoine Troudeau had sought to do when he discarded Shiloh in search of a wealthier conquest.

Hawk's father, John Fletcher Logan, had *used* his Indian bride and his Apache connections to improve his financial status. Then he had abandoned the Apache people before the soldiers closed in around them and he never looked back.

A gust of cold wind slapped Hawk in the face, jostling him back to the present. This was not the time to dredge up hurt and resentment. It was dark. It was wet and cold and the footing was treacherous. One misstep and he'd be buzzard bait. Which would leave Shiloh alone to hobble over the stone crest, while dodging bandits intent on disposing of an eyewitness.

Gritting his teeth in anticipation of another battle with the horses, Hawk forged ahead. Sure enough, the animals set their feet stubbornly when he urged them to scrabble downhill into Sundance Canyon.

Exasperated, Hawk glanced skyward. "Can't at least one thing come easy tonight?"

Thunder boomed in the distance. Hawk was pretty sure that translated as *no.*

Shiloh didn't realize how attuned she'd become to her surroundings until she noticed Hawk's masculine silhouette outlined by a flash of lightning. She sagged in relief. At least she didn't have to contend with a hungry predator or those bloodthirsty bandits on this dark and stormy night.

"Are the horses all right?" she called out as Hawk approached.

"You mean other than being perturbed at me for forcing them to become mountain goats? Yeah. They are tucked out of the rain…and now it's your turn."

Shiloh pushed away from the boulder and balanced on her right leg. She gasped in surprise when Hawk swooped down to pick her up. "Absolutely not!" she protested, squirming in his arms. "I can walk…well, limp at least."

"I doubt you weigh more than a hundred pounds dripping wet," he insisted as he carried her up the trail. "You'll have to handle the difficult stretches of the path, but until then save your strength."

Shiloh resented the fact that she was forced to put her life in a man's hands. It went against the grain that she actually savored the security and comfort of being cradled against the solid wall of Hawk's chest. She shouldn't enjoy the feel of his sinewy arms encircling her.

Wasn't it just last week that she'd made a pact with herself to avoid physical and emotional contact with men? And here she was, depending on this brawny Apache knight to provide for and protect her.

But this is a rare exception, she convinced herself. She was weak and injured—in unfamiliar terrain and turbulent weather. She would have offered aid and comfort to Hawk if the situation were reversed. When she was functioning at full capacity again she would be self-reliant and independent. Until then—

"Time to prove what you're made of, Shi," Hawk challenged, breaking into her thoughts. He set her carefully on her feet, but wrapped his hand around her elbow for support. "I'll hoist you up beside me after I'm standing on the overhanging ledge."

Shiloh watched him lever himself up and over the angular slab of stone, then extend his hand to her. She reluctantly reached out to him—and broke her promise of never depending on a man again.

She grimaced as she braced herself on her injured arm and skinned knees, but she did what she had to do to drag herself onto the rough slab of rock. She drew in a fortifying breath and mentally prepared herself to repeat the process twice more. When Hawk slid one arm around her waist and the other beneath her knees, she didn't object.

Exertion made her light-headed. Worse, the blow to her skull caused bouts of nausea at unexpected moments—like now.

When she felt Hawk's heartbeat pounding against her shoulder she squirmed for release so he could catch his breath. "Want me to carry you awhile?" she teased.

"Yeah, don't know why I should have to do all the work," he said between gasping spurts of breath. "Just because your ankle is swollen twice its normal size is no excuse for slacking off." He tossed her a wry glance. "So tell me, how long do you plan to milk my sympathy? Until I have a stroke?"

"Yes. Then I will have repaid you for scaring two dozen years off my life and getting me into this predicament."

Shiloh was relieved to realize that, thanks to Hawk's teasing, she was regaining her playfulness and self-assurance. But of course, this wasn't the same as following proper protocol at a social ball. She'd felt ill equipped to play the role of a Southern aristocrat in New Orleans. Yet, here on the edge of nowhere, where only the basic rules of survival applied, she didn't have to be anyone except herself.

Hawk wasn't a sophisticated suitor trying to make a grand impression on her—or vice versa. He was the competent companion who accompanied her from one misadventure to the next. They didn't have the time or the need to put on airs. They had their hands full just trying to stay alive.

"Break's over," Hawk said before he scooped her up again.

Several minutes later Shiloh nearly squeezed the stuffing out of him in tense anxiety because he set her on her feet on the highest peak of Ghost Ridge. The wind buffeted her, threatening to launch her from her perilous perch. Dark though it was, she could see the spooky silhouettes of boulders that created eerie formations rising from the inky-black depths of the chasm. Her fear of height broadsided her and her heart leaped into triple time, making it difficult to breathe.

"I've got you," Hawk whispered against the side of her neck. As reassurance, he tightened his grip on her waist. "In daylight this is an awe-inspiring view because you can see for miles. It's little wonder that my people believe this is where the guardian spirits congregate to oversee the world."

"I'll take your word for it," she said, keeping her eyes squeezed shut. "Can we get on with this before I lose what nerve I have left?"

"Just so you know, Shi, you've impressed the hell out of me," he confided. "You've met every challenge like a trooper."

"Not that I've had a choice," she replied, begrudgingly pleased with his compliment. She forced herself to open her eyes and survey the dark precipice. "I appreciate the fact that you returned to rescue me. You're still a man, of course, and I'll continue to hold that against you," she added wryly, "But I'm willing to overlook that basic flaw. For now."

"You'll be cursing me in the next breath," he foretold. He gestured toward the drop-off that had unnerved the horses earlier. "You'll have to put faith in me and leap into my arms, Shiloh. There's no other way since you sprained your ankle."

Shiloh swallowed uneasily when she glanced down where he pointed. Her stomach dropped twelve feet.

"This isn't going to be one bit of fun," she said.

Chapter Five

⁂

Morton DeVol swore foully when he slipped on the slick boulder and his rifle went flying. Everett Stiles reached out to lend a hand and pulled him upright.

"How the hell did that redskin son of a bitch get those horses so far up that slope?" Morton wondered aloud. "I don't see him or the woman anywhere. Where'd they go?"

"Dunno," Everett muttered as he anchored himself to a scraggly tree. "But he must know a way out of this pile of rocks."

Morton braced his feet then swooped down to retrieve his rifle. "After we get back to camp and this rain lets up we're gonna scout around to see what's on the west side of this canyon. That Injun ain't gonna get away with our money and live to tell about it. Neither is that woman."

"You'll hear no complaints from me," Everett mumbled as he retraced the difficult route that led nowhere. "I was hopin' they'd both fall and save us some trouble. Guess not."

* * *

Forty-five minutes after Shiloh worked up the nerve to jump off the ledge and allow Hawk to catch her, he halted outside the cave tucked beside a tumble of monolithic boulders and scraggly junipers. This place had been a familiar haunt for Apache warriors that sought vision quests and communication with their guiding spirits.

Hawk had been through several initiation rituals at this site. He remembered the personal pride and sense of dedication he had experienced in those early years as a warrior.

But that had changed drastically, tragically, with the arrival of the army.

Deliberately, Hawk shook off the memories that transformed from good to bad. He grabbed his pistols from one of the saddlebags and focused on the dark entrance to the cavern. "Wait here. I'll make sure the cave isn't occupied by unfriendly varmints."

The moment he ducked inside the overhang, he heard a faint rustling noise that put his well-honed senses on full alert. He hunkered down so he wouldn't provide a large target then he inched toward the north wall where he had previously stockpiled torches, matches, campfire logs and eating utensils for emergency visits. Like this one.

Hawk groped for the box of matches, kept his trusty pistol handy, and then lit the torch. On full alert, he pointed his weapon toward the spot where he'd heard an unrecognizable noise. He tensed when he noticed the sprawled form lying beside the opposite wall.

A six-shooter was aimed right between his eyes.

"Damn, Hawk, am I ever glad to see you," came the low, panting voice. "I can't believe my luck."

Hawk was on his feet in a single bound, rushing toward his injured brother. "Fletch, what the hell are you doing in Texas?" He squatted down on his haunches then gestured toward the bloody wound on Fletcher's thigh. "Did you bring this with you from Colorado or pick it up when you got here?"

Fletcher grimaced as he propped himself against the wall. "I zigzagged the wrong way when I accidentally stumbled onto a gang of bandits, while I was tracking a fugitive into Texas," he rasped in obvious pain. "That was two days ago."

Hawk frowned worriedly as he examined the wound that was in need of a thorough cleansing and fresh bandages. Judging by Fletch's hollowed eyes and chalky pallor he was damn lucky to be alive.

"Hang on for a few more minutes," he murmured as he gave his brother a comforting pat on the shoulder. "We have a guest outside. An injured one. The woman's name is Shiloh."

"A woman?" Fletch choked out, eyes popping. "*Your* woman? You have a woman? When did this happen?"

"She isn't *my* woman and she is never going to be," Hawk insisted quickly. The prospect of romantic involvement between him and Shiloh went without saying. So why had he felt the need to deny it? he wondered.

"I only met her this morning," he elaborated. "I should warn you that some French dandy left her nursing a broken heart recently and she is intolerant and wary of all men."

Fletch sighed heavily. "Difficult to be on my best behavior for her benefit when my leg hurts like a son of a bitch. But I'll try not to offend her too much."

While Fletch made an effort to rearrange the tangle of black hair that drooped in his face, Hawk spun toward the exit. He needed to get Shiloh settled in for the night and take a closer look at Fletch's wound. If infection set in on either of his patients, it could be a long few days.

Hawk halted outside the cave to expel a long-suffering sigh. Shiloh, obviously impatient, had dismounted and balanced on her good leg. She had unfastened all the saddlebags and had them draped over her good shoulder.

"That took long enough," she said crankily. "Did you have to wrestle a bear for ownership of the cave? I don't think I could be any wetter than I am and my teeth are chattering to beat the band."

"And you're in a good mood, too, I see." Hawk teased as he scooped her into his arms and then reversed direction.

"Sorry. The cold and dampness is settling in every sore muscle and is burning every scraped inch of skin," she admitted. "A decent night's sleep should do wonders for my disposition."

Hawk carried her inside then watched his brother's stubbled jaw drop to his chest when he got his first look at Shiloh. She gaped in astonishment when she saw Fletch propped against the rock wall.

"Shiloh, this is my brother, Fletcher Hawk." He set her carefully on her feet. "As you might have guessed, this is where the Hawks come to roost when they're in trouble."

Shiloh nodded a silent greeting to the brawny man who looked to be suffering from his injury. He was about as pale as a bronze-skinned man could get and the stubble on his jaws was as thick as Hawk's. Although the family resemblance was obvious, Fletch's eyes were blue. His shoulders were as broad as Hawk's and his legs as long and muscular. He also wore a dark shirt and breeches like his brother.

"What happened to you?" she asked as she limped forward.

"I ran into a nest of outlaws." Fletch absently rubbed his injured leg. "I took two of them down and kept them there. I winged another one, but the two survivors got away. Not before plugging me in the leg." He frowned in annoyance as he stared at his wound. "I must be losing my touch, Hawk. Four to one odds were never a problem before."

"You're getting older," Hawk taunted playfully as he dumped the saddlebags in the corner. "You have to take that into account."

"Old? Hell…er…heck. Pardon, ma'am," he said as he darted Shiloh a quick glance then stared at his brother. "I'm two years younger than you."

"Yes, but you were *born* old," Hawk teased.

Fletcher's ashen face puckered in a mock scowl. "Don't know why I'm so glad to see you. You always were a nuisance."

"Don't know why I'm glad to see you, either, *pest.*"

Shiloh smiled at the teasing exchange followed by affectionate smiles. It granted her insight into the man that had held himself at an emotional distance most of the day. Rough and tough though Hawk was, he was still capable of affection—for his brother, at least.

The interaction reminded her of the camaraderie that existed between her and her big brothers. They had delighted in tormenting her, too… Until their parents died and her brothers convinced themselves they were responsible for protecting her. It was then that they focused on teaching her dignified manners and frowned on her hoydenish ways.

Then they sent her off to New Orleans with instructions to snag herself a sophisticated husband among the Southern gentry. If they hadn't had her best interest at heart, she'd have clubbed them over the head for trying to make her a proper lady. It would never happen. She'd discovered women in proper society were denied the freedom she thrived on.

"I'll bring in the rest of our belongings," Hawk volunteered. "Shiloh, will you build a fire?"

She shivered from the chill. "With pleasure."

Hawk grabbed the matchbox and an armload of logs then dropped them near the entrance. When he disappeared from sight, Shiloh stacked the logs as her brothers had taught her.

"That's not the Apache way," Fletch commented. "Palefaces don't know beans about smokeless fires that don't attract unwanted attention. Spread out the logs a bit, Shiloh, and arrange them in a circular fashion."

"And naturally the *Apache* way is the *right* way," she countered, tossing him an impish grin.

He returned her smile. "It is, if you don't want the cavern to fill up with smoke and force us out into the rain."

Shiloh took his suggestion and rearranged the logs. To her amazement the fire burned clean, giving off little smoke.

"Where are you from, Shiloh?" Fletch asked as he massaged his injured leg.

"She won't say," Hawk answered for her as he entered, laden down like a pack mule. "She's afraid I'll ferret out her last name and hold her for ransom."

"Smart woman." Fletch tossed her an approving

smile. "It's nice to finally meet a female who has enough sense to keep her mouth shut occasionally."

"She's skeptical and cautious because she thinks I'm part of the outlaw gang I infiltrated three months ago," Hawk elaborated. "Even when I flashed my badge she didn't believe me. She thought I had stolen it, along with this…."

He fished into the saddlebags to retrieve the stacks of bank notes. Fletch's eyes widened in astonishment.

"When I made off with the bandits' loot, Shiloh presumed I took it for personal gain."

"Considering our mixed heritage, what else would you think?" Fletch focused his resentful gaze on Shiloh.

"Now wait just a blasted minute!" Shiloh snapped as she lurched toward Fletcher. Pain and weariness made her irritable and sensitive. "As I told your brother, it isn't his heritage that makes me wary. It's being male. But after he saved my life a couple of times I *have* revised my low opinion of him. Somewhat, at least. But just because you're brothers doesn't mean I'll take your word. I'd expect you to vouch for him."

"Well, at least I've been forgiven for the nearly unpardonable sin of being born a man." Hawk snapped out the padded bedroll, then gestured for Shiloh to make use of it.

She shook her head. "Fletcher needs the added comfort of soft bedding more than I do."

Offended, Fletch glared at her. "And let a woman sleep on the rock floor? Hawk and I might not have been taught the polished manners of white aristocrats, but we sure as hell—heck know better than that!"

Although the thought of sleeping on bedrock made her cringe, Shiloh knew Fletch was in worse condition.

Grabbing the unlit torch to serve as her cane, Shiloh snatched up the bedroll then hobbled over to Fletcher. She shook out the padded pallet then stabbed her finger at it.

"Don't argue with me," she said in a no-nonsense tone. "Hawk can attest that I'm a grouchy shrew. You don't want me to harp at you the whole livelong night, I assure you."

Hawk chuckled when she skewered her face into a witchlike scowl. "Meanest damn female I ever met," he said, giving his brother a wink and a grin. "Almost as mean as me, in fact. Better not tick her off if you know what's good for you."

"Well, if you insist." Fletch's breath sighed out appreciatively as he settled on the soft pallet and propped his head on the saddle.

"I'd give a month's wages for some whiskey," Fletch murmured. "Damn outlaws stole my bottle, my rifle and my horse. The bottle and rifle can be replaced, but my horse is like a personal friend and I take serious offense to that."

Hawk's smile faded and he stared grimly at his ailing brother. "Did you remove the bullet?"

Fletch shook his head. "I tried, but the pain kept making me pass out before I could dig deep enough."

Shiloh watched Hawk grab his dagger, then hold it over the campfire. He set it aside to fish out the whiskey then handed it to Fletch. Although she had been reluctantly impressed with Hawk's skills and abilities in the wilderness, her admiration doubled while she watched him prepare to perform primitive surgery. By all indication, this wasn't the first time he'd dug out a bullet.

Wanting to help, Shiloh limped over to sink down gingerly beside Hawk.

"Go away, woman," Fletch demanded tersely. "You don't need to see a grown man cry or hear him scream."

"Nonsense, I *live* to see men in agony." She handed him a twig to bite down on. "Get on with it, Hawk. This should be the most fun I've had all day."

Fletch grabbed the whiskey and took another guzzling swallow, then he thrust the bottle at Shiloh. "Pour this over the wound and I'll scream bloody murder. Guaran-damn-teed."

Shiloh glanced at Hawk, who nodded grimly. When she dribbled whiskey on the angry red wound that Hawk exposed by ripping the seam of the breeches, perspiration popped out on Fletch's forehead. The color seeped from his face. Shiloh took pity on him and offered him another drink, which he readily accepted.

"If foul language offends you, close your ears," Hawk suggested as he tore open another portion of his brother's breeches to grant better access to the wound. "There are no curse words in the Apache dialect. But Fletch learned plenty of them in English."

"Curse away," Shiloh invited as she patted Fletch's rigid shoulder. "Whatever gets you through the surgery. My delicate sensibilities aren't all that delicate. Compared to the genteel ladies in New Orleans I'm a hoyden."

Although Shiloh began feeling light-headed the moment Hawk probed for the bullet, she told herself that exhaustion and her own injuries were responsible. But no matter how faint she felt, she was going to be right here to aid Hawk and console Fletch while he moaned, swore foully, and then passed out so Hawk could stitch him back together.

Sighing heavily, Hawk sank down cross-legged and watched Shiloh apply the poultice then bandage

Fletch's leg. He gave her high marks for assisting him, even when he could tell that she had come close to passing out herself a time or two. She had also teased Fletch playfully and put him at ease before the surgery began.

This is one hell of a woman, he mused as he watched her brush her palm over Fletch's clammy forehead to check for fever. Hawk didn't want to like her and admire her, but he did. He didn't want to desire her, either, but his traitorous body reacted each time they touched.

With all that was going on around him, that was not a complication he wanted to contend with. He kept telling himself that he was reacting to her because he'd been a long time without a woman. He almost had himself convinced. Almost.

"Do you think your brother happened onto one of the outlaw factions that you *claim* the Rangers are trying to apprehend?" she asked.

The jolt from staring into those thick-lashed green eyes nearly stole his breath. His gaze dropped to her lush lips. And damn it, he wanted to kiss her so badly that his insides twisted into tight knots.

What was wrong with him? He usually had more willpower and didn't give women much thought except in the heat of a passionate moment. But he'd spent numerous hours with Shiloh, seeing her at her best, worst and every mood in between. She affected him, got to him—like it or not. Which he didn't.

Scowling at his sudden lack of common sense and the warm flood of sensations prowling through him, Hawk surged to his feet. "Yes, I suspect Fletch stumbled onto part of the crime syndicate that has been plundering this area of Texas. Hopefully, he can identify the two men who got away." He reached down to draw Shiloh to her feet. "Now, let's have a look at your ankle and arm so you can get some shut-eye."

To his disbelief, Shiloh pushed on tiptoe to plant a kiss on his lips. It was another hit-and-run kind of kiss that granted him just enough of a taste to drive him crazy.

"Thank you for getting us to safety," she murmured.

He frowned disconcertedly at her as he backed away. "You need to stop doing that."

The look of rejection and embarrassment that flooded her enchanting face left Hawk cursing himself up one side and down the other. That was a thoughtless remark, considering her recent bout with unrequited love. She was stepping from behind her cautious shell and his self-preservation instincts had him snapping at her. He wished he could remain unaffected by her.

"I like it too damn much," he felt compelled to admit. "*I* might turn into a threat to you if you don't watch out. You tempt me and you need to understand that. Don't push your luck."

She angled her head to study him for a contemplative moment. "You're just trying to make me feel better about myself, aren't you?"

"Just back off before I do something I'll regret and you despise me for it. I want us to walk away as friends when this is over."

It was killing him the way she stood there balancing on her good leg, searching his gaze and his expression, trying to figure him out. Damn it, he really wanted to wring that bastard's neck for making her so wary of anything a man said to her.

Another poignant moment passed while she stared at him and he battled the urge to *really* kiss her, to satisfy this maddening craving he wished he didn't feel for her.

"I've been a cynical termagant most of the day and I still tempt you? Ha!" She smirked. "I look like something the cat dragged in from the rain."

He managed a grin. "Amazing, isn't it? There's just no accounting for some men's tastes."

A faint smile pursed her lips, making her eyes sparkle. Lust sucker punched him again. He needed to stay away from her. But he also needed to treat her wounds. He was stuck with touching her, breathing her scent, until he completed the necessary tasks. Damn, this really was his unlucky day.

"My family owns a ranch north of here. It sits on the banks of Echo River," she confided unexpectedly. "My brothers are Gideon and Noah Drummond. Gid is about your age and Noah is a year younger than Fletch. They have smothered me and tried to overprotect me since our parents died when I was ten.

"Frank Mills, the rancher we believe is responsible for hiring the gunslinger that impersonated a Ranger, is our nearest neighbor," she went on to say. "Which is another reason Noah and Gid packed me off to Louisiana to stay with my aunt and cousin. Frank expressed an interest in courting me last summer and my brothers wanted nothing to do with Frank."

The thought of that conniving rancher putting his hands on Shiloh had Hawk swearing under his breath.

"Of course, Noah and Gideon didn't have to discourage me. Frank Mills is pompous and overbearing. I would never consider his marriage proposal. I have decided to become a spinster so any proposal would be wasted on me." She smiled wryly. "I might even *enjoy* carrying the reputation of the meanest female you ever met."

That impish grin just about did him in—again. Hawk reared back the instant he felt himself leaning impulsively toward her. "Make yourself comfortable, hellion," he said as he rose from his crouch. "I'll tend the horses."

She looked around. "Where are you going to sleep, Hawk?"

His gaze dropped to the empty space beside her. Desire hit him right between the eyes—and straight south of his belt buckle.

"I'll bed down by the mouth of the cave, in case unwanted visitors show up," he said, clearing his throat.

Wheeling around, Hawk walked outside to blow out his breath. He felt edgy, restless and he was battling another half-dozen emotions that he didn't dare identify. He'd been a hell of a lot better off when Shiloh purposely needled him and was outwardly suspicious of his motives. Now she was offering the basic rudiments of friendship and he wasn't sure he could be satisfied with that. Not when he was hard and needy— which had become his typical response to her.

Plus, he had his brother to worry about now. Fletch needed medical attention. And what the devil was Fletch doing in Texas anyway? True, bounty hunting occasionally took him out of Colorado, but Fletch was careful not to be seen too often with Hawk, for fear someone might identify them as the missing Apache renegades who had disappeared from the reservation a decade ago. Surely by now that wouldn't be a concern. He hoped.

Hawk didn't know if they still had prices on their heads in New Mexico, but he wasn't planning to cross the border to find out. He was satisfied where he was—living and working in the shadow of Ghost Ridge—the only home he'd ever known.

By the time Hawk reentered the cavern Shiloh had shed her damp clothes and snuggled beneath the quilt. Fletch was out cold. The whiskey he'd consumed to counter the pain would keep him sedated until morning, Hawk predicted.

Hawk sprawled out by the campfire, using a saddlebag for his pillow. His clothes were damp. His body was on fire because forbidden visions of Shiloh kept chasing each other around his head. If the guardian spirits were smiling kindly at him, he would get a good night's sleep.

Thankfully, he dozed off a few minutes later. But the memory of Shiloh's curvaceous body molded intimately to his, much as it had been while they were rolling through the reeds to dodge bullets by the river, filled his mind.

Luckily, in this erotic fantasy there were no flying bullets....

And Shiloh wasn't wearing a stitch of clothing....

His eyes popped open in middream. Hawk ruthlessly tamped down his body's fierce reaction to the forbidden fantasy.

But it still turned out to be a long, hard night.

Chapter Six

At dawn, Shiloh levered herself onto her elbow and scraped the wild tangle of auburn hair from her face. She glanced around then stared at the dim light filtering into the entrance. The fire had died during the night, leaving a chill.

Her focus shifted to the exit. Hawk was up and gone. Fletcher was sprawled on the pallet, oblivious to the world.

Shiloh smiled faintly, recalling last night's conversation with Hawk. She shouldn't care that he admitted he wasn't completely immune to her. Nevertheless, it did please her immensely. His begrudging confession restored a smidgen of her feminine pride and self-esteem.

Of course, only a naive fool would make more of Hawk's comment than he actually meant, she cautioned herself. Close proximity accounted for his supposed attraction to her. If she incited his lust, it was only because she was female. It wasn't personal and she wasn't going to let it get more personal than a few experimental kisses, either.

She had no intention of trying to charm Hawk. Not that she was very good at it. In comparison to Cousin Bernice and her friends in New Orleans, Shiloh was ashamedly outclassed when it came to luring a man beneath her spell.

Besides, Shiloh wasn't sure what she felt *for* him, felt *about* him. Gratitude? Certainly. She would be dead and gone if not for his daring rescues. Friendship? Yes…and no. She had tried to regard him as a brother, but that didn't feel right, either. Then he had kissed her and they had taken turns planting swift kisses on each other's lips—after a series of narrow escapes that had her blood pumping and her heart pounding. Then Hawk had called a halt, just when she was beginning to feel comfortable with the sensations he stirred in her, comfortable initiating physical contact with him.

Shiloh shook her head, bewildered by the riptide feelings surging through her. She couldn't believe she was actually disappointed to hear Hawk say they should dispense with kissing and hugging.

What was the matter with her? She should be relieved… Shouldn't she? Of course, she should.

Her befuddled thoughts trailed off when Fletch moaned, then rolled onto his side. "Aw, damn, my leg feels like it's on fire," he said to no one in particular.

Shiloh modestly grabbed her clothes and hurriedly dressed beneath the concealing quilt. She hopped over to unfasten the bandage on Fletch's thigh. Sure enough, the wound was still angry red and swollen.

"Not good, huh?" Fletch said hoarsely. He propped himself up to survey his leg. "Damn, it looks as bad as it feels."

"I'm sure Hawk is gathering ingredients for a curative," she said, striving for an encouraging tone.

"Or contemplating amputation," Fletch muttered dismally. His face etched with pain, he propped his back against the wall then tried to shift his leg. "Son of a b—" He clamped his mouth shut. "I think *dead* might feel better than this."

"Probably so. But where is the fun in that?" Shiloh offered him a sip from the canteen. "Would you like to nibble on pemmican or hoecakes?"

Fletch shook his shaggy head then grabbed his pistol when muffled noises near the cave entrance caught his attention. When Hawk appeared, Fletch sagged in relief. "I hope you found a miracle poultice. I could use one right about now."

Hawk set the rabbit he'd snared and dressed beside the ashes of the campfire. "As a matter of fact, yes." He directed Shiloh and Fletch's attention to the cactus roots, horehound stems, wild peppermint, willow leaves and mesquite tree sap. "One miracle cure coming right up."

"Grandfather would be proud," Fletch murmured as he absently rubbed his aching leg. "But I'm not sure even he had a remedy to counteract this kind of infection."

Hawk hurried over to inspect the wound. Obviously he didn't like what he saw, either, because he frowned in concern. "As soon as I get the rabbit roasting on the fire and make coffee we'll tend your leg."

He turned his attention to Shiloh. "Spirit Springs is a warm water basin down the hill. Even with the drizzling rain, it's still refreshing. I tried it out earlier. You can bathe there if you like."

Shiloh wanted to hug the stuffing out of him for the considerate offer. Then she reminded herself that she was going to keep her distance. She wasn't interested in unattainable men like Antoine or Hawk. She wasn't interested in any physical or emotional contact with any man these days, she promptly reminded herself.

"That sounds wonderful." She came awkwardly to her feet to balance on her makeshift cane. "I'll get the fire going while you mix up your concoction, witch doctor."

Shiloh noted that Hawk was all business this morning. No ornery teasing. No wry smiles. He cast her impersonal glances and made impersonal comments while tending to his duties.

She *wasn't* disappointed, she told herself. Why should she be? This is what she wanted, too. She had to learn to ignore the whisper of her reckless heart and her body's reactions.

After the campfire flared to life, Shiloh skewered the meat and put it on to cook. Hawk combined ingredients in the small wooden bowl he'd rooted from his saddlebag. He had obviously inherited the tools of his grandfather's trade. She wondered if Fletch practiced Apache medicine—when he wasn't the injured patient. Probably.

Several minutes later Hawk set aside the bowl of ingredients and came to his feet. "Ready, Shi?"

When she nodded eagerly, he scooped her up then carried her outside. She sat stiffly in his arms, thinking of anything except the clean scent of him, the feel of his muscled arms encircling her as he carried her downhill.

He set her on her feet then laid a pistol beside the hollowed out limestone basin where steamy water formed an inviting pool. "Fire off a signal at the first sign of trouble," he instructed. "I'll give you an hour to bathe. More, if that's what you want."

"Thank you." She sighed appreciatively and stared at the bubbly pool as if it were heaven. "I'll be here until I shrivel up like a prune. I can't remember wanting anything more than a good, warm soaking."

"*I* can," he mumbled before he pivoted on his heels and left her to her bath.

Shiloh enjoyed her leisurely bath, despite another downpour. The steamy pool relieved her aches and pains and the solitude was most welcome. She tested her bruised pride and was startled to discover that the unrequited affection she thought she'd felt for Antoine wasn't as poignant as it had been the first two days after she fled from New Orleans.

My, wasn't that amazing, she mused as she submerged in the pool to avoid another cold rain shower. No doubt, the arduous task of staying alive had overridden the memories of finding Antoine in a compromising situation—in the boudoir assigned to Aimee Garland, the daughter of one of New Orleans's wealthiest merchants.

"Shiloh!"

Her thoughts evaporated when Hawk called out to her. Shiloh paddled across the pool to retrieve the clean clothes from her carpetbag. "Give me a moment, please."

Exasperated with the constant rain, Shiloh muttered at the fact that she couldn't stay dry for more than five minutes. Living in the wilds was certainly a challenge. Out here in the back of the beyond, all the simple conveniences that she had taken for granted at home were luxuries.

"Ready or not, I'm coming down," Hawk announced.

She finished buttoning her blouse as he veered around a slab of stone that was three times as wide and twice as tall as he was. He stopped short, looked her up and down, and then glanced the other way.

His behavior confused Shiloh. He had told her that she tempted him—simply because she was female and available, no doubt. Yet, he refused to make eye contact with her for more than a few seconds. His behavior was so unlike Antoine's and the other Southern gentlemen that she'd met at the palatial balls that she didn't know what to make of it. Despite what Hawk had said last night, she didn't think he could be more disinterested in her than he was now. The demoralizing thought hammered at her feminine pride.

"C'mon," Hawk said impatiently as he swung her up into his arms to take pressure off her swollen ankle. "I need you to help me cauterize Fletch's wound before we feed him breakfast. The infection worries me and the poultice I mixed up will need time to take effect. I don't think Fletch has much time before gangrene sets in."

Shiloh braced her arms around Hawk's neck as he followed the winding trail to higher elevations. She told herself that the shivers assailing her were the result of the chilling rain, not the feel of Hawk's masculine chest and washboard belly brushing rhythmically against her ribs and hip.

Then she made the mistake of recalling the impulsive kisses they had shared. Unwanted warmth spread through her body like a flash flood. Blast it, what was there about Hawk that triggered such spontaneous reactions? He didn't seem the least bit affected by her. His jaw was clenched as he made the climb with her cradled in his arms. His gaze remained straight ahead, watching where he stepped so he wouldn't trip and send them both sprawling.

She was simply another responsibility, a part of his job. That realization did nothing for her feminine pride, either.

By the time Hawk set Shiloh on her feet and handed her the new cane he had made from a small cedar tree he was more than ready to get her out of his arms. Damn it, for a man who had spent years practicing self-discipline and cautious restraint he still had one hell of a time remaining immune to the sight of Shiloh's damp clothes clinging to her curvaceous figure. He'd taken one look at her while she stood beside the pool and poof! He'd gotten hot and bothered in nothing flat. Pretending she didn't affect him was an exercise in self-control. One of too many exercises already.

Hawk knew his interest in Shiloh was ill-advised. He was on a personal and professional crusade. Once they reached the Ranger camp she wouldn't be his responsibility and he'd have no future contact with her. One of his coworkers could deliver her home. He had a job to do—and he couldn't do it when he was constantly distracted by this fascinating female, who probably wouldn't have given him a second glance if fate hadn't tossed them together and left them living in each other's pockets.

Murmuring a quiet thank-you, Shiloh tried out her new cedar cane. She limped toward Fletch who had propped his shoulder against the stone wall to hold himself upright. He still looked pale and gaunt, but he managed a smile of greeting. Shiloh asked herself how two men—who looked so much alike, who were both the picture of rugged masculinity—could set off two drastically different reactions in her.

She looked at Fletch and felt something akin to brotherly concern. Yet, when she looked into Hawk's midnight-black eyes and stared too long at his full, sensuous lips, forbidden desire rippled through her.

Frustrated, Shiloh tried to shrug off the sensations and focus on the upcoming task of cauterizing the wound. She felt Fletch's forehead and found him a bit warmer than normal, but not as hot and clammy as he'd been the previous night.

"Are you sure you want to watch this procedure?" Fletch asked as he massaged his aching leg.

"Sure, torturing a man is one of my favorite things," she teased saucily. "I do so love to see men suffer, you know."

Fletch chuckled as he glanced at his brother. "Not much sympathy forthcoming from this lady." His expression sobered as he focused on his festered leg. "Might as well get on with it, I guess."

"You know I really don't wish any misery on you, don't you?" Shiloh murmured when Hawk strode off to sterilize his blade. "I'm as eager for you to be back on your feet as I am to be there myself."

He nodded and smiled wryly. "All the same, better *you* than *me* under the knife. Too bad we can't switch places."

Shiloh knew Fletch was trying to keep the conversation light, even though he was dreading the inevitable pain. She looped her arm around his rigid shoulder to give him a comforting pat.

"What brought you back to Texas, Fletch?" she questioned as a means of distraction.

"An assignment gone bad." He turned his head to meet her gaze directly. He made Shiloh his absolute focus when Hawk sank down with glowing knife in hand. "I also needed time away from my job. Plus, I wanted to visit my brother again…. Ouch! Damn it, that hurts!" His roar echoed around the cavern when hot steel seared his tender flesh.

"Keep it down," Hawk cautioned. "There are outlaws lurking about. We don't need unwanted guests right now."

Shiloh winced when Fletch grabbed hold of her unexpectedly, as if he needed something to squeeze while Hawk cauterized the festering wound. His arms clamped onto her like a vice. She wrapped both arms around him as he tucked his head against the side of her neck and swore ripely—but quietly. She could feel beads of perspiration forming on his forehead and upper lip. She could smell smoldering flesh.

Fletch's body shook and he cursed several more blue streaks—most of them directed at Hawk. Then Fletch nearly came unglued when Hawk dribbled whiskey over the wound. Fletch bit down on his bottom lip until it bled, then huffed and puffed for breath.

"Sorry, little brother," Hawk murmured. "Now, tell me about this assignment gone bad. Anything I can do to help?"

"Yeah," Fletch said with panted breaths. "Help me track down my double-dealing ex-assistant who tried to have me assassinated before he made off with my bounty money."

"You must not be any better at selecting assistants than I am at selecting beaus," Shiloh commented.

"Apparently not. That's the first and last time I plan to work with a partner, unless it's with Hawk," Fletch said hoarsely. "He's the only man I trust not to betray me. I followed my ex-partner to Texas because he once mentioned he had family near Cerrogordo. I figured that would be a good place to start my search."

"What's his name?" Shiloh asked as she clutched Fletch's trembling hand in her own. "Maybe I've heard of the family."

"Grady Mills."

Shiloh's suspicious gaze locked with Hawk's. "Small world," she murmured.

"Ain't it, though," Hawk agreed. "Makes me wonder if Frank Mills's previous run-in with the law is hereditary. He and Grady might share the same crucial character flaws."

"If Grady is as unscrupulous as Frank, it's a wonder you didn't end up with a bullet in your back," Shiloh told Fletch as she offered him a sip of water.

"Damn near did," Fletch muttered. "It wasn't from Grady's lack of trying. That traitorous bastard is going to spend a few years behind bars…or take up permanent residence at the cemetery. His choice."

"I wonder if Frank has a connection to the gangs that are preying on folks in this part of Texas," Shiloh remarked while Hawk smoothed the fresh poultice over Fletch's thigh.

"You read my mind," Hawk murmured.

She wished she could. She wanted to know if Hawk was assailed by the same kind of thrilling sensations she experienced when they touched. And, bad idea though she knew it was, she would like to have a larger sampling of his kisses—ones that lasted long enough to determine if the pleasure she sensed awaited her was real or imagined.

No, you don't want to know that! the sensible voice inside her head shouted. *He has heartbreak written all over him, same as Antoine does. Don't be a glutton for punishment.*

While Hawk and Fletch spoke quietly, Shiloh removed the juicy meat from the fire. She glanced back at the two men, exasperated that her gaze went magnetically to Hawk. When he glanced in her direction, she averted her gaze and wished she could fly home with great haste. Back to her familiar world and to her brothers. Away from this compelling attraction that was headed nowhere.

Two days later, while Hawk was hunting food, scouting for trouble and gathering more herbs for his curatives, Shiloh played nursemaid to Fletch.

"So…have you realized yet that Hawk isn't the thieving mercenary you first thought he was?"

Shiloh stared pointedly at the stack of stolen money in the corner. The exasperating truth was that Shiloh had wanted to think the worst about Hawk because, right from the start, she found herself liking him a little too much. If that made sense. Unfortunately, it made perfect sense to her. Doubting his integrity was another method of protecting her wounded heart. After her humiliating ordeal with Antoine, the last thing she needed was to find herself intrigued by the first man who crossed her path. Unfortunately, Logan Hawk was as unattainable and wrong for her as any man could get. If she had any sense, she wouldn't let herself forget that.

"I'm willing to concede that he probably is a Ranger," she said belatedly.

"Damn right he is," Fletch insisted. "I'd be a Texas Ranger, too, if not for past complications—"

"Which he told me about." She came to her feet to balance on her improvised cane.

Fletch's stubbled jaw dropped open and his blue eyes popped. "He told you about our past?"

She nodded. "He confided that you two sneaked from the reservation.... And I'm very sorry that you had to split up indefinitely to avoid capture."

Fletch braced himself on his elbow then struggled to his feet to test his tender leg. "It's been long enough now that I'm hoping to join Hawk's battalion, no questions asked. I'm as anxious to track down the men responsible for killing our mentor and friend as Hawk is." His troubled gaze swung to the mouth of the cave, as if he were staring through the doorway of the past. "There's nothing left to hold me in Colorado or New Mexico now. I plan to remain in Texas indefinitely. This is our childhood home, bittersweet memories and all."

"Well, look who finally decided to get up."

Shiloh started at the sound of Hawk's deep baritone voice rolling toward her. The man moved like a shadow. Which, considering his profession, was probably a good thing.

"I'm ready to test my leg and get some fresh air," Fletcher announced. "After being cooped up for so many days, I have a severe case of cabin fever."

Shiloh felt the same way. She was going stir-crazy and having Hawk underfoot wasn't helping.

"I'm hoping to leave here shortly before dark," Hawk announced as he watched his brother lean heavily on his makeshift crutch. "The outlaw gang left the east canyon and my instincts tell me that's not a good thing. We need to get moving, but if you aren't up for a downhill hike we can hold out until tomorrow night."

Shiloh cringed at the thought of being chased by those vicious ruffians again. In their presence, being a woman didn't afford her any special privileges—and she had a mending wound on her arm to prove it.

Fletch forced an enthusiastic smile that Shiloh doubted he felt. "I feel a dozen times better than I did when I dragged myself up here. I'll be ready at dark."

"I think I'll take advantage of the warm springs once more before we leave," Shiloh murmured when she realized her betraying gaze had settled on Hawk's broad chest and horseman's thighs—again.

Braced on her cane, Shiloh limped from the cave, resigned to the cold drizzle that settled over Sundance Canyon, battling her star-crossed infatuation for a man who, after tomorrow, she probably wouldn't see again.

Chapter Seven

"A penny for your thoughts, big brother."

Hawk snapped to attention when he realized his gaze had followed Shiloh until she disappeared from sight. One more day, he silently chanted. She would be out from underfoot and he wouldn't be fighting this constant distraction.

"Okay, a nickel," Fletch upped the ante when Hawk didn't respond immediately.

"I'm anxious to rejoin my company and get back to the business of tracking these outlaw factions so we can locate the clever mastermind," Hawk replied belatedly. "Which should lead me to information that might also point me in the direction of the men responsible for killing Archie Pearson."

A knowing smile quirked Fletch's lips as he limped around the cave to work the kinks from his stiff body. "Not to mention the relief of getting a certain green-eyed spitfire out of sight and out of mind. Or will it be a disappointment rather than a relief to have Shiloh gone?"

Hawk scowled and said nothing as he poured himself a cup of coffee.

"Admit it," Fletch challenged. "Shiloh piqued your interest. Of course, a man would have to be dead a week not to react to a woman with her beauty and spirit." He waggled his eyebrows suggestively. "Maybe I'll look her up after I have two good legs under me so I can court her properly."

"No, you won't." Hawk shot to his feet to halt his brother's stiff-legged stroll around the cave. "She's on the rebound because some silver-tongued Frenchman took advantage of her in New Orleans. She's lost faith in men and isn't going to trust another man until she learns to trust her own instincts again. She needs time to recover. She doesn't need you, me, or any other man pursuing her right now."

"Or maybe she needs a man to prove to her that some of us are more loyal and reliable than others," Fletch countered. "Sometimes the best way for a woman to forget the treachery of one man is to snuggle up in the arms of another man. Believe it or not, I can be a very comforting soul when I try."

Hawk was ready to go for his brother's throat… until he noticed Fletch's wry grin and realized he was purposely baiting him.

"It's obvious to me that you're attracted to her," Fletch said as he detoured around Hawk. "I think you're both trying a little *too* hard to ignore the sparks you set off in each other. Stop fighting the feeling."

"Stop trying to put stupid ideas in my head," Hawk grumbled. "We don't have a damn thing in common and society would frown on any connection between us." He stared meaningfully at his brother. "Do I need to remind you that most whites have an aversion to our mixed heritage?"

The wry smile on Fletch's weather-beaten features

turned upside down. Hawk wasn't sure, but he suspected his brother had faced a similar situation in the recent past.

"Who was she, Fletch?" Hawk questioned perceptively.

It was Fletch's turn to scowl and glance the other way. "Doesn't matter anymore. Elaina and I were doomed from the onset. She died trying to protect me from Grady's treachery. That's the reason I want that bastard swinging from a rope."

"I'm sorry for your loss," Hawk commiserated.

"Like you said, some lines aren't meant to be crossed. You're probably wise to keep your distance from Shiloh. Nothing can come of it."

Even when Fletch verbalized what Hawk knew to be true, a part of him yearned to throw caution to the wind and pursue his unprecedented feelings for Shiloh.

Very bad idea, he told himself as he strode off to replace the supplies he kept in the cavern for the kind of unseen emergencies that brought him to Sundance Canyon on occasion.

A quarter of an hour before the scheduled departure from the cave, the clouds parted, providing a spectacular view of Sundance Canyon, with its lush green valley, wild tumble of rocks and wildflowers waving in the breeze. Shiloh could almost visualize Hawk and Fletch practicing their survival skills in the Apache camp and bounding around the intriguing rock formations that inspired the imagination.

After the threesome crossed an overhanging ledge that towered above a winding creek on foot, Hawk assisted Shiloh onto his mustang. She tensed when he swung up behind her. The feel of his muscled chest and thighs pressed familiarly against her sent her heart into rapid staccato.

Shiloh gnashed her teeth. It wasn't a bit fair that she was so aware of him, so fascinated by him—while he seemed to have no difficulty controlling unwanted feelings for her. Shiloh nearly leaped out of her skin when he leaned in closer to ask if she was holding up all right during their winding downhill jaunt. His warm breath caused gooseflesh to pebble on her neck and then stream down her spine. Her body burned each place they touched and his appealing scent kept clogging her senses. She was so frustrated with her traitorous body's reaction to him that she wanted to scream.

"Is there some reason why we need to be riding double?" she said through gritted teeth.

"Because I don't trust your skittish mare at night," he murmured against her neck. "She's been dodging shadows since I forced her up and over Ghost Ridge."

Forbidden desire sizzled through her as his touch and scent overwhelmed her. She cursed herself soundly for entertaining the impulsive urge to turn in his arms and kiss the breath clean out of him.

"We'll reach the Ranger camp by midnight," he reported.

"Good. I'll be ready to give my injured arm and ankle a rest," she said, her voice a little on the unsteady side.

Shiloh half collapsed in relief when he straightened away from her and granted her more breathing space. She glanced heavenward, watching a canopy of stars wink to life, grateful for the reprieve….

And suddenly gunfire erupted to the north and the peaceful evening shattered like glass.

"Get down!" Hawk commanded as he leaned protectively over Shiloh. "Fletch! Are you up to a fire-fight?"

Fletch's reply was the rapid-fire eruption of his pistol that found its mark on one of the five riders thundering after them. Hawk fired directly at the spark and trickle of smoke that rose from one of the distant pistols. He heard a yelp before the second silhouette tumbled from a galloping horse.

To his relief, the last three riders veered sideways, giving up the chase. He suspected the bushwhackers were the gang he'd infiltrated. It was just like Morton DeVol to retreat when he risked becoming the casualty of a shoot-out. The only life that cutthroat valued was his own.

Les Figgins glanced over at his boss, Morton DeVol, then stared at his fallen cohorts. "We need to bury Joey and Hank properly," he insisted.

"You wanna bury 'em? Go ahead," Everett Stiles snorted. "I ain't wastin' my energy."

Les looked to Morton for support and found none forthcoming. He made the crucial mistake of saying, "Maybe you'd be more helpful if I tracked down those Rangers that have been dogging our trail for months and tell them—"

Les Figgins's voice fizzled out when the pistol blast hit him from close range. He stared incredulously at the smoldering flames on his vest and felt the icy chill of death settle over him.

"Never had no tolerance for a snitch." Morton holstered his pistol and watched Figgins keel off his horse to join his fallen comrades. "Never did like a devious redskin, either," he added, staring at the riders that disappeared into the night.

"We'll find that thievin' Injun eventually," Everett said as he reined back in the direction they'd come. "I ain't chasing him now that he's picked up reinforcements. Whoever his sidekick is, he's as accurate with a six-shooter as that damn redskin."

Biding his time, Morton DeVol turned back toward camp. He'd catch up with that bastard and cut him to pieces, he promised himself. That wicked thought put a smile on his lips and then he reminded himself that he'd have to send word to the ringleader to report that his band of five men had been reduced to two.

Forty-five minutes later, Hawk drew his mustang to a halt to signal the guard posted a mile from headquarters. When he walked the horses into camp several bushy heads popped up from the pallets spread around the campfire. It was probably because Shiloh's auburn hair caught flame in the flickering light, he surmised. Every man in camp was vividly aware that a shapely female was riding double with him.

When Hawk dismounted, the seven Rangers that had bedded down for the night shot to their feet and raked their hands through their ruffled hair to make themselves more presentable. It was a damn good thing his coworkers slept in their breeches. Otherwise, they would have embarrassed themselves when they surged toward Shiloh like high tide.

Hawk rolled his eyes at the doting attention Shiloh received the instant she set foot in camp.

"What the devil did you expect?" Fletch asked in Apache dialect. "That your friends wouldn't notice what you and I have had trouble ignoring? Beautiful women always attract attention. It's a fact of life, Hawk."

Hawk stared disapprovingly at the Rangers then focused on his brother. "My cohorts don't have to be so *obvious,* do they?" he replied in Apache. "I'm surprised they haven't slipped in the pool of their own drool. How can men that don't bat an eye at riding into a hellish firefight turn into mush when a woman shows up? Where's their self-restraint?"

Fletcher barked a laugh. "Did I just hear the pot call the kettle black? You've ogled her plenty yourself."

Hawk shot his taunting brother the evil eye. "I never did like you much, you know. Pain in the ass since the day you could walk and talk. I haven't had a moment's peace since."

"Never liked you much, either," Fletch teased right back. "Always bossing me around…. Now help me off this horse. My leg is throbbing something fierce and I need to lie down before I fall down."

While the Rangers lined up for introductions to Shiloh, Hawk helped Fletch dismount. He grabbed the bedroll, anxious to get Fletch off his injured leg. In the distance Hawk could hear the murmur of Shiloh's voice, which was followed by the eruption of male laughter. He looked at Fletch then sighed in dismay. "These besotted Rangers are giving all men everywhere a bad name. I expected more from them."

"Maybe all this preferential treatment Shiloh is receiving from your friends will restore her faith in men," Fletch remarked.

"Doubt it," said Hawk. "I don't think her man-hating days are over yet."

By the time Hawk had Fletch resting comfortably and applied a fresh poultice to the wound, one of the Rangers had lifted Shiloh from the saddle. Hawk watched Cameron Armstrong and Abram Ballard half carry her to the campfire so she wouldn't have to put pressure on her tender ankle.

Alien sensations twisted through his belly. Was it jealousy? Possessiveness? What in the hell was wrong with him? These Rangers were his trusted comrades in arms, who guarded his back as often as he guarded theirs. Why should he be annoyed if they stumbled all over themselves trying to make a good first impression on Shiloh?

He shouldn't be, he told himself. It was their business how they responded to the unexpected arrival of a woman.

Grinning, Commander Ben Tipton ambled up to Hawk. "When we asked Shiloh how you two met she said you dropped out of the sky and tried to drown her. Then you left her as an open target for the outlaw gang. Which is how she got her arm injured." Ben snickered. "She has quite an imagination, doesn't she? What's the real story?"

"Unfortunately, she isn't kidding." Hawk watched the men help her settle onto one of the pallets then deliver coffee and hoecakes for her midnight snack.

Ben's fuzzy gray eyebrows shot up. "You nearly *drowned* her?" he chirped, appalled.

"Well, not on purpose." Hawk gave Ben the condensed version of his departure from the outlaw's hideout and his unexpected encounter with Shiloh.

Ben stroked his bristly mustache. "Quite the eventful few days you've had." His curious gaze slid to Fletcher. "By his looks and the style of his clothes I'd say the man is a relative of yours. Yes?"

"My brother, Fletch," Hawk affirmed. "He's been in Colorado tracking hard-core cutthroats for bounty and working as a detective for the railroad, stage lines and ranchers. Fletch's partner betrayed him while working a case. He tracked the man to Texas. Unfortunately, Fletch stumbled onto one of the gangs we're trying to apprehend. He disposed of two bandits, winged the third and he can identify the ones that made off with his Appaloosa horse."

Ben's thick brows rose another notch. "And that's how he got shot?"

"Yeah, but since we look alike, I'm wondering if the two survivors of the gang he encountered might think we are one and the same. No doubt, they plan to rejoin the other bands and swap information about a certain 'gun-toting half-breed.'"

Ben nodded pensively. "Which means you and your brother will become marked men. These elusive high-waymen might even decide to lie low and let things cool down around here." Ben blew out a frustrated breath. "We're having one hell of a time locating the bandits. These crime factions are too well coordinated to be working independently."

"I couldn't agree more," Hawk replied.

"Did you have any luck figuring out how these gangs contact each other and who is coordinating their raids?"

Hawk shook his head. "I was accepted into the gang with wary caution and offered no privileged informa-tion. No outsiders entered camp to parley. Morton DeVol, the outlaws' ringleader, occasionally struck off alone. He'd return to announce 'the boss' had decided precisely where and when the next raid would take place. It was impossible for me to track DeVol because the rest of the men kept close tabs on me."

"We need a stroke of luck to break this case wide-open," Ben grumbled. "Seems like we've been chasing our tails for four months with nothing to show for it. I've instructed the men not to answer too many questions when we ride into Cerrogordo to restock supplies, for fear we might tip someone off. We always seem to be a step behind the robbers and damn if I can figure out why. We're missing a key clue."

"Shiloh reminded me of the trouble we had with Frank Mills, the rancher that allegedly hired a gunman to pose as a Ranger," Hawk commented. "Then Fletch told me that he'd been partnered with a man named Grady Mills who double-crossed him before clearing out. Probably headed to Texas."

Ben glanced up sharply and frowned. "You think Frank and Grady might be in cahoots?"

"Yes, I think a man as sly and cunning as Frank Mills might have a brother or cousin with the same lack of integrity. Sending one of our men to reconnoiter Mills Ranch, and to see who comes and goes, might give us a lead and clear up some of our confusion."

"Good idea," Ben replied.

"Fletch can identify the two men who shot him and stole his horse while he was tracking Grady Mills. I can identify the men in the gang I infiltrated." Hawk glanced in the direction they'd come. "I think DeVol and his men tried to ambush us earlier tonight. With any luck, the men Fletch and I shot off the saddle won't get up again."

Ben gaped in alarm. "Was Shiloh endangered?"

"I was her shield of defense," Hawk assured Ben.

"Glad to hear she was in good hands, but the ordeal still might have her suffering nightmares."

Hawk smiled wryly. "I think the lady is tougher than she looks. At least that's my impression.

"I think we should establish surveillance in town as well as Mills Ranch," Hawk recommended.

"If it gets some results I'm all for it," Ben replied. "Beats the hell out of showing up to talk to victims and witnesses *after* they've been robbed and shot. A couple of our men investigated cattle rustling north of Cerrogordo two weeks ago. Another stage holdup occurred west of town last week. We need more men on patrol." He glanced sideways at Fletch. "Do you think your brother might join us? We could use another good man. If he can ride and shoot as well as you can I'll swear him in right now."

"There's just one thing, Captain," Hawk said hesitantly. "You need to know—"

Ben flung up his hand to forestall him. "Don't tell me anything I don't want to know about you and your brother. I have some speculations of my own and I have had since you joined up. But you've proved your worth so many times that I really don't give a damn who you or Fletch were or what you did before we met you. I prefer to judge a man's worth on how he handles himself during a fight against lopsided odds. You've passed the test with flying colors scores of times already. I predict Fletch will, too."

"Thanks for the vote of confidence," he murmured.

"You're welcome." Ben grinned wryly. "Now, is there anything else you feel compelled to divulge before I swear in your brother?"

Hawk pursed his lips and shrugged. "No, I guess not."

"Good. Keeping things simple is my personal and professional motto," Ben stated.

When Ben strode away Hawk turned his attention to Shiloh. The Rangers had formed a semicircle in front of her and were questioning her about her visit to New Orleans. She was treating them to a detailed account of the bustling port and the elaborate soirees she'd attended. The Rangers seemed enthralled by the elegant side of life that was a world away from their dangerous forays in the wilderness.

Hawk couldn't picture himself strutting about town with the stylishly dressed aristocrats Shiloh described. Not that he and Fletch fit in anywhere, he mused as he watched his friends blatantly dote on Shiloh. But he would stick out like a sore thumb in New Orleans society.

Considering his associates' fawning fascination with Shiloh, Hawk doubted he'd have trouble convincing *any* Ranger to escort her home the following morning. More than likely *all* of them would leap at the chance to spend time alone with her.

Better any of them than me, he assured himself. He'd tested his self-restraint to the limit already.

"If you don't mind I'd like to get some sleep," Hawk heard Shiloh say to her doting admirers. "My ankle is throbbing." She glanced hopefully at Hawk. "Do you have some of that soothing poultice to spare?"

Hawk stifled the stirring need that her smile provoked. One look at her and he reacted. Hell! What happened to the unflappable willpower he'd spent thirty years cultivating?

He was turning as sappy as the other Rangers and he refused to let it happen. Repeating that mantra, Hawk strode off to fetch the salve. When he returned, he had to shoulder past his friends who still hovered around Shiloh as if she were visiting royalty.

"You're sleeping over here." He gestured toward a tree located apart from the bedrolls encircling the campfire.

He didn't know what possessed him, but he scooped

Shiloh up in his arms and clutched her protectively against him. He inwardly cringed when the men gaped at him.

"I can walk under my own power," Shiloh protested when she noticed all the speculative glances that came their way. "This isn't necessary, Hawk."

"I didn't want you tripping over my coworkers who can't seem to take their eyes off you." He cast the men a pointed stare. "Shiloh should be rested up by tomorrow morning. Surely you can wait until then for more bowing and scraping."

When Hawk walked off Shiloh frowned curiously. "Just how long have these Rangers been in the field? You would think I am the first female they'd laid eyes on in a year."

"They have been around women more than I have the past three months," he replied. "But then, you're prettier than most. Rangers or not, they're still men. Who wouldn't be easily beguiled when you grace a man with your dazzling smiles?" He cast her a teasing glance. "If you didn't want their attention you should've scowled at them the way you scowled at me."

"If they knew me as well as you do, they would run screaming in the opposite direction," she predicted.

When the bite of possessive jealousy finally eased up, Hawk grinned at her. "If you won't give me any grief tonight I promise not to tell them what you're *really* like."

He set her on her good leg then handed her the cane for support. Shiloh shivered and told herself—for the forty-eleventh time, damn it—that it was because of the evening chill, not because of the tingles of pleasure provoked by Hawk's touch.

"Now that I've seen that you're a respected member of this battalion and you've turned in the stolen money I want to officially apologize for thinking the worst about you."

Hawk shrugged casually then rolled out her padded pallet. "I didn't blame you for being suspicious."

"Will you be taking me home tomorrow?" she asked as he steadied her arm while she sank awkwardly onto the pallet.

"Someone else will be delegated that task."

Shiloh was annoyed with herself for feeling disappointed. She shouldn't care who escorted her home, so long as she reached the ranch quickly. She was anxious to get on with the rest of her life, one that would not include courtships. She had always taken an active interest in managing the ranch and she intended to devote even more time to that from now on.

The only problem would be convincing her brothers that she wanted to accept more responsibility and that she wasn't interested in a husband. She had to convince them that it wasn't their mission in life to find her a suitable match.

"Is there anything else you need tonight?" Hawk asked, itching to put some space between them before he did something stupid—like bed down beside her, supposedly for her protection. Which was ridiculous because more than a half-dozen sharpshooters and skilled fighters surrounded them.

"No. I'm fine." She glanced at Fletcher, who had conked out like a doused lantern. She gestured toward the shiny badge lying beside his two pearl-handled peacemakers. "Your commander must have leaped at the chance to sign up another lawman. If Fletch is half as skilled as you are he will make a fine addition to this battalion."

"I'll tell him you said so."

Shiloh frowned at Hawk's brisk tone. "You've been standoffish lately. Did I do something to annoy you?"

Yes, you live. You breathe. You arouse me when I want to feel nothing, he thought to himself. But he said aloud, "No. It's just been a long three days. I could use some shut-eye. Good night."

Shiloh snuggled beneath her quilt and watched Hawk gather an armful of tall grass to make his pallet, since Fletch was using the spare bedroll. With Fletch ten feet away to her left and Hawk ten feet away to her right, she was insulated from the well-meaning but overeager Rangers who had showered her with such rapt attention.

She couldn't figure out why Hawk was acting protective toward her while they were in the Ranger encampment. Although she vowed not to become romantically involved with men again, the Rangers seemed harmless enough. She really hadn't minded their collective company because it took her mind off her silly notions about Hawk.

She recoiled instinctively when Hawk's hand curled around her foot. She propped herself on her elbow to watch him unwrap the bandage then apply more soothing poultice. From beneath lowered lashes, she studied his masculine profile in the flickering campfire.

He was definitely an impressive male specimen— if a woman were inclined to fantasize about him. He was also an amazing survivalist—if a woman found herself in need of protection. And being in the circle of his sinewy arms provoked feelings of comfort and invincible strength.

Not to mention a host of arousing sensations that Shiloh refused to let herself think about right now.

The moment Hawk completed the task, Shiloh murmured a quiet thank-you then closed her eyes. She listened to Hawk stretch out on his pallet, heard him expel an audible sigh. She suspected he was tired of tending to her and was anxious to have her out from underfoot so he could resume his duties.

A part of her felt insulted, rejected and disappointed by the impersonal attitude. She preferred to see the professional lawman facade crack to reveal the sometimes playful and sometimes vulnerable personality that drew her against her will. In addition, she was oddly pleased that he didn't treat her with the same doting attention of the Rangers. She would have lost respect for him if he catered to her as if she were a fragile princess perched on a pedestal....

Her eyes snapped open and she propped herself up to stare at the glowing campfire while she contemplated that disturbing thought. He allowed her to be herself, allowed her to test her limits instead of pigeonholing her because she was a woman.

"Something wrong?" he questioned quietly.

When she felt Hawk's intense gaze on her she squirmed in her skin. "No. Everything is fine. Peachy, in fact."

And it was—or so she tried to convince herself. Tomorrow she would be on her way home after her six-month absence. Noah and Gideon were not going to ship her off again, either.

She'd be home to stay and Hawk would be out of her life. No more complications. No emotional turmoil. No temptation to deter her from her new role as a spinster who was well pleased with the new direction of her life.

Chapter Eight

Shiloh came awake with a start at daybreak the next morning. Three Rangers—Virgil, Henry and Arthur, if she remembered their names correctly—were standing over her with a cup of steaming coffee and biscuits. She glanced to the right to note that Hawk was up and gone. She glanced to the left to see Fletch grinning in wry amusement.

"We thought you might like to start off the day with fresh brew, ma'am." Bowlegged Virgil sank down on his haunches to hand her a tin cup that had his name scratched on it.

"Artie and I had the same notion," Henry said as he hunkered down to offer her warm biscuits.

Shiloh smiled gratefully. "That's very kind of you, but please enjoy your coffee. I need to…um…" She shifted self-consciously.

"I'll be glad to accompany you," Artie spoke up. "This way, Miss Shiloh."

Feeling like a spectacle in a camp full of men, Shiloh followed Artie into the bushes near a narrow stream so she could see to her needs. It was sweet really, the way the Rangers treated her with the utmost respect and consideration. They had dragged out their best manners and were eager to please. It was soothing balm after her dealings with Antoine.

Yet, here she was secretly yearning for the attention of a man who seemed anxious to get her off his hands. As Hawk said, Sometimes there was just no accounting for some people's tastes. Certainly, she had made a critical error in judgment when she fell for Antoine Troudeau's practiced charm. Once he was out of her life she'd made a pact to avoid romantic entanglements. But fate put her on a collision course with Logan Hawk. Ironic, wasn't it? And maddening.

Muttering at her foolishness, Shiloh emerged from the underbrush. Sure enough, three bodyguards were waiting for her. Five minutes later one of the other Rangers—Herman was his name—handed her a plate heaping with more biscuits and gravy. Then he kerplunked down beside her to inquire about her night's sleep.

While Shiloh enjoyed her meal, the other men joined her to watch the sun splash its vibrant colors across the horizon. After so many consecutive days of clouds and rain, the sun was a welcome change. When she made mention of that aloud all the men bobbed their heads in agreement.

And that's when she realized what it was about Hawk that drew her unwilling interest. He didn't cater to her and agree with her, just to please her. He was also a bit ornery, just as she was when the mood struck. He was as disinterested in getting involved in a dead-end liaison as she was. He didn't try to put his best foot forward to make a good impression and neither did she.

Hawk was just Hawk. His job was his life. You could

take him or leave him—it didn't seem to matter one way or the other to him. Never once in their brief but action-packed acquaintance had he tried to impress her.

And that's what impressed her most, confound it!

"Here, ma'am, let me take that for you." Samuel Hampton, the tall, lanky Ranger, plucked up her empty plate then retreated to fill her cup.

"You don't suppose an injured *man* could get a cup of that fresh brew to wake him up, do you?"

The men turned in unison to glance at Fletch who had braced himself on his arms to sit upright.

"We weren't formally introduced last night, but I'm Hawk's brother, Fletch," he declared. "I met up with one of the gangs you're chasing and ended up with a bullet in my leg. I'd give my good leg for a cup of that hot coffee."

Shiloh rolled to her knees to extend her fresh cup to Fletch. "Here, take mine," she insisted.

And that's how Hawk found her when he rode into camp. All the Rangers, except Fletch—were staring at Shiloh's curvaceous backside while she was braced in a suggestive position. Lust and possessive jealousy lambasted Hawk simultaneously. He growled like an irascible grizzly.

Hell and damnation! He'd taken his turn at standing guard and spent most of his time listing all the sensible reasons why Shiloh should remain off-limits to him. He had even dreamed up another dozen excuses in an effort to keep an emotional distance. But now he couldn't remember one reason why he shouldn't succumb to lust while he stared at her shapely backside.

Hawk cleared his throat—loudly. His coworkers jerked to attention and then glanced guiltily at him. As well they should have, the shameless lechers. He knew what every damn one of them was thinking, too, and he wanted to shoot the whole lot of them for fantasizing about Shiloh.

Dismounting, he strode toward the cluster of lollygagging Rangers. By that time, Shiloh had handed off her cup and sunk back on her pallet. She glanced up to nod a greeting and he got lost in those expressive green eyes that were surrounded by long, sooty lashes. Another jolt of need hammered at him so he wheeled toward Fletch to distract himself.

"Are you feeling better this morning?"

Fletch nodded and grinned knowingly, then sipped his coffee. "Yep, how about you, big brother?"

Hawk shrugged evasively. He didn't announce that he was going to be a much happier man when Shiloh and her guide rode from camp so he could get back to business as usual.

"I found three bodies after last night's ambush attempt."

Fletch's eyes widened in surprise. *"Three?"*

"One of them was shot at close range," Hawk said grimly. "My guess is that Les Figgins complained about something. DeVol doesn't deal well with criticism or suggestions."

"Well, that lessens the number of bandits we have to track down," Fletch said.

"And I'm anxious to get my hands on DeVol and Stiles." Hawk turned toward the other Rangers. "Does anyone want to volunteer to escort Shiloh home?"

Every arm—save Hawk's and Fletch's—shot up simultaneously. Hawk rolled his eyes at the overzealous responses. Hawk would sacrifice his own life to protect any of these men, and he trusted them with his life.

Yet, he didn't trust any of them in Shiloh's company because the entire battalion had been panting and drooling over her since she set foot in camp.

Hell of a dilemma, thought Hawk. He didn't want anyone to accompany Shiloh home, but he was hesitant to do it himself. He didn't need to be in on the decision making so he lurched around to fetch a cup of coffee and a plate of biscuits. Captain Tipton could make the choice.

"Hold up, Hawk," Ben Tipton called out.

Hawk pivoted to face the commander.

"Seems to me that since you and Shiloh are already acquainted and have adjusted to having each other underfoot that *you* should be the one to escort her home."

No! I don't trust myself with her! he thought. Aloud he said, "I think my time would be better spent tracking the two men that survived the confrontation with Fletch. Now that we have a possible headquarters site at Mills Ranch to check out, I might be able to glean valuable information for this case."

"No doubt," Ben said. "But protecting our Texas citizens is our foremost concern. Don't you agree?"

"Of course, but every man here is capable of providing an escort for Shiloh," he pointed out reasonably.

Hawk's gaze swung briefly to Shiloh. Although she tilted her curly auburn head to a proud angle, he could see the hurt glittering in her eyes. Not that she wanted him near her again, but neither did she want him to embarrass her by refusing escort duty in front of an audience of Rangers. Damn it, he was unintentionally trouncing on her feelings. She'd had enough of that lately, thanks to that French Casanova from New Orleans. But this was about his self-preservation and fighting the maddening temptation she presented to him.

"Fine." He tried very hard to keep defeat from seeping into his voice—and didn't quite succeed. "If Shiloh is agreeable then I'll gather some supplies and we can head northwest when she is ready to leave."

Disappointment showed on the Rangers' faces as they turned and walked away.

"Could you have looked and sounded less pleased with the prospect of accompanying me home?" Shiloh muttered as she surged upright to test her ankle. "But not to worry, Hawk. As soon as we reach familiar territory, I'll make my own way. There is no need for me to detain you longer than necessary. You can veer off to scout for Fletch's bushwhackers and confiscate his stolen horse while I make the last leg of the journey *alone.*"

"Shi—"

She wheeled to stare squarely at him. Her eyes flashed in irritation. "Did you have to make it sound as if you were grasping any excuse to avoid spending more time with me? I'm just recovering from Antoine's hurtful rejection. But thank you so much for making me feel about two inches tall in front of the other men."

"I didn't mean to embarrass you."

"*You didn't mean to?* Well, *that* makes me feel so much better," she smirked. "And just so you know, I wasn't all that enthused about riding off with you, either. But I do have enough common decency not to let your coworkers think I found you unpleasant or offensive!"

"I said I was sorry," Hawk huffed out.

"Stick your apology where the sun doesn't shine," she muttered before she spun around and hobbled off to pack her belongings on her horse.

Hawk heard his brother's quiet chuckle behind him.

He glared over his shoulder. "If you think that conversation was funny then your sense of humor is skewered," Hawk growled.

"Watching that spitfire turn you inside out and backward is the most fun I've had in weeks." Fletch lifted his cup in toast. "Her tongue can lay a man's hide wide open." He grinned broadly. "But more amazing is that you two set off all sorts of sparks and ignite fires in each other. I find that very interesting."

"I don't want fires burning in my wake," Hawk grumbled as his gaze magnetically shifted to Shiloh.

"Too late, big brother," Fletch said, snickering. "It's too damn late."

Shiloh ignored Hawk for the first two hours of their overland jaunt. Clearly, she'd become too sensitive to rejection after her dealings with Antoine, and her ill-fated fascination for Hawk made her touchy. Listening to Hawk's attempt to pawn her off on another escort earlier that morning had cut to the quick—and she hadn't gotten over it yet.

"How long is this cold-shoulder routine going to last?" Hawk asked a half hour later.

Shiloh flung her nose in the air. "Until I die. Or you die. Whichever comes first."

"I'm sorry I offended you," he murmured as he led the way toward the tree-lined creek to water the horses and take a lunch break.

"You can offend me any time you please, but not when there is an audience. Understood? You cannot imagine how difficult it was for me to hold my tongue and not flail you alive in front of your coworkers!"

"I'm surprised you restrained yourself," he mocked.

Shiloh twisted in the saddle to glare poison darts at

him. "We were among your peers. It was common courtesy. Something you obviously know nothing about."

"Too true," he surprised her by agreeing. "I didn't grow up learning society's protocol and practicing dignified manners. *Savage* and *heathen* are the words whites usually use to describe my kind. The fact is that each civilization has its own set of rules and customs. In fact, if you were living in an Apache village, your tendency to speak your mind and contradict a man every time you feel like it would earn you a private tepee on the edge of camp and a reputation as a woman possessed by evil spirits."

"Speaking my mind in the presence of gentlemen, who consider women too dense and uneducated to have an opinion, has gotten me in trouble in the *white* culture," she informed him. "I might be a misfit but I see no reason to kowtow to men who think it's their natural-born right to lord over me."

To her surprise, Hawk chuckled. "So that's why your brothers are trying to marry you off to someone miles away in New Orleans. Out of sight and out of earshot, much to their relief, I suspect."

The teasing remark caused Shiloh to frown thoughtfully. Had Hawk hit upon the underlying reason why Gideon and Noah had packed her off to stay with her aunt and cousin in New Orleans? Had she become too outspoken, too hoydenish, too confrontational? Obviously.

"Before you get bent out of shape again," he put in hurriedly, "I was only teasing you, although I probably shouldn't have." He shifted restlessly on the saddle then flung her a fleeting glance. "You're not that bad, Shiloh."

"Not that bad?" she repeated in offended dignity.

"The point is that every Ranger in camp would have leaped at the chance to exchange places with me so he can spend time alone with you." He stared at her momentarily, then glanced the other way. "How many more hopeless admirers do you need following at your heels to reassure you that you appeal to all men everywhere?"

"For your information, Chief Know-It-All, I don't feed on masculine attention," she said huffily. "That is not how I define myself or count my worth in the world. I have no desire to be a man's financial acquisition or trophy bride—"

Shiloh blinked, startled, when he thrust up his hand abruptly and halted his horse. His attention shifted to the thick underbrush. After a moment he motioned for her to follow closely behind him.

"Furthermore, I am inexperienced at coquettish games, which obviously made me an easy target for a man like Antoine, who relies on his calculated charm and skills of seduction," she said in a quieter voice.

Hawk gnashed his teeth when the vision of some French dandy, decked out in expensive velvet waistcoats and ruffled shirts, popped to mind. He could imagine Shiloh being lured in by that suave predator. The thought of the man touching Shiloh familiarly, claiming her innocence like a prize, made his blood boil.

And damn it, she did have every right to be bitter, wary and angry, he mused. She had been manipulated and carelessly discarded. Any so-called gentleman who treated a lady so callously deserved to be poisoned, shot and hanged.

Hawk volunteered to mete out the various punishments.

"That's one of the drawbacks of being born into an

affluent family," Shiloh went on to say as she ducked beneath a low-hanging limb. "You never know if a man is interested in you or your inheritance. Antoine was content to court me for a time. Fool that I was, I thought it was my dazzling personality that attracted him." She gave a disillusioned snort. "Turns out that I have no charm and the men in my social circle—and else-where—aren't to be trusted."

"Don't be so hard on yourself." Hawk grinned dev-ilishly. "That's what I'm here for, or so you claim."

Hawk dismounted to let Dorado drink his fill in the stream. He lifted Shiloh from the saddle. The moment he placed his hands around the trim indentation of her waist awareness sizzled through him and he cursed his helpless reaction to her.

Her hands clamped on his forearms to steady herself as he lowered her to the ground—and he wanted to keep going down until she was on the grass beneath him so he could mesh his aching body to her lush contours then help himself to a generous taste of that sassy mouth.

"I swear, men aren't worth the trouble they cause women." Her voice grew husky when she met his gaze directly.

"And vice versa," he said, telling himself to let her go before he fell beneath this forbidden spell and did something reckless. But his leaden feet refused to re-treat. He stood there holding on to Shiloh, staring into her beguiling face, hungering to devour her tempting lips—for starters.

He wasn't sure who broke eye contact first. It might have been a draw. Whatever the case, he stepped back as she stepped sideways. He didn't know if she glanced at him because he was making a monumental effort *not* to look directly at her.

It always got him in trouble.

"You'll probably want to stretch out and take a load off your ankle while you have the chance," he suggested, his voice two octaves lower than normal. "I'll grab your bedroll." Which he did quickly. "This will be a short stop for a cold meal. Tonight we'll find a place to bed down that's off the beaten path."

"Whatever you say, you're the expert frontiersman." She accepted the bedroll and snapped it out beside the stream. "But you don't have to pamper me, Hawk. My ankle is feeling much better and I can keep up with your pace. I know you're eager to get me off your hands and concentrate on your assignment. And I'm anxious to get home."

Get her off his hands? A lot she knew! He wanted her *in* his hands more than he wanted to draw breath. But he still had enough sense left to avoid that dangerous pitfall. Surely he could control his basal needs for the two-day journey. Considering the various and sundry ordeals he'd endured the past two decades this should be a piece of cake.

The murmur of voices sent Hawk's senses to full alert. He snatched up the bedroll Shiloh had spread out, then draped it over the saddle. Tying the horses to a stripling, he grabbed Shiloh's hand to lead her up to the rise of ground overlooking the creek to locate the unidentified travelers. When he tried to pick her up to take the pressure off her ankle, she shook her head adamantly. She made a stabbing gesture with her hand, silently ordering him to lead the way while she limped along behind him.

A moment later Hawk reached back to hook his arm around Shiloh and draw her to a halt at the point where the narrow path descended from the sandy knoll to the creek bank. His brows furrowed when he recognized the two men that were squatted down, filling their canteens.

"They match your brother's description," she whispered against his ear.

Hawk nodded, willfully ignoring the tantalizing tingles her warm breath evoked. "The description matches the horses, too." He indicated the muscular brown and white Appaloosa. "That's Fletch's horse and I intend to get it back."

"So how do you want to handle the situation?" she questioned as she surveyed the area. "I'm a fair shot with a rifle and pistol, thanks to my brothers."

"Have you ever shot a man before?"

"No."

"Then let's not make this your first time."

Hawk inwardly cursed the fact that he had Shiloh underfoot right now. Ordinarily he would wing the outlaws and apply a few scare tactics to get them to talk. Threatening to resort to Apache torture usually loosened the tightest lips.

"I know what you're thinking," she murmured against his ear again. "I'm in the way. I'm preventing you from doing your job. So just pretend I'm not here. I can find my way home."

Pretend you aren't here? Now there was a laugh. He could feel her, breathe her, see her. It was impossible to ignore a woman who had such a fierce impact on a man's senses.

Furthermore, she wasn't functioning at full capacity and his conscience refused to let her ride off alone.

Hawk held position while the bandits—one of whom kept his arm in a sling after his run-in with Fletch—mounted their horses. He wasn't surprised the hombres were headed the same direction he was. Which meant their headquarters were near the area where Shiloh lived. Hawk couldn't help but wonder if her brothers were involved in the outlaw rings and if they had sent her to Louisiana so she wouldn't be suspicious of their activities. It wouldn't be the first time unsuspecting family members had been kept in the dark about crime sprees.

"There has to be a connection between these outlaw factions and the string of ranches along Echo River," Shiloh said perceptively. "My money is on Frank Mills."

Hawk hoped she was right because it would break her heart if her brothers were involved.

After they reversed direction to retrieve their tethered horses, Hawk picked up Shiloh and set her in the saddle.

"I'll lag behind," she offered. "I know you want to apprehend the men who shot your brother and stole his horse."

He mounted his mustang. "Yes, I do. But not at your expense. You've suffered enough because of me already."

He could tell that he was in for a heated debate when she tilted her chin and stiffened her spine. "Fine, if you won't leave me behind then I'll assist you however I can. I can serve as bait if you like. But I refuse to hamper you and I insist on helping."

Hawk glanced at her, exasperated, as they followed the bandits at a cautious distance. "But if you suffer needlessly, Captain Tipton and your brothers will have my head."

She tossed him a challenging smile. "And here I thought you called no man master, Oh Great Apache Warrior."

"That's because the son of a bitch hasn't been born that I'll bow down to," he quickly assured her, then cursed himself for his snappy retort that gave too much of himself away.

She studied him pensively. "I accidentally hit an exposed nerve, didn't I?"

Hawk blew out his breath. "Yeah, Fletch and I got fed up with the lording soldiers at the reservation. They delighted in taunting our people and calling us no-account savages. They tried to break our spirit by telling us that we were less than human and that all redskins should be annihilated, not penned up like cattle. They molested our women and sold them, as well as our children, on both sides of the border as slaves for extra profit. Too many times the fort commanders looked the other way when it happened."

"I'm sorry. I have been growling and complaining about Antoine's betrayal, but that is nothing compared to what you and your people suffered."

Hawk forcefully shoved aside the bitter memories of those hellish days on the New Mexican reservation at Bosque Redondo, where rancid meat and daily doses of scorn were the rule, never the exception. He turned his attention to the two men that trotted northwest, then dug into his saddlebag for pemmican to curb Shiloh's and his appetites until supper.

"I would have preferred to take a lunch break as planned," he said as he handed food to Shiloh.

She shrugged indifferently. "I don't mind eating on the go if it will lead you to the bandits' hideout. I for one would like to know how close these thieves are to our ranch."

Hawk inwardly grimaced, wondering if the masterminds were right under her nose.

"If Frank Mills is involved," she went on to say, "I want to see him punished for his cruel treatment of the two Mexican sheepherders that got in his way."

For the next few hours Hawk and Shiloh followed the brigands at a discreet distance. Shiloh knew Hawk was itching to overtake the outlaws, but he refused to because of her. And she was sorry to say that sitting in the saddle for so many hours was making her ankle throb again. Finally, she could endure no more. She reached over to tap Hawk on the shoulder.

"Why don't you ride ahead and leave me behind to make camp for the night."

He glanced at the strained expression on her face then stared at her ankle. "You're in pain, aren't you? You should have said something earlier."

Shiloh grumbled sourly when Hawk snatched up her mare's reins. He glanced this way and that before heading straight east at a fast clip that sent pain shooting up her leg.

"There's a place nearby that will make a suitable camp. It's a mite close to the watering hole where predators sometimes lurk, but the higher elevations make it easy to spot incoming intruders."

"But the bandits are getting ahead of us," she objected as he led her in the wrong direction.

"I'll use a shortcut to catch up with them after I've stashed you away for safekeeping."

Nothing like being extra baggage, Shiloh thought dishearteningly as Hawk trotted up the tree-choked hillside that opened onto a secluded plateau. She sighed appreciatively when she spotted the stream below. She could use a good soaking to ease her throbbing ankle and cleanse the wound on her arm. Being left behind wasn't going to be as disappointing as she first thought.

Hawk hurriedly set her to the ground then thrust one of his six-shooters into her hand. "Sound carries a long way out here in the wilds, but use the weapon to protect yourself from trouble. I'll be back as soon as I can. Take care of yourself so I don't have to worry about you the entire time I'm gone."

To her surprise, he dropped another hit-and-run kiss to her lips before he bounded back into the saddle.

"I thought you said you didn't want any more kissing and touching." She frowned warily. "Is this your idea of a goodbye kiss, because you're not coming back? If it is, then tell me now so I won't worry about what happened to *you*."

"I'll be back," he promised as he shifted uneasily in the saddle, then looked the other way. "Kissing you seems to have turned into an impulsive habit. I'll try not to let it happen again. It's not good for either of us."

"I couldn't agree more," she said before he shot off like a flying bullet.

Shiloh brushed her fingertips over her lips, wondering why those snippet tastes of him left her hungering for… She dropped her hand to her side and told herself to be sensible.

She was not going to hold Hawk in higher regard than the rest of his gender. If she could resist Logan Hawk's rugged masculine appeal then she could resist any man.

Unfortunately, somewhere along the way, she had become the slightest bit intrigued by Hawk. Of course, she'd cut out her tongue before she admitted any such thing to him. She was not going to get her foolish heart broken again, she told herself determinedly.

Spinning about, she limped toward the creek to soak her head and recover her common sense.

* * *

Shiloh lounged in the shallows of the creek until dusk. Her arm and ankle felt considerably better. She'd had the chance to relax, after being surrounded by men the past few days. But Hawk still occupied her mind.

She still hadn't figured out what that certain something about Hawk was that lured her against her fierce will.

With Antoine, it had been his polished manners and refined good looks that first captured her interest. Of course, he had turned out to be a superficial, calculating scoundrel—which proved that you couldn't judge a man's character by the cut of his expensive clothes and his blue-blooded pedigree. However, with Hawk…

Shiloh sighed, frustrated. Hawk was everything Antoine was not. He was rough-edged, hard-nosed, straightforward and brimming with character and integrity. At least that was how she perceived him. But her attraction to him was still as ill-advised as her short-term infatuation for Antoine.

Could she ever trust her instincts? Was she one of those unfortunate women who was attracted to men who were completely wrong for her? Or was she simply a miserable judge of men? Was she destined to always make the worst choices?

Discarding her troubled thoughts, Shiloh donned clean clothes then limped along the creek, gathering fallen branches and driftwood to start a fire. Recalling what Hawk had said about the place being a favorite haunt for varmints Shiloh kept her pistol handy as she sidestepped uphill.

Back in camp, she circled the stack of dry branches with stones—arranging the campfire in the shape of a skillet, as Hawk had done, so he could adjust the heat while cooking. She absently tucked the pistol in the saddlebag, along with the spare set of clothing, then grabbed the matchbox. She was about to strike a match to the fire when she heard a low warning growl nearby.

Her mare nickered uneasily then strained against the tether. Shiloh noticed the wild look in the mare's eyes as it sidestepped. The horse pricked up its ears and its nostrils flared, indicating that trouble was sneaking up on them.

Another ferocious growl rolled toward her from the opposite direction. The hair on the back of her neck stood on end. An eerie sensation rippled through her. Shiloh snatched up one of the tree limbs to use as protection, wishing she had kept the pistol handy. Rising from a crouch, she inched toward her jittery mare and the saddlebag containing the six-shooter....

Chapter Nine

Shiloh's blood ran cold when she saw several pair of predatory eyes reflecting in the last rays of sunset. She nearly leaped out of her skin when she became alarmingly aware that a pack of wolves had picked up her scent.

Curse it! If she'd had time to get the fire going, perhaps the lobos would have backed off and left her alone.

A spine-tingling howl shattered the silence. Shiloh's heart catapulted to her throat. She glanced every which way at once, anticipating an attack.

"Get out of here!" she snarled in her most intimidating voice.

Her harsh tone obviously wasn't an effective repellent because a trio of ominous growls wafted through the gathering darkness. Her mare half reared, jerking frantically against the tether. Shiloh moved closer to the prancing horse, hoping to retrieve her weapon.

Frissons of fear seeped through her when she heard the rustling in the tall grass on the perimeter of camp. The lobos were creeping up on her, causing her panic to escalate. Shiloh had witnessed the destructive damage left by wolves on her ranch. The Drummonds had lost calves to hungry lobos that clipped the hamstrings of cattle, brought them down and devoured the feast.

The gruesome vision prompted Shiloh to hurriedly root around in the saddlebag to grab the pistol.

A frightened gasp burst from her lips when three adult wolves that looked to be at least six feet long and heavyset appeared in the clearing to her left. Shiloh recoiled when the animals crouched and bared their teeth. Behind her, the frantic mare bolted sideways, unintentionally knocking Shiloh off her feet.

The pistol went flying and the wolves crept closer. With a sense of urgency, Shiloh surged to her feet, hoping to grab the mare's reins and climb aboard. But the horse backed away from her. Hurriedly, she tried to work the tight knot loose on the reins. She finally managed to untie the horse, but the mare bounded sideways before she could pull herself into the saddle. Shiloh yelped when the panicky horse nearly jerked her arm from its socket as it plunged forward.

She held on to the reins for a few seconds, but the pressure on her ankle forced her to let go. Scowling, she watched the mare beat a hasty retreat from the wolves.

The yipping of young pups mingled with the clatter of departing horse hooves. Her only hope was to retrieve the pistol that lay near the unlit campfire.

When Shiloh crept forward, the circling wolves closed in around her. She tried to breathe over the thundering pulsations of her heart, which was trying to beat a hole in her chest. Shiloh did her best to rest her weight on the balls of her feet so she could be prepared to launch herself in any direction in case of attack, but her injury made her clumsy.

Sinking into a crouch, Shiloh reached for the pistol. She didn't know if the lobos could smell fear, but if they could, she knew she was giving off the scent. She reminded herself that Hawk probably wouldn't bat an eyelash at being surrounded by a pack of snarling wolves. He had probably been in so many life-threatening scrapes that nothing fazed him.

Well…it sure as hell fazed her, much as she hated to admit it. Her mouth was so dry she could barely swallow. Her arm shook as she reached for the discarded pistol. Her legs wobbled and she didn't trust them to hold her up while she made a run for it.

It's now or never, Shiloh chanted silently as she gathered her courage. Her wary gaze leaped from one vicious-looking predator to the next. She reminded herself that her brothers had taught her to be reasonably accurate with a rifle and pistol, but rapid-firing accuracy had never been her forte. She wasn't sure how she was going to fend off the pouncing wolves while she was crouched on the ground—hoping to make herself a smaller target.

Grabbing a quick breath, Shiloh dived toward the pistol. Her abrupt movement was like a signal for the lobos to attack. She shrieked involuntarily as the wolves sprang at her with those glittering eyes and fanged jaws that promised torture and death.

Shiloh rolled over and bounded to her knees. Clutching the weapon in both hands, she fired wildly. The snarling beasts retreated briefly, but lunged at her again. Their jaws snapped like steel traps that could crush bone and muscle with horrifying ease.

When the largest of the lobos gathered itself then sprang toward her, she yelped reflexively. Her life flashed before her eyes as the beast, its lips curled and its fangs bared, hurtled through the air. Panicked, Shiloh jerked the pistol into firing position—and screamed bloody murder when the oversize wolf landed on top of her....

Hawk heard the unnerving shrieks in the distance, heard the clatter of an approaching horse. He didn't know what kind of trouble Shiloh was in, but fear—the likes of which he hadn't experienced since childhood—went all through him and settled like a stone in the pit of his belly. Teeth gritted, he gouged his mustang into its swiftest pace, forcing the three horses he had confiscated from the unsuspecting outlaws to race along in his wake.

When Shiloh's mare appeared from the darkness, Hawk rode straight at it, forcing it into a skidding halt. Hurriedly, he tied the wild-eyed mare to the saddle on his brother's Appaloosa then raced headlong toward the elevated meadow where he had left Shiloh to fend for herself.

And obviously that had been a mistake, he mused, imagining all sorts of disasters that might have befallen her.

Another blood-curdling scream echoed in the darkness, followed by the sound of a discharging pistol. Hawk nearly suffered heart seizure as he splashed through the stream and headed toward the haunting echo of Shiloh's voice.

Then he heard the growls and snarls and he knew what kind of trouble she was in.

Pistol drawn, the reins clamped in his teeth and his rifle cradled over his left elbow, Hawk plunged into camp. Two mangy wolves and three pups swept back and forth in the clearing as Hawk thundered toward them. His heart all but ceased beating when he saw the adult male lobo sprawled on top of Shiloh's motionless body, its wooly head lying beside her exposed neck.

Swearing profusely, he took down the two snarling lobos with two well-aimed shots, which caused the pups to turn tail and run. Hawk was off his horse in a single bound.

Shiloh was sprawled lifelessly on the ground, the six-shooter lying at her fingertips. There was just enough twilight left for him to see the bloody stains that spread across the front and the right sleeve of Shiloh's shirt.

"Shiloh!" he roared as he gave her a jostling shake. "Damn it, if I got you killed I'll never forgive myself!"

Desperate, he tried to revive her, but she didn't respond. Hands shaking, he grabbed the scruff of the wolf's neck and dragged it aside. His eyes popped when he saw the alarming extent of the bloodstains on Shiloh's shirt.

"Dear God!" he breathed shakily.

Suddenly her eyes flew open and she clawed wildly at him, screeching at the top of her lungs. He wasn't sure which one of them was more startled. Her, when she realized he wasn't the big bad wolf come to gobble her alive. Or him, because she had come back to life when he was certain that she had lost so much blood that she had breathed her last breath.

Hawk grabbed her wrists before she scratched out his eyes. "It's me!" he all but yelled at her, then gave her an abrupt shake to bring her to her senses.

Her wild-eyed gaze fixated on him. "Oh, God!" she gasped. "I thought I was a goner for sure."

Hawk nearly tumbled backward when Shiloh

lurched upward to fling her arms around his neck. She buried her head against his shoulder and bawled her head off to relieve the terror pulsing through her. Hawk let her vent for a few minutes while he rocked her gently and whispered words of reassurance. But he knew he couldn't delay much longer before he inspected her bloody wound. She was operating on raw emotion at the moment, but any second now her survival instincts would shut down and she'd collapse.

"You're okay, sweetheart," he murmured compassionately. He didn't think she was okay, but he didn't have the heart to tell *her* that. "Just lie back and let me check your wounds."

She seemed reluctant to let him go, seemed perfectly satisfied to anchor herself to him and let him encircle her in his arms. But time was wasting and Hawk was anxious to see how much damage the lobo had done.

"If not for you I would be wolf bait right now," she choked out as she slumped on the ground. "How am I ever going to repay you for all the times you've saved my life?"

He wasn't sure he could save it this time because a wolf bite always carried the possibility of rabies and there was so damn much blood! Lord! He couldn't imagine how he'd feel if he had to watch Shiloh die. The world just wouldn't be the same without this lively, feisty spitfire in it.

"Don't go crazy on me, honey," he cooed as he raked her tangled hair away from her peaked face. "I have to unbutton your shirt to examine the wounds."

As if she just realized what a bloody mess she was, she glanced down at her torso, swallowed bravely then nodded.

Hawk reached over to strike a match to the camp-fire she had built earlier, hoping for more light. While the flames flickered to life, he hesitantly unfastened her blouse. He braced himself, expecting to see gnawed flesh on her throat and shoulder. But there wasn't a bloody gash on her anywhere. Not even a scratch!

His jaw dropped open while he stared at her creamy skin and watched the quick rise and fall of her bare breasts.

Damn, this was far more than he needed to see if he didn't want to be tormented by erotic dreams.

Bewildered, Hawk snatched his hand away from her, but his betraying gaze remained transfixed on her concave belly, taut nipples and full breasts. It took a moment to regain enough sense to jerk her stained blouse back together.

Hurriedly, he sank down beside her to examine the motionless wolf. When he rolled the animal onto its back, he noted the wound to the neck that had suc-ceeded in dropping the beast in its tracks—precious seconds before it went for Shiloh's throat.

"Hell of a shot you got off at the last possible mo-ment," he praised as he gestured at the wolf.

"W-what?" Shiloh blinked dazedly, and then glanced from Hawk to the shaggy beast.

She couldn't remember what happened after the lobo launched itself at her and, staring death in the face, she'd fired off one desperate shot. But she could feel the throb on the back of her skull that left her dazed and nauseous. Frowning, she levered herself onto her elbow to examine the back of her head.

"When the wolf dropped down on top of me, I must have slammed my head against one of the stones I gathered to encircle the campfire," she mused aloud.

Hawk reached behind her neck to feel the knot at the base of her skull and came away with blood on his fingertips. He gestured toward the wolf. "You shot him in the throat before he went for yours." He stared grimly at her. "Otherwise, things would have turned out much differently. All this blood on your clothes belongs to him, thank goodness." A faint smile curved his lips. "You did well, Shi."

She half collapsed in relief. "Another challenge met and conquered," she said then stared curiously at him. "How do you deal with this kind of danger and fear on a daily basis? I nearly had a stroke when those wolves moved in for the kill and my panicky mare refused to let me mount up before it thundered away."

"You get used to it," he said with a lackadaisical shrug that belied what he was feeling.

The truth was that, although he dealt with danger regularly, the prospect of riding into camp and finding Shiloh dead had rattled him to the extreme. He had accepted the inevitability of his own death years ago and had even cheated death several times. But Shiloh was another matter altogether. His fear for her left his heart pounding furiously. There was also a noticeable tremor in his hands.

Shiloh pushed herself into a sitting position to see the other two adult wolves sprawled on the ground. "Impressive shots. But if it isn't too much trouble, could you drag all these carcasses out of sight?" She shuddered in revulsion. "I'm probably doomed to nightmares as it is. I don't need the visible reminders lying an arm's length away."

Hawk surged to his feet to do her bidding. Then he rounded up the horses and tethered them near camp.

Shiloh frowned, bemused, as he ambled back to her.

"Isn't stealing the bandits' horses going to make it obvious that you're on their trail?"

"That's the point," he replied. "I wanted to give them a taste of being hunted and preyed upon. I'm hoping that by playing cat-and-mouse with them that they'll panic and try to go to ground so I can locate their headquarters." He smiled wryly. "Besides, it seems fitting for horse thieves to have their mounts stolen. If they're afoot, it will be easier to catch up with them after I deliver you home."

Shiloh sidled closer to the campfire and plucked at her bloody shirt. "I don't recall wolves being so aggressive toward humans when I was a child. It seems there have been more attacks the past few years."

Hawk's jaw clenched as he squatted down beside her to brew coffee. Bitter memories flooded over him, but he tried to keep anger from seeping into his voice. "We have the white man to thank for the lobos's and coyotes's more aggressive tendencies. When the hide hunters slaughtered buffalo, they left the skinned carcasses in their wake. Wolves, coyotes and panthers became gluttons for the excessive amounts of meat at their disposal. After the hunters destroyed the great herds that were the Indian's mainstay the predators turned to cattle and to man to satisfy their ravenous eating habits."

"And your people went hungry while the hide hunters got rich and the predators got fat," she murmured.

Hawk nodded. "Even before the arrival of the hide hunters, fear and respect for wolves, coyotes and panthers were a part of Indian legend," he informed her. "In fact, I grew up hearing the story of the great shaman that knows how to call in the wolves, and becomes one himself to fight evil spirits. Another legend tells about the medicine man that changes form to prowl with panthers during the dark of the moon. According to the tale, the beasts scream in warning of their coming. They are said to stalk the darkness during the nights of a thousand eyes."

Hawk came agilely to his feet. "I better see what I can round up for a meal."

Shiloh plucked distastefully at her soiled clothing. "I'm going to take another bath." She snatched up the discarded pistol. "I plan to have this weapon within easy reach…just in case."

Hawk smiled wryly as he watched Shiloh limp away. Although she had proved that she could hold her own reasonably well in the wilds, the incident with the wolves had taught her another valuable lesson: Be prepared for anything and everything.

Too bad *he* hadn't been prepared for the tantalizing sight of her creamy skin and luscious curves and swells when he examined her for wolf bites—and found not one bloody wound, only tantalizing feminine flesh. Hawk muttered when Shiloh's image—bared to the waist—exploded in his head. Although he was sincerely relieved that she had escaped a painful attack he had not needed to see what he was trying so damn hard not to touch intimately.

Fate, that cruel bastard, just kept tormenting him by keeping this irresistible female underfoot.

Scowling, Hawk stalked off to hunt for supper. If he could have trusted any of his coworkers with Shiloh, he wouldn't be here with her right now.

Then some other man would have pulled open her shirt to check for wolf bites—and got an eyeful of exquisite feminine beauty.

The unacceptable thought had Hawk muttering and

scowling all over again. He didn't need to see Shiloh half-naked and he sure as hell didn't want the other Rangers to, either.

Willfully, he shook off the forbidden images floating in his mind and told himself that he had enough willpower to resist temptation for the next two days. He would take Shiloh home, pick up the bandits' trail and hope they led him to their hideout. He hoped like hell it wasn't Drummond Ranch.

"Two more days," Hawk chanted. A man could endure just about anything for two days, couldn't he?

Shiloh felt ten times better after bathing and cleaning her clothes. However, she was still as jumpy as a grasshopper, ready to bolt at the slightest sound that suggested danger. It didn't help when she heard coyotes yipping in the distance, but thankfully, she didn't stumble upon any varmints that posed a threat.

Hawk was still hunting when Shiloh returned to camp. She decided to fish into his saddlebags to help herself to a sip of his whiskey. Ordinarily, Shiloh didn't indulge, but she had discovered during primitive surgery on her injured arm that whiskey served to calm her nerves.

She definitely needed to calm her nerves after the harrowing days she had endured. Plus, having Hawk peel open her blouse then gape at her had shaken her to the very core.

And what really shook her was that she liked having his eyes on her, even if she had felt self-conscious. But then, she reminded herself that she and Hawk had been living in each other's pockets for several days and he had seen her with her wet undergarments sticking to her like paint and that he had seen her in the best and worst of moods—not to mention everything in between. The long and short of it was that there were very few secrets left between them. She felt more comfortable with him than with any man she'd ever met.

Shiloh took a sip of whiskey and wheezed when it burned its way down her throat. From her recent experience, she knew the first few sips took her breath away, but she vowed to get past that stage to reach those numbing sensations that sent her frustrations drifting off in the wind. She took another drink as she propped herself against her saddle to stare at the hypnotic flames of the fire.

A few minutes later, her jittery nerves gave way to lethargy. Ah, this was much better, Shiloh mused as she took another sip. She wasn't leaping apprehensively each time shadows shifted. She didn't have to be tense and on guard because she knew Hawk was nearby and he hadn't failed her yet.

A lopsided smile quirked her lips as she helped herself to another drink. She'd almost died earlier that evening and she had managed to stave off disaster until Hawk arrived to provide reinforcement. Considering the week she'd had, she was beginning to think that it was important to live in the moment, because the future was extremely uncertain, especially out here in the wilderness where two-legged and four-legged predators lurked.

Shiloh asked herself what regrets she'd have if today were her last day on earth. She would miss her brothers, certainly. And, of course, her friends in town and her relatives in New Orleans. She would also miss Hawk, she mused as she sipped freely on the whiskey.

All sorts of erotic sensations wafted through her when an arresting vision of Hawk leaped to mind.

Those sensations intensified when she remembered their brief kisses and the titillating feel of his muscular body pressed closely to hers on occasion….

"Damn, woman, are you drinking to forget you almost died or are you celebrating the fact that you're still alive?" Hawk gave her a disapproving stare as he approached the campfire.

Shiloh poured more whiskey into the tin cup then offered him a smile. At least she presumed she did. Her nose and her facial muscles were so numb she couldn't be certain. In addition, her eyes refused to keep up with her when she turned her head too quickly.

"You better go easy on that stuff," Hawk warned as he placed the quail he'd cleaned and dressed on the fire. "It will go straight to your head, especially if you don't have food in your belly."

"It's taking the edge off my frazzled nerves," she said, surprised by the slur in her voice. "Want some?"

"Nice of you to offer since it's my stash," he teased as he accepted the bottle she extended to him.

He took a big swig, hoping the liquor would take the lusty edge off his thoughts. He had barely been able to concentrate on snaring food for supper, while visions of Shiloh's luscious body danced in his head.

In order to drown that tormenting thought he took another guzzle before handing the bottle back to Shiloh.

She refilled her cup then stared at him so intently that he squirmed in his skin. "What's-a-matter?" he asked.

"I was just thinking about those times you kissed me and I kissed you…all too quickly."

Hawk grabbed the bottle and guzzled another drink. "That's not a safe subject. Let's talk about something else."

She shook her head and his helpless gaze settled on the glorious mane of hair that caught flame in the light, making his fingers itch to test the silky texture of the long tresses that spilled over her shoulders. Hawk inwardly groaned in torment then helped himself to another sip of liquor.

"I was sitting here listing all the things I would miss if I hadn't survived the wolf attack," she commented in a slurred voice.

"I don't want to talk about *that* prospect, either," he said before he took another swig.

She went on as if she hadn't heard him. "Guess what I wouldn't want to miss if I sailed off to the Hereafter?"

"I give up. What?" he said impatiently.

He silently applauded when the effects of the whiskey kicked in. A few more drinks on an empty stomach and he wouldn't remember that he wanted Shiloh in the worst way.

She rolled onto her hands and knees, her green eyes dancing in the firelight. The smile she flashed him was so alluring that he felt himself leaning involuntarily toward her. It was damn scary how thin his veneer of self-control was when he was with her. And how hard it was to think of anything except how much he wanted her.

"I don't wanna leave this world, wonderin' what it'd be like to *really* kiss you," she mumbled. "Not just one of those hit-and-run kisses. I want a slow, deep kiss so I can get a thorough taste of you."

Need pelted him like a Gatling gun when she inched ever closer and he got a whiff of her fresh clean scent. *Don't do it, you fool!* The voice of reason railed at him. *There are some things a sensible man doesn't need to know…or feel…. This is at the top of your list!*

"Kiss me like you mean it, Hawk," she entreated as he stared into those jewel-green eyes and those inviting Cupid's bow lips.

Chapter Ten

Despite that well-meaning voice echoing in his brain, he didn't retreat when Shiloh's lush mouth slanted over his. He breathed her in, tasted her deeply and buried his fingers in those shiny tendrils so he could hold her head at just the right angle to explore the hidden recesses of her mouth.

He heard her moan softly, felt her arch toward him then loop her arms around his shoulders. His body caught fire and burned everywhere her body touched his. He was so aware of her, wanted her to such extremes that he ached and throbbed with hungry desire. Even breathing became a chore because his accelerated pulse was pounding against his rib cage so hard that his lungs threatened to collapse.

Sweet mercy! The intensity of the impact this woman had on him was frightening!

"Mmm…that's more like it," she mumbled when he came up for air. Her head tilted sideways and an impish grin pursed her kiss-swollen lips. "I've definitely been missing out. We need to do that again." Her hand drifted down his neck to the buttons of his shirt. "I want my hands on you, too."

When she leaned in, Hawk dodged her kiss and her experimental touch. His lusty body rained down a raft of salty curses for avoiding her, but he had just enough common sense left to call a halt before it was too late. "This is not a good idea," he bleated. "Besides, I need a bath."

"Go take one," she said as she sank down to retrieve her cup. "I'll be waiting for you to get back." She cast him an encouraging smile—and it hit him so hard that he swayed on his knees. "I like the taste and feel of you, Hawk. I want more."

When he felt himself reaching for her, he knotted his fists at his sides and made himself stand up and turn away from her. He was so hard and aching that a cold bath was all that would save him from doing something he would later regret. He shook his head to clear the lusty haze from his brain and promptly reminded himself that Shiloh wouldn't be voicing those outrageous comments, if not for partaking of whiskey to forget the hair-raising encounter with lobos.

Hawk had experienced that same high-flying intensity, followed by the downward spiral of emotions after battles. He recognized the sense of recklessness that consumed Shiloh. The desire to reaffirm that you survived made you eager to make the most of every moment.

But she would regret becoming physically involved with him when she came to her senses, Hawk thought realistically.

Inhaling a fortifying breath to get his unruly body under control, Hawk peeled off his clothes on the way down to the creek. He expelled a groan when the cool water sizzled on his overheated male anatomy. Thankfully, his sanity returned after he soaked his head.

Damn good thing that he had walked away from Shiloh when he did. Otherwise, they might be locked together in the heat of lust and she would regret it later.

The image of her naked body moving familiarly against his blazed across his brain like a shooting star. Hawk thrust his head underwater again, hoping to douse those vivid images before they set off another round of maddening sensations.

He had to think about something else. Like his injured brother. Like his departed mentor and friend and the restitution Hawk wanted to deliver to those murdering thieves that terrorized the area.

When he regained some measure of control, he emerged from the creek to dress in clean clothes. He would like to linger for another half hour to make sure he had his head back on straight and his lusty body under wraps, but there was food cooking and Shiloh was already three sheets to the wind. He didn't dare leave her alone for too long.

Hawk breathed a gusty sigh of relief when he returned to camp to see Shiloh draped sideways over the saddle that served as her pillow. Her eyelashes lay like butterflies against her creamy cheeks. The half-empty bottle sat at her fingertips.

Another jab of lust hit him hard and fast. He could think of a dozen interesting ways to wake Shiloh up— all of which involved his roaming hands and wandering lips greeting every inch of her silky flesh.

Stop torturing yourself! came that sensible voice— one that he was really getting tired of. His noble conscience refused to let him have one bit of fun—not with her, at least.

Wheeling around, Hawk checked on the meat roasting on the fire then strode off to unsaddle all the horses and check the contents of the extra saddlebags. He frowned pensively when he fished out two stacks of bank notes. His heart thudded against his ribs when his fingertips closed around the familiar pearl-handled dagger with the initials A.P. inscribed on it.

Rage and frustration overcame him as he surveyed the knife that had once belonged to the Indian Agent that had given the Hawk brothers refuge after their escape from the hated reservation in New Mexico. He couldn't swear that the two men were responsible for Archie Pearson's death, but he would dearly love to tie them up and extract information from them—Apache style. Unfortunately, that would mean exposing Shiloh to the brutality involved in his job or leaving her alone again to confront the two outlaws. He felt much too guilty for not being on hand to protect her from her recent mishap already. First he'd get Shiloh to safety then track the outlaws he'd left afoot.

"I'll have the truth someday soon, Archie," Hawk promised the vision floating above him. "Justice will prevail. It's the only way Fletch and I can repay you for your kindness now."

After dragging the saddles to the ground, Hawk walked back to the fire. He cast a glance at Shiloh who was still sprawled on her pallet. Squatting down, Hawk retrieved the meat and coffee. He nudged Shiloh gently to rouse her, but she simply moaned and curled up beside him. Idiot that he was, he dropped a kiss to her lips, then asked himself what the hell he thought he was doing. It had taken a cold bath to calm him down after their last sizzling kiss.

To his dismay—or pleasure, he wasn't sure which— she responded to his kiss then glided her arms around his neck to snuggle even closer to his sensitized body.

Another jolt of fiery desire scorched him and he gnashed his teeth.

Damn it, he and this woman had no future and she deserved more than a fleeting moment in the wilderness. Why couldn't he remember that when he got within five feet of her?

"I can't think of a better way to wake up," Shiloh murmured drowsily. "Kiss me again, Hawk."

"No. Sit up and eat," he demanded gruffly.

She crinkled her nose at his terse command then levered herself upright. Hawk set the plate between them. "I found my friend's knife when I checked the desperadoes' saddlebags."

"I'm sorry." She stared quizzically at him as she munched on the tender meat. "Who was this friend of yours, Hawk?"

"Archie Pearson was the Indian Agent who tried to persuade the government officials to let my people establish a reservation in the Apacheria in Texas instead of splitting us up and shipping us off to New Mexico and Indian Territory," Hawk explained. "He was our spokesman and loyal friend to the Apache, unlike too many agents that swindle from their charges for personal gain."

Hawk smiled fondly as he continued. "Archie also granted Fletch and me refuge when we fled from Bosque Redondo. He gave us clothing and money to tide us over until we found work. He put in a good word for me with his friend at Ranger headquarters in Austin and sent Fletch off with a letter of recommendation to a law official that hired him as a railroad detective."

"I can understand why you feel a deep sense of devotion to him," Shiloh murmured.

Hawk gritted his teeth against the bitterness and

pain he had experienced when he learned of Archie's senseless murder. "I stopped by to see Archie eight months ago, but raiders had been there first. They ransacked the ranch, stole his food and belongings and shot him."

"I'm truly sorry," Shiloh whispered as she reached over to clutch his hand consolingly.

He tried to shrug off the burning resentment, but it was still there, still roiling beneath his pretense of calm control. "That was another hard lesson I had to learn. Nothing is forever and bad things often happen to good and decent people. Evil and brutality aren't the least bit selective about where they strike."

He glanced at her momentarily. "Take you, for instance. You did nothing to deserve the hell you've been through this week. You were simply at the wrong place at the wrong time." He stared meaningfully at her. "I don't want to make things more complicated between us than they already are."

Shiloh nibbled on her meal, her head downcast. "So you are saying that kissing me again isn't simple?"

"Yes… I mean no…." Hawk raked his hands through his hair when her luminous gaze locked on his.

"Which is it?" she wanted to know.

"Both," he said on a deflated breath.

"What is wrong with living in the moment once in a while?"

"Because you and I are treading on dangerous ground and I don't want things to get complicated," Hawk insisted. "The sooner you're home with your brothers—" provided they weren't behind this thievery "—the better off you'll be."

And that was a fact, he told himself sternly. Shiloh was on the rebound because she'd lost her heart to a silver-tongued opportunist. As much as Hawk desired Shiloh—and his need for her was as hot as hell blazing—he'd be damned if he became her consolation prize. He might be considered a second-rate citizen by whites, but he refused to be a substitute for the man Shiloh really wanted. He still had his pride, damn it.

"I suppose you're right," she replied, battling the sting of rejection. Why was it, she wondered, that the men she found appealing felt no fond attachment to her? First Antoine, the cad. Now Hawk. She'd practically thrown herself at him earlier, ready to cast caution to the wind. But he'd backed off. The infuriating man!

"If I stripped naked in front of you and offered myself to you, with no strings attached, you'd probably tell me to put my clothes on," she muttered under her breath.

"Come again?"

Shiloh waved off his curious frown. "Never mind. It isn't important." *Just my injured pride taking another beating.*

She stretched out on her pallet and turned her back on Hawk. She stared into the darkness, trying to convince herself that it was only the reckless side effects of whiskey that provoked her to seduce Hawk—unsuccessfully. If she had been in full command of her senses she wouldn't have kissed him as if she was about to die and he was her last wish.

She probably should thank him for refusing her reckless invitation. As he said, he'd be out of her life by tomorrow.

Shiloh frowned as her eyes drifted shut. *Gone tomorrow.* The troubling thought echoed in her mind.

She'd become accustomed to seeing Hawk the first

thing in the morning and the last thing at night. She hoped that having him gone wouldn't take some serious getting used to.

Blast it, when had she gotten emotionally attached to him? She certainly hadn't meant to, she mused as she drifted into whiskey-induced sleep.

Eerie pinpoints of light flickered in the darkness as a pack of wolves stalked toward the dying coals of the campfire. Panthers, black as a moonless night, crept up in their wake. Forming the outer circle of imminent peril were the ruthless bandits that made it a policy never to leave eyewitnesses to testify against them.

Muffled thunder rolled like a forewarning of danger. Warning growls and piercing screams filled the air. Shiloh scrambled onto her hands and knees, desperate to locate the pistol she had dropped earlier. Terror clogged her throat, making it impossible for her to cry out in alarm, as dozens of ominous shadows and glowing eyes converged on the campsite, ready to gobble her alive.

When one of the prowling beasts launched itself at her, she clawed at it wildly. Her horrified scream finally broke from her throat when she saw the other fanged predators moving in for the kill. Another howl of terror burst from her lips as she tried to wrest free of the oppressive weight bearing down on her. Cold chills shot down her spine when she saw the man-eating beasts transform into the ghastly apparitions of men....

"Shiloh, damn it, wake up! It's me. Hawk!"

She heard the deep voice rolling toward her, as if through a long winding tunnel. But her survival instincts kept her on full alert, prompting her to fight for her life.

"Open your eyes and look at me!"

She was afraid to, afraid the mystical phantom beasts that changed from men to monsters on a whim were trying to play a trick on her.

"Shi, can you hear me?"

When she was jerked upright abruptly and clamped tightly in unyielding arms, her eyes flew open. She glanced at the glowing coals of the campfire, bewildered and confused. There were no glowing eyes floating above the tall grass, no fanged beasts waiting to tear her to shreds, no armed gunmen lined up like a firing squad behind the lobos and panthers.

Her breath gushed out as she stared into Hawk's concerned expression. "Dear God!" she said with a seesaw breath.

"That must have been one hell of a nightmare." He stroked her back, easing the riveting tension that claimed her. "I thought I'd never get you to wake up. I probably have claw marks on my face and bruises on my belly where you pelted me."

"I'm sorry." She raked her hands through her tangled hair and dragged in a steadying breath. "It was—" she shuddered at the vivid images "—awful. I had nightmares as a child when my parents died in the fire, but this…" She breathed deeply and told herself to stop shaking. "This seemed so real. The wolf attack this evening, those legends about phantom lobos and panthers you mentioned and the threat of the outlaws wanting to silence me so I couldn't identify them, all got tangled up with a bit too much whiskey," she deduced.

Shiloh told herself to move away from the comforting circle of Hawk's arms because he didn't want her. But the aftereffects of the unnerving nightmare held her solidly in place and she shivered uncontrollably.

NO POSTAGE
NECESSARY
IF MAILED
IN THE
UNITED STATES

BUSINESS REPLY MAIL
FIRST-CLASS MAIL   PERMIT NO. 717-003   BUFFALO, NY

POSTAGE WILL BE PAID BY ADDRESSEE

HARLEQUIN READER SERVICE
3010 WALDEN AVE
PO BOX 1867
BUFFALO NY 14240-9952

LAS VEGAS
GAME

*Just scratch off
the gold box with a coin.
Then check below to see
the gifts you get!*

YES! I have scratched off the gold box. Please send
me my **2 FREE BOOKS** and **gift for which I qualify**. I understand
that I am under no obligation to purchase any books as
explained on the back of this card.

349 HDL EFV2   246 HDL EFZ2

FIRST NAME	LAST NAME

ADDRESS

APT.#	CITY

STATE/PROV.	ZIP/POSTAL CODE

(H-H-06/06)

7	7	7	Worth TWO FREE BOOKS plus a BONUS Mystery Gift!
🍒	🍒	🍒	Worth TWO FREE BOOKS!
🔔	🔔	♣	TRY AGAIN!

www.eHarlequin.com

Offer limited to one per household and not
valid to current Harlequin Historicals®
subscribers. All orders subject to approval.

r Privacy - Harlequin is committed to protecting your privacy. Our policy is available online at www.eharlequin.com
pon request from the Harlequin Reader Service. From time to time we make our lists of customers available to

When she felt his chin resting on the crown of her head, felt his hand glide from her rigid shoulder to the curve of her hips, her lingering fear gave way to tantalizing sensations that heated her chilled flesh from inside out.

Shiloh heard an inner voice whispering, *Live for the moment because you never know which moment is going to be your last. Take whatever Hawk will give you without any expectations.*

Spurred by desire and an overwhelming need for protection and comfort, Shiloh tipped back her head and arched upward to brush her lips over his. She felt his splayed hand coast over her abdomen then settle on the swell of her breast. Pleasure rippled through her. Passion flared to life like a match set to dry kindling.

Enthralled by the sensations flooding through her, she leaned into him, aching for more. She was amazed that what she felt for him far exceeded the naive infatuation she had developed for Antoine. But comparing the two men was laughable because they were at opposite ends of a spectrum.

Antoine was all for show—like an expensive tailored suit designed to dazzle and impress guests at an elaborate ball.

Logan Hawk was a rugged, invincible warrior. He was the man she wanted on her side, by her side when trouble broke out. He was also the man she wanted to introduce her to passion because in all likelihood she would never allow herself to be this vulnerable to a man again.

With that thought drifting in her mind, Shiloh looped her arms over his sturdy shoulders. She kissed him for all she was worth, silently assuring him that she wanted this embrace to be the beginning of a fantasy, not the end of her harrowing nightmare. She heard him groan deep in his throat, felt his arms contract around her.

Even when she told herself that any woman could satisfy the need she had aroused in him, she still experienced a gratifying sense of feminine power. Nothing had prepared her for any of these unique sensations and ravenous needs that overwhelmed her.

When Antoine had taken her in his arms and kissed her, it had been pleasurable. But it was nothing like being consumed by Hawk's embrace. Whatever she thought she felt for Antoine was nowhere near the tidal wave of intense pleasure that cascaded over her when Hawk crushed his sensuous mouth against hers and stole the breath from her lungs.

She was astonished that he seemed as frantic and desperate as she felt. Her heart was hammering like a tom-tom and her breath came in panting spurts. Her body sizzled and burned when his hand cupped her breasts and his thumb brushed against her turgid nipple. When he bent to suckle her through the fabric of her blouse, a wobbly moan tumbled from her lips. Shiloh swore she was melting beneath his hot mouth and there was nothing she could do to prevent it.

Nothing she *wanted* to do to prevent it.

"Hawk?" Her voice was filled with wonderment and aching need. "I want you…."

Hawk squeezed his eyes shut and battled valiantly for control, but it was slow in coming. He eased away from her and asked himself what the sweet loving hell he thought he was doing. This was not one of the occasional women who came and went from his life when he wanted to scratch an itch. This was Shiloh, someone he had come to know and like—because of her feisty nature and independent streak that sometimes drove him crazy but always intrigued him. She was someone who had come to matter to him, someone who deserved more than a quick tumble on the ground.

"The wanting is just lust talking," he told her in a raspy voice that he barely recognized as his own.

"Then I'm all in favor of listening," she replied recklessly. "You need to know that I am very determined to have my way with you, Hawk."

When she rubbed provocatively against him he wanted to throw back his head and howl at the moon. Sweet mercy! This green-eyed siren was driving him to complete distraction. She tasted like heaven and felt like an angel—all soft and smooth flesh…and not quite attainable to a man like him.

The words *forbidden, taboo* and *off-limits* flittered through his mind without taking root. But that was because his heart wasn't listening to the good sense sent down by his brain. The truth was that he wanted Shiloh as he had never wanted anything else in life. Hell, he hadn't known it was possible to want someone as much as he desired her. Even when he knew she was on the rebound, he still wanted her. Even when he knew that he wasn't the right kind of man for her, he still craved her. He had nothing to offer her that she didn't have already, but none of that seemed to matter when she was warm and willing in his arms.

They were alone in the dark of night, far away from the condemning eyes of society. He had spent too many waking hours trying to resist her lure, trying to remain professional and impersonal. It hadn't worked worth a damn, though. Every time Shiloh faced disaster or suffered pain, it affected him to the extreme.

He had grown accustomed to caring for her, protecting her. He was constantly drawn by the alluring sight of her, by the sound of her voice, by her vivacious personality. She made him feel more alive than he'd ever felt, made him want to yield to the tempting and dangerous emotions she called from him.

He wanted her. The undeniable truth was that he had wanted her since the very first time he laid eyes on her.

Now here she was, confiding that she wanted him, too, whether it was best for them or not—and he knew it wasn't.

But consequences be damned....

Hawk lost the inner battle he'd been fighting when she kissed him as if she was starving to death for another taste of him. Her fingertips drifted across his bare chest and his defeated groan must have encouraged her because she raked her nails down his belly.

Need, intense and forceful, struck like a physical blow. Her touch made him hard and aching in the time it took to draw breath. He tried—and barely managed—to exhibit some restraint when her lips drifted down his shoulder to skip lightly from one male nipple to the other. When her adventurous hand skimmed over the waistband of his breeches he couldn't breathe because need throbbed heavily, tormentingly inside him.

There was no hope for it, he realized defeatedly. Shiloh set off so many wild sensations and triggered so many emotions that he didn't know which feeling to fight first. He couldn't remain immune to her touch when she set him on fire and fanned the flames with each tantalizing kiss and caress.

He was pretty sure that she was going to be the exception to every rule he had made about remaining detached and uninvolved, whether it was in business or pleasure. Because *not* feeling, *not* responding to her was impossible.

He groaned in unholy torment as her warm lips skimmed over his chest, making him melt into a puddle of helpless desire. "Damn, woman, what are you doing to me?"

"Whatever I wish," she murmured impishly. "Do you mind so much, Hawk?"

"Mmm…" was all he could get out when her mouth returned to his and he drowned in the intoxicating taste of her.

He absorbed her alluring fragrance and felt ravenous hunger engulf him. He wanted her out of her clothes—now. He wanted to kiss and caress every satiny curve and contour of her body until he knew her by touch and taste. He wanted to feel her respond to his touch and lose himself in the fire of desire that billowed around him.

To that end, he unfastened her blouse and bared her satiny flesh to his appreciative gaze. He pressed his lips to the swanlike column of her throat, felt her pulse racing in accelerated rhythm. When he cupped her breasts in his hands and teased her nipples with thumbs and fingertips, a soft moan tumbled from her lips. He smiled in satisfaction when she trembled beneath his tender touch and he realized he had given her pleasure.

She whispered his name as his lips skimmed the taut peaks of her breasts then he flicked at them with his tongue. He felt her nails spike into his back as he suckled her gently, aroused her and drew her from one plateau of dizzying pleasure to the next.

Hawk had never dedicated so much time to pleasing a woman, never felt the need or the desire to explore a woman's body so thoroughly. But anything less than complete devotion to Shiloh's pleasure was unacceptable to him. He should have fretted over why that seemed so important, but he was too enthralled with seducing her—one kiss and caress at a time—to puzzle it out. Too caught up in the power he seemed to hold over her and mystified by her uninhibited responses to him.

"Sweet mercy!" Shiloh panted as he eased her back to the pallet then hovered over her. "I can barely breathe."

He kissed her and she realized she didn't have to breathe. All she needed was the taste of him to survive. He had lifted her into another realm where erotic sensations prevailed. The feel of his hands and lips drifting unhurriedly over her body was driving her crazy. She couldn't control the fervent desire that burst alive inside her like fireworks. She couldn't satisfy the maddening needs that he incited in her. He made her feel wild and desperate, impatient and reckless.

Her breath hitched and her heart skipped a beat when his hands and lips whispered over her rib cage. A coil of heat knotted inside her when he loosened the band of her breeches and slowly but deliberately eased them off her hips. Shiloh told herself that she probably should be embarrassed when he tossed aside the last of her clothing and she lay naked and exposed to him. But the look of masculine appreciation gleaming in his midnight eyes made her feel desirable, special.

Although Antoine had left her feeling unwanted and insecure, Hawk made her feel alive and empowered… and yet enslaved by the unrestrained passion he incited in her. Her thoughts scattered like buckshot when his hands drifted back and forth over her inner thighs. Her breath broke when his warm lips flitted over her abdomen then drifted lower.

Shiloh forgot to breathe—didn't care if she ever did again—when he stroked her intimately with his thumb. Wild hunger raged through her quivering body. Fiery sensations shot into her very core with each slow, deep penetration of his fingertip. Never in her life had she experienced such a phenomenal craving, such a desperate need for a man. But she wanted Hawk like an addict craved a mindless obsession.

And she wanted him *now,* before white-hot desire caused her to burst into flames.

"Come here," she demanded frantically.

"Not yet," he whispered as he lowered his head. "I want to taste you completely...."

Shiloh was unprepared for the hot, spiraling sensation of pleasure that riveted her body when he kissed her intimately. Uncontrollable spasms rocked and buffeted her. She shamelessly arched toward his erotic kiss, felt his fingertip tracing her secret flesh then gliding inside her to set a seductive rhythm that drove her insane with wanting all over again.

Hawk shuddered with barely restrained need when he felt the hot rain of Shiloh's desire on his lips and fingertips. Answering heat throbbed heavily through his sensitized body, burning him inside and out. He had never known a woman could be so responsive, had never dared such intimacy before.

Yet, for some reason he couldn't seem to be satisfied with anything less than watching and feeling Shiloh come apart in his arms. He wanted to know what pleasured her, wanted to know her in every way imaginable. Wanted her to know him just as well. And when he came to her, he wanted to share the same intense pleasure, share the same frantic breath, the same uncontrollable need.

For sure and certain he didn't want Shiloh to mistake him for that low-down, conniving scoundrel that she had fallen in love with. He wanted *his* face to be the one she saw above her, *his* touch to be the one that set her aflame.

"Please…" she cried out in frantic desperation.

"Look at me," he commanded as he eased between her legs.

Her long lashes swept up, her green eyes glowing with the ardent passion he had ignited inside her.

"Who do you see, Shiloh?"

"A tormenting devil who is taking his hellish time about satisfying all these wicked cravings he set off." A smile pursed her lips as her hands glided up his chest to settle on his shoulders. "Are you going to make me beg all night?"

"No, I just wanted to make sure you aren't pretending I'm someone else."

Shiloh cupped his ruggedly handsome face in her hands and brought his head steadily toward hers. She was so wildly desperate for him, so entranced by the sensations leapfrogging through her body that it didn't dawn on her that Hawk needed the reassurance that he wasn't her consolation prize.

She couldn't think. Period. She simply desired.

"I need you," she panted. "*Now,* Hawk. Make the empty ache go away."

When he lifted her hips to his and thrust forward, she tensed. The unexpected pressure of his masculine invasion took her by surprise, dimming the pleasure that shimmered inside her. Alarmed, confused, she stared up at him.

And he stared back. "Shiloh?" he choked out hoarsely.

There were a dozen questions in his voice, in his eyes, as he went absolutely still above her. The realization that he was her first lover sent his thoughts spinning like a cyclone. "I presumed—"

"*I* thought all good Rangers dealt strictly with facts," she murmured wryly. "Presumptions always get you in trouble."

She shifted beneath him, restless, curious and so naturally seductive that he felt another jolt of desire ricochet through him. She moved again, as if silently assuring him that she still wanted him, wanted the passion he offered. He felt the fragile barrier of innocence give way as he moved instinctively toward her, trying to be as tender as possible.

He had never been a woman's first time—hadn't expected to be Shiloh's, either. An unexplained sense of possessiveness overcame him as he buried himself deeply within her then gently withdrew. He felt her lush body caressing him inwardly. The unparalleled pleasure she gave him played hell with his noble attempt at self-control.

Burning alive in the passion she stirred in him, he wrapped her legs around his hips and plunged into her again. To the hilt. He made himself wait until she adjusted to the feel of their bodies locked intimately together as one pulsing essence.

And then the most incredible smile spread across her lips. It was like watching a radiant rainbow arc across the heavens. It blinded him, dazzled him and stole his breath.

"The next time a wild renegade drops from the sky I won't be in such an all-fired rush to escape him." She stared up at him as only Shiloh could—curious and straightforward. "Is there more?"

"Plenty," he assured her, feeling a devilish grin spread across his lips. "I'll be all too happy to show you."

He moved gently within her, although it was damn near killing him to maintain such a slow, deliberate pace while his male body was making frantic demands on him. He watched her luminous eyes sparkle with desire, saw her lips part with wonder as they rocked together then apart, setting a cadence that took him higher, deeper and then left him spinning out of control in a way he never had before, and might never again.

Breath-robbing pleasure bombarded him when he felt Shiloh shudder and contract around him. The biting pressure of her nails on his back indicated that she was attempting to anchor herself against the mind-boggling sensations that consumed her. Consumed him. She clutched at him as desperately as he held on to her when waves of ecstasy drenched them both. Shimmers of indescribable release swamped him as he toppled off some unseen ledge that he'd never toppled off before.

And suddenly he was drifting through a dark, unfamiliar universe where time knew no measure and pleasure was without boundaries. It seemed to take forever for Hawk to breathe normally again, to think again.

Marshaling what was left of his energy he eased away. He gathered their scattered clothes and helped Shiloh wiggle back into hers, then she helped him into his.

"I'd prefer to have you spend the night naked in my arms," he murmured huskily, "but it's better to be ready to get up and get moving in case of trouble."

She nodded drowsily as she snuggled up against

him and burrowed her head against his shoulder. "I'd rather have you naked in my arms, too," she confided before she dozed off.

Hawk's worst fear was being so satiated that he slept like a trusting child. He'd made it a habit to sleep with one eye open and both ears tuned to danger. But try as he might, he couldn't overcome that tempting sense of peace and security that blanketed him while he and Shiloh cuddled in each other's arms. He slumped against her, finding that his dreams had taken up exactly where erotic reality left off.

Hawk had been in some tight scrapes in his life, but he was damn sorry to say that he'd consumed enough liquor the previous night to be caught completely off guard the next morning when the barrel of a shotgun jabbed into his neck. Two men grabbed his feet and jerked him off the pallet.

Outlaws, no doubt, he mused as he appraised the ferocious glares directed at him. Five ragtag men, their faces rimmed with the stubble of whiskers, snarled viciously. Refusing to be intimidated, Hawk snarled back.

"Do me a favor and try to make a run for it, you worthless son of a bitch!" the man with the shotgun hissed as he crammed the weapon against Hawk's throat and growled maliciously.

Hawk didn't attempt to wrest free while the men dragged him away from the campfire. If that weapon went off, he wasn't about to take a chance on Shiloh being shot. Everything inside him rebelled. He squirmed for release when he saw another dark-haired scoundrel swoop down to jostle Shiloh from the whiskey-induced sleep that made her slow to rouse—and even slower to react.

Every protective instinct inside him exploded to life. When Shiloh mumbled intelligibly, unaware of the danger she faced, Hawk knew he needed to get to her quickly. His arm shot upward to knock aside the shotgun barrel stuck in his neck. He reared up to plant his fist in the nose of the man who had clamped hold of his right ankle.

Pained howls and foul curses erupted around him as he shook off the other would-be captor. Hawk vaulted to his feet to deliver a right cross that packed enough wallop to send the man standing in front of him staggering backward into a graceless sprawl in the grass.

Shouts went up around him, but Hawk ignored them in his haste to reach Shiloh before she was dragged off to be molested and abused. Her befuddled gaze locked with his momentarily—and then his eyes went out of focus because the butt of the shotgun slammed against the back of his skull.

Hawk hit his knees, fighting the dizziness that swam before his eyes. When he tried to launch himself at the man who hoisted Shiloh to her feet another sharp blow connected with his head, causing him to pitch forward in the grass.

Hawk cursed himself soundly for failing Shiloh and then he collapsed, oblivious to the world.

Chapter Eleven

Dazed and disoriented, Shiloh tried to shake off the cobwebs that clogged her mind and swore never to ingest whiskey again. The hangovers were murderous!

"What the devil do you think you're doing?" Shiloh croaked as she watched her two scraggly-looking brothers drag Hawk's unconscious body to the nearest tree.

"We're hanging the son of a bitch that kidnapped you…and only God knows what else he's done," Gideon Drummond muttered as he glared murderously at his unmoving captive.

"Wake up that bastard," Noah Drummond ordered one of the three cowboys that had volunteered to ride in the rescue brigade. "I want him to know what's going on when we leave him dangling from the end of a rope. He's going to feel his neck stretched out before he dies."

"Stop it!" Shiloh railed—unintentionally inflicting agony on her sensitive head. Nauseous though she was, she abruptly jerked free of Noah's grasp. "You are not going to hang him!"

"You're sorely mistaken, little sister," Gideon growled. "If you don't want to watch it happen then take a walk."

Shiloh tried to reach Hawk, who had been tossed over a horse and had a noose draped around his neck. She was ten feet away when George Porter, one of their ranch hands, splashed water on Hawk's head, rousing him to consciousness.

In the next instant, Hawk was lashing out with his hands and feet to land blows that sent the cowboys standing on either side of him leaping out of his reach. Shiloh noted, amazed, that not only did Hawk put up an impressive resistance, but he was a force to be reckoned with, despite the odds. The consummate fighter, she mused, awed.

"Shiloh, run!" he shouted as he pulled his head from the noose.

When several shotguns snapped into firing position, threatening to blow Hawk out of the saddle if he tried to escape, Shiloh thrust herself in front of him like a shield.

"Move, damn it," Gideon bellowed at her.

"Make a run for it," Hawk ordered, glaring defiantly at his captors.

Shiloh waved her arms in expansive gestures. "This man is a Texas Ranger," she told her bloodthirsty brothers. "If you shoot him or hang him then you'll have to answer to *his* brother and a battalion of law officers."

Her comment met with disbelieving stares and silence.

Then Noah growled and said, "I don't give a damn what he *claims* to be. He kidnapped you and he is going to suffer the consequences!"

Shiloh braced her fists on her hips and stared down her mule-headed brothers. "You have jumped to the wrong conclusion. Logan Hawk didn't abduct me. He *saved* me from a shoot-out with outlaws." She indicated the bandage on her arm and purposely omitted the fact that *he* was the reason she ended up in a shoot-out with outlaws in the first place. "Then he rescued me from the fall I took down the side of a mountain." She called their attention to her tender ankle. "Last night he saved me from being devoured by a pack of wolves. He deserves a medal for his heroics, not a hanging."

Apparently, Gideon was unfazed by Hawk's honorable deeds. He glowered at Hawk and said, "He was sharing your bedroll and *that,* by God, is punishable by death!"

"Amen to that, brother," Noah chimed in as he cast Hawk the evil eye.

Brother? Hawk's head snapped up and he glanced between the two scruffy-looking, green-eyed men that were only a few inches shorter and perhaps twenty pounds lighter than he was. Earlier, Hawk had been too busy trying to avoid a hanging so he could rescue Shiloh to notice the Drummonds' family resemblance.

But now he noticed. "Oh, hell," he muttered.

"You can say that again," Gideon sneered ominously.

"*Hell* is exactly where you're headed," Noah vowed spitefully.

"Been there," Hawk shot back, refusing to back down from the two men who glared at him with mutinous disapproval. "The devil sends his regards, by the way."

The caustic remark earned him a few more menacing stares, which Hawk ignored. He was accustomed to being instantly disliked because of his bronzed skin, raven-black hair and midnight-colored eyes. He critically assessed the Drummond brothers and their companions. All five men were in desperate need of a clean set of clothes, a haircut and a shave.

His previous suspicions rose to the surface as he fixed his condemning gaze on Noah and Gideon. "I won't be surprised to learn that your ranch is one of the outlaw hideouts we're searching for. Did you parley with your two horseless friends this morning?"

Shiloh whipped around to stare at him in disbelief. "Are you suggesting that *my brothers* are mixed up with this spree of robberies, killings and rustling? That's preposterous! *You* are jumping to as many ill-founded conclusions as *they* are!"

"There are five of them and they're armed to the teeth," Hawk pointed out reasonably. "They also look as ragtag and unkempt as the gang I infiltrated."

"That's because we've been scouring the countryside since the day we rode into Cerrogordo to discover that Shiloh had returned, but left her luggage at the blacksmith shop and rented a horse to make the last leg of her trip home unescorted." Noah swiveled his head around to glare reproachfully at his sister. "And I would dearly like to know what you're doing back in Texas, gallivanting around here alone. Apparently your damnable independent streak got you in serious trouble." He glared at Hawk, indicating that *he* was the serious trouble she had gotten into.

"We were worried sick about you," Gideon snapped. "We were afraid the absolute worst had happened." He, too, focused his venomous gaze on Hawk. "Which appears to be true."

"Why *are* you back in Texas?" Noah demanded. "And why didn't you inform us that you were coming home?"

Hawk saw Shiloh wince. But to her credit, she tilted her head, squared her shoulders and said, "We will get to that explanation later. What's important right now is that you apologize to this Ranger for nearly hanging him unjustly."

She half turned to focus her disconcerting frown on Hawk. "And you can apologize to Noah and Gideon for presuming they are bandits."

"So sorry," Hawk said in a tone that wasn't the least bit apologetic. He slung his leg over the saddle horn then hopped to the ground.

This was not the way he had planned to introduce himself to Shiloh's overprotective brothers. They were smart enough to realize that he and Shiloh had become a mite too familiar with each other—hence sleeping on the same pallet. Judging by the censure in their eyes, they were going to hold that against him until the day he died—which would have been today if they had had their way.

Of course, Hawk didn't blame them for what they were thinking. He was never going to forgive himself for abandoning his good sense last night and surrendering to forbidden temptation. He had predicted that he would regret his reckless impulse later.

Sure enough, he did.

"I suppose you want to see my badge," Hawk said as he glanced from one annoyed brother to the other.

"Damn right we do," Noah let him know in a hurry.

Hawk strode over to fetch his boot, then dug out the silver star. "And no, it isn't stolen. I earned it the hard way and I have the battle scars to show for it. Captain

Benjamin Tipton, my coworkers and my brother, Fletch, can vouch for me if you still doubt my identity."

"After the incident with Frank Mills and his hired imposter you can bet we plan to check on you," Noah insisted.

"I'm really sorry about this," Shiloh murmured when she and Hawk began to gather up their belongings. "My brothers are usually courteous and respectful. As I told you, they are a bit overprotective where I'm concerned."

"At least you have someone who cares," he replied as he tossed his saddlebags over his mustang. "Now that you're in good hands, I think it's best if we part company. I don't want to lose track of the bandits I left traveling on foot."

Shiloh felt her heart drop to her feet. She'd known this moment was inevitable, had even anticipated getting back to a life that was familiar to her. However, after last night she was feeling… Well, she didn't know exactly *what* she was feeling. Not that it mattered because Hawk's brisk comment made it glaringly apparent that he was anxious to get her off his hands. He was on a personal and professional mission and she was only a distraction, a night of reckless passion that he allowed himself before he went merrily on his way.

Although the realization cut to the quick, she put on a bold front, just as she had done when Antoine jilted her. And hadn't that become a disturbing pattern in her life? Being jilted by one man and then another? Which reaffirmed her belief that her lack of charm, personality and character made her as resistible as a woman could possibly get.

Shiloh hauled in a bracing breath and rallied around her bruised pride. She thrust out her hand, vowing to appear as impersonal and unaffected as Hawk seemed to be. "Thank you for your protection and assistance, Mr. Hawk. I am indebted to you. If there is anything my brothers and I can do to help you—"

"Speak for yourself, Shi." Noah smirked, his expression indicating that he didn't care to have any further association with Hawk, Texas Ranger or not.

Shiloh shot her brother a silencing glance then continued, "I will be glad to do whatever necessary to bring the desperadoes to justice. Don't hesitate to ask for assistance in tracking the outlaws."

"Hesitate," Gideon grunted sarcastically, then sent Hawk another dour glance. "But thanks so much for toting our little sister home."

"Yeah, and nice knowing you…temporarily," Noah said flippantly.

"C'mon, Shiloh." Gideon held the reins to her horse so she could mount up. "Thanks to this time-consuming search we are a week behind schedule on ranch chores. We've probably lost a few more head of cattle and horses to rustling while we were riding all over creation looking for you."

"I'm sorry I've caused so much trouble," she told her brothers. "I never meant to be a burden or inconvenience to anyone." *Hawk included.*

Shiloh cast Hawk one last glance before she followed her brothers and the cowboys from camp. He never changed expression, not even once. You would have thought she had made the same impact on his life as a fly buzzing by.

He was probably wishing her a silent good riddance while she was wishing they'd had the opportunity to repeat last night's passionate performance. Did their tryst mean nothing to him? Had she pleasured him at all? Would he have wanted her again, as she wanted him, if her brothers hadn't intruded?

None of that matters, Shiloh told herself resolutely. *This misadventure is over and done.* That was the way she wanted it because she had vowed not to think in terms of a lasting liaison with Hawk. She had only wanted to live in the moment…and she had. The moment had come and gone. Now it was time for her life to return to normal.

Without a backward glance Shiloh rode away, knowing Hawk was breathing a gigantic sigh of relief because she was finally out of his hair for good.

The demoralizing thought pricked her pride, but she stiffened her spine and reminded herself that she had known going in that Hawk was never going to be a part of her life.

Hawk watched the entourage disappear over the hill and felt a strange emotion well up inside him. It was different from the knot of grief that consumed him when he watched his mother and grandfather die from their fatal wounds shortly before the clan was marched off to Bosque Redondo. It was different from the frustration and sense of loss he experienced when Archie Pearson became the helpless victim of robbery and murder.

No, this was an unfamiliar emotion that Hawk couldn't define…and was hesitant to examine too closely.

He was accustomed to a solitary life of tracking criminals for the Rangers and he expected nothing more. But the loneliness he experienced when he was left behind in camp beat anything he'd ever known. He felt lost and restless, unsure how to adjust to being by himself for the first time in almost a week.

Which was ridiculous because he was on a crusade to keep the two thieves that he had left afoot under surveillance and hope they gave him a productive lead to follow.

Muttering at the odd feelings coiling inside him, Hawk grabbed the reins to the spare horses then rode away. Even though Shiloh was in the caring and capable hands of her brothers—and he hoped to hell they weren't involved in the criminal activity plaguing the area because it would sure enough break her heart—he missed her already.

Get back to business, the sensible side of his brain lectured him. But he felt as if he'd left things unsaid between Shiloh and himself this morning—although he hadn't the foggiest notion what he was supposed to say after experiencing the most amazing interlude of passion. And he sure as hell couldn't tell her *that.*

Noah and Gideon's unexpected arrival had prevented a repeat of last night's tryst—which was definitely for the best. Plus, it had saved him from an awkward, morning-after conversation. So maybe it was good that her brothers showed up when they did.

Shiloh's unexpected arrival in his life had been as spectacular as her departure. First a wild splash and then a near hanging, he mused wryly.

An hour later Hawk spotted the two hombres who were tramping across a meadow where a herd of horses and cattle grazed. He waited while the two men cut out two horses from the herd then managed to move in close enough to hop on bareback.

Following at a cautious distance, Hawk veered off to check the brands on the cattle. A suspicious frown furrowed his brow when he spotted the Triple D brand on the livestock's hips. Either the men had randomly stolen Drummond horses or they knew where to locate replacement mounts…because there was a secluded hideout on Drummond land where the gang leaders met to organize upcoming robberies.

That disconcerting thought kept spinning around Hawk's mind as he followed the brigands right smack-dab across Drummond property.

"Have you calmed down enough yet to tell us what the blazes you're doing back in Texas unannounced?" Noah questioned, as he, Shiloh and Gideon rode abreast.

"And then you can explain what possessed you to share a pallet with that half-breed Ranger," Gideon added in the same irritated tone of voice.

Shiloh angled her chin to meet their disapproving stares. She had rehearsed her explanation several times, hoping to maintain her objectivity and composure when she confronted her brothers. Amazing how much easier it was to confide in them, after plunging from one disaster to another with Hawk as her companion and protector.

The excitement and threat of danger had never stopped while she was with Hawk. Now she understood why nothing seemed to faze him. His life was a series of life-threatening challenges and he was trained to cope with whatever adversity came his way.

Just as he was probably accustomed to bedding a woman and then going his way without a second thought or any sentimental attachment whatsoever.

The demoralizing thought stung like a wasp, but Shiloh refused to react in front of her brothers.

She shifted restlessly on the saddle as the procession followed Echo River toward the ranch house to the northwest. "The fact is that I fancied myself in love with one of Cousin Bernice's acquaintances. He discarded me in favor of a young lady with a larger inheritance," she announced, pleased with how steady her voice sounded. She was also amazed that the sting of angry humiliation and bruised pride were no longer hounding her.

When had that happened?

"He discarded you?" Gideon parroted as he stared at her in shocked disbelief. "Who is this fool? He couldn't have selected a better marriage prospect than you. And how much of an inheritance and dowry does the idiot think he needs at his disposal? Yours is nothing to sneeze at!"

Shiloh smiled at her brother's fierce loyalty to her. "Antoine Troudeau is an aristocratic sponge that relies on the hospitality and generosity of others to gain entrance into New Orleans society. I didn't discover that until it was too late."

Noah frowned warily. *"Too late?* Exactly what does that mean? And if it means what I think it means then how long will it take me to reach New Orleans to defend your honor by blowing the Frenchman to pieces?"

Shiloh was greatly relieved that she hadn't lost her innocence to that silver-tongued adventurer who was short on integrity and character. Instead, she had offered herself to Hawk, knowing that he wasn't going to be her husband, permanent lover or an integral part of her life.

So what did that say about her morals? And again, what was there about Hawk that made her break her own rules to satisfy the overwhelming desire he inspired in her?

Shiloh decided to reply to her brother's comment rather than contemplate the reasons for her reckless abandon last night. "I only meant that I *thought* I was in love with Antoine. I realized, too late, that he was a mirage of practiced charms," she explained. "I suspect the same thing happened to Aimee Garland. Except he probably compromised her, in hopes of attaching himself to her fortune and forcing her father to announce a betrothal that would set Antoine up for life."

"At least you showed sensible restraint," Gideon said, then studied her pensively. He glanced around to make sure the cowhands were still out of earshot. "Now, would you mind telling me why you and that supposed Ranger were snuggled up under the same quilt?"

There was a biting edge to Gideon's voice and a stony expression on Noah's face while they waited for her response. Shiloh decided there was no time like the present to inform her brothers of her plans for her future, and then explain her state of mind the previous night after her near-death experience. She intended to set the record straight, once and for all, so she could get on with her new life—immediately.

"As I said, I was attacked by wolves while Hawk was confiscating his brother's stolen horse from the two bandits he was tracking. He arrived in camp to drop two wolves after I shot the one that tried to eat me alive. I was rattled and unnerved by the ordeal so I helped myself to Hawk's stash of whiskey to recover my composure. I drank a bit too much and nodded off."

Her brothers muttered and scowled, but they didn't interrupt.

"When nightmares about the incident awakened me, Hawk offered me a shoulder to lean on. We were exhausted and we unintentionally fell asleep on the same pallet."

That was the truth, she reminded herself. She simply omitted that private encounter in which Hawk taught her the meaning of passion. If anyone was to blame for their midnight tryst it was she. Of course, her brothers would refuse to believe that. They would prefer to blame Hawk because they had gotten the wrong impression when they first met him.

"No matter what the reason or the excuse, it did not bode well for our hired hands to see you snuggled up with a man," Gideon replied tersely. "That is exactly how rumors that can ruin a woman's reputation get started."

Shiloh sighed appreciatively when she spotted the stone-and-timber ranch house in the panoramic valley a mile away. *Almost home.* Back to where she should have been allowed to stay in the first place. It certainly hadn't been *her* idea to go husband hunting in Louisiana.

"Rumors are of no concern to me," she said belatedly.

"They should be if you want to protect your upstanding reputation," Noah countered. "Gideon and I care."

Shiloh stared at one brother then the other. "I do not want either of you trying to find me a suitable match," she declared firmly. "Once was more than plenty. The fact is that I have decided not to marry. At all. Ever. I intend to share more of the responsibility in managing our ranch, too."

"*What?*" Noah and Gideon crowed in unison.

"You heard me." Shiloh thrust out her chin and stiffened her spine. "I think marriage is overrated for women. And thanks to you, I've learned what it's like to enjoy freedom and independence during my upbringing. I am not interested in the restrictions proper society places on women like Cousin Bernice. I don't want any part of it."

"You're blaming *us* because you've decided to be a spinster?" Noah croaked, frog-eyed.

"I'm not blaming anyone for anything," Shiloh corrected. "Least of all the two of you. You raised and cared for me after Mama and Papa passed on. I am only saying that you needn't feel responsible for marrying me off because I *don't want* to be married off."

"I think you're just soured on men because of your dealings with that Antoine character," Noah surmised. "You can't judge all men by the mistakes of one man."

"That's what Hawk said and I realize now that he and you are right. I was bitter and resentful, but I'm over that now," she declared with a dismissive flick of her wrist. "I simply want to live by my own rules in Western society."

Noah and Gideon exchanged glances that suggested they wanted to debate that issue, but decided to pick their battles with her. "There's no rush and no need to be rash about your decision," Gideon said diplomatically. "You can always reconsider if you meet someone who changes your mind."

She thought perhaps she had already met that special someone, but she refused to harbor any illusions about Hawk reappearing in her life. Whatever fond attachment she had developed for him—and she refused to examine her feelings for him too closely—she knew they were one-sided.

A pragmatic and sensible woman should adapt the nonchalant attitude men adhered to when it came to trysts and such. She told herself that passion was purely physical and short-lived. She cautioned herself to keep her emotions separate from the breathless passion she had discovered with Hawk. Like him, she had taken what was offered in the moment that was a spontaneous space out of time and reality. If she were smart, she would consider their tryst an experimental introduction to physical passion—and nothing more.

"So...have we seen the last of that Texas Ranger?" Noah asked, watching her all too closely.

"I expect so," she said carelessly. "Unless his investigation can be furthered by any information you might contribute. That and my eventual civic duty to identify the outlaws in court to make sure they pay penance for their many crimes."

"Too bad Logan Hawk didn't bother to question us when he had the chance," Gideon said as he halted his horse beside the hitching post near the corrals. "We came across several suspicious characters while searching for you." He gave her a meaningful glance. "Don't venture off by yourself again, Shi. The area is more dangerous than it was when you left. Noah and I were frantic to find you because we imagined all sorts of horrible fates befalling you."

"I'm sorry," she said contritely. "I really didn't mean to worry you. I should have notified you of my arrival, but I was embarrassed and hurt by Antoine's betrayal. I needed time to compose myself before I encountered you. I simply ran into unforeseen trouble on my way home from Cerrogordo."

"I'll say you did," Noah snorted. "That fiasco ought to be more than enough excitement to last you a lifetime."

"One would think," Shiloh murmured as she dismounted.

Despite her firm resolve, the memory of her secret tryst with Hawk followed her inside the house and remained like an unwanted guest that refused to go away.

Chapter Twelve

Hawk frowned suspiciously as he watched the two bandits dismount from their stolen horses then duck into a far-flung line shack that sat inside a grove of cottonwood trees. He wasn't absolutely certain whose property the cabin sat on, but he had the unshakable feeling that it was well within the borders of the Drummond's sprawling ranch—land that once belonged to the Apache, land he had roamed uncontested until the white man decided to stake their claim.

He cast off the bitter thought and tethered the horses.

Two hours later, no one else had arrived at the secluded shack and neither of the men had exited. Hawk cautioned himself that the endless, solitary hours required for surveillance were dangerous duty for a man with too much on his mind and too much time on his hands.

Although he'd vowed not to give that adorable spitfire another thought, he couldn't get her off his mind. Visions of curly auburn hair, vivid green eyes and a luscious body kept dancing in his head. He craved her still…and that scared the living hell out of him.

Scowling at himself, Hawk lay down on a knoll of grass that allowed him a clear view of the shack. Retrieving his field glasses, he watched and he waited. Then he waited some more.

Four hours later darkness descended and still no one came or went from the shack.

He snapped to attention when it dawned on him that he had seen two pigeons flutter into the cupola atop the cabin. One bird flew off a short time later.

"Well, I'll be damned." A wry smile pursed his lips as he retreated to the place where he had left the horses to graze.

No wonder these outlaw gangs were so difficult to tie together, he mused. The mastermind didn't *have* to meet at a central headquarters if he didn't want to. He cleverly contacted gang members by carrier pigeon.

Now all Hawk had to do was find out if the brothers Drummond had birds in *their* belfry.

For Shiloh's sake, he hoped not.

Shiloh frowned warily when she heard the sharp rap at the front door. It was long past dark and she had come downstairs to join her brothers in the parlor. When Noah opened the door, she gaped in surprise at Hawk, who loomed on the porch. She noticed that he didn't bother to glance in her direction, just kept his gaze fixed on Noah and Gideon.

Despite her vow to put her encounter with Hawk behind her, her traitorous body responded to the unexpected sight of him. Something about him called out to her, no matter how valiantly she battled against those warm tingles that rippled down her spine.

"You cleaned up better than expected," Hawk said as he studied Noah and Gideon critically.

"Are you lost?" Noah questioned, ignoring the back-handed compliment.

"Hardly. This land was part of the Apacheria, long before you land-grabbing palefaces showed up to steal it from us," Hawk said sourly, then invited himself inside.

His onyx gaze still didn't drift to Shiloh.

"I want to ask you and your brother a few questions." He bore down on the brothers Drummond. "Like why the bandits I've been tracking are holed up in a line shack near the western boundary of *your* property."

Shiloh stared incredulously at Hawk. So did her brothers, she was relieved to note. To her, that indicated innocence. However, it didn't appear to sway Hawk's low opinion of her brothers.

"That line shack sits empty most of the time," Noah said.

"I haven't stopped there in weeks," Gideon declared.

"Well, somebody sure as hell has." While Noah and Gideon bristled in offended dignity, Hawk tossed out his next question. "How many carrier pigeons are caged in your attic?"

Shiloh stared blankly at him. "What does that have to do with anything?"

"Plenty." Hawk's intense focus riveted on Noah. "Are you going to answer the question or should I ask your brother?"

"We don't keep homing pigeons," Gideon snapped.

"Good, then you won't mind if I take a look for myself."

Without waiting permission, Hawk strode toward the staircase then disappeared from sight. He returned five minutes later. His expression was neither pleased nor relieved that he'd found nothing but cobwebs, extra furniture and old trunks in the attic.

"Now, if you're satisfied," Noah remarked smugly, "perhaps you would like for us to offer you a description of the men and their horses that we happened onto while we were trying to locate our missing sister last week. Then maybe you will be inclined to tell us why you need to know if we house caged pigeons."

Shiloh couldn't keep silent for another second because it went against her basic nature. "Were you able to question the two bandits that shot Fletch?"

"No." Hawk cast a quick glance at her then looked away.

She wanted to pound him over the head for treating her like a nodding acquaintance when they had become so much more. She presumed Hawk was trying to leave the impression that their connection hadn't been the least bit personal. At least she *hoped* that was his motive. Otherwise, she was going to be insulted that he was acting as if she wasn't there—and counted for nothing.

"I kept surveillance on the two hombres for several hours before it dawned on me that carrier pigeons entered and left the shack. Carrying messages, no doubt. I didn't want the men to alert their cohorts to my presence so I didn't approach them." He stared pointedly at Noah and Gideon. "You were my first two suspects so I came here first."

Gideon snorted. "Thank you so much for your faith in our integrity."

Hawk shrugged a broad shoulder. "As far as I'm concerned, you're as guilty as you presumed me to be when you tried to string me up by the neck."

Noah had the decency to wince. "We told you that

we were in an emotional whirlwind because we couldn't find Shiloh. Naturally we assumed you were up to no good when we found the two of you—" He flung up his hand when Shiloh opened her mouth to tell him to shut his mouth. "She assured us that you were only consoling her because of her near-death experience and her wild nightmares."

Consoling her? Is that what folks called wild, incredible passion these days? Hawk cast Shiloh a discreet glance. He wasn't sure if he was annoyed or relieved that she hadn't told her brothers the whole truth about what happened between them.

Furthermore, he couldn't tell by the carefully guarded expression on her face if she was pleased or dismayed to see him standing in her elegantly furnished parlor after they had parted company abruptly this morning.

Not that her reaction to his arrival made a damn bit of difference, he tried to convince himself. He was here on official business and that's the only reason he'd shown up.

"Shiloh informed us that your Ranger battalion suspects there is a connection between the four criminal factions preying on this area." Gideon gestured for Hawk to take a seat on the fancy chair that looked as if it cost more than he made in a month's salary.

Hawk declined the offer, noting the difference between his bare-bones existence and the luxuries that surrounded the Drummonds. "That's right," he said, casting his comparisons aside. "I can identify men from two gangs, but there are at least two other factions targeting local ranches, banks and stage lines. They're on the move constantly."

Hawk listened attentively while Noah and Gideon

offered detailed descriptions of the men and their mounts that they had spotted through their spyglasses while searching for Shiloh.

"We saw four men camped out north of Cerrogordo," Noah reported.

"There were five riders camped southwest of town," Gideon informed him. "None of the men appeared to be cowboys affiliated with nearby ranches. When we were certain Shiloh wasn't in their camp we rode off to search elsewhere."

Hawk ambled over to pluck up a piece of stationery that sat on the walnut desk. "May I?"

"Of course," she said generously.

"I'd like to send a message to Captain Tipton so the Rangers can concentrate their efforts on the area near town. Considering the methods of operation for the gang I investigated, I predict another well-orchestrated strike soon," Hawk said. "I'd like to press your most trustworthy employee into service to deliver a message and my brother's horse to Ranger camp. I need to stay here and keep an eye on the two fugitives. I also want to reconnoiter Frank Mills's ranch."

"I'll see that George Porter delivers your message and the horse," Noah promised. "He's an old, trusted cowboy who has been here since our parents homesteaded this place."

Hawk wrote out a brief message, then handed it, face-up, to Noah, in case he was suspicious of what Hawk included in the letter. "Shiloh can give directions to Ranger headquarters since she spent one night there."

When Hawk turned to leave Gideon said begrudgingly, "If you'd like to spend the evening here, we can…furnish a room. We…uh…we're grateful for what you did for our sister."

Hawk inwardly winced and purposely avoided glancing in Shiloh's direction, for fear his expression might reveal telltale emotions to her brothers. He doubted the brothers Drummond would offer him the slightest hospitality if they knew his idea of comforting their distraught sister hadn't ended with a consoling pat on the shoulder.

Leaving the Appaloosa and two spare mounts for the courier to return to headquarters, Hawk exited the grand three-story home that testified to the Drummonds' success in ranching—at the Apaches' expense. If the house wasn't a prime symbol of the drastic difference between his lifestyle and Shiloh's, Hawk didn't know what was. No doubt about it, they'd grown up in drastically different worlds.

But still…

His gaze fixated on the shapely silhouette that appeared on the second-story balcony. Hawk cursed himself soundly when his heartbeat picked up at the sight of Shiloh. Forbidden yearning streamed through him, turning him hard and aching in the time it took to blink.

"Well, hell," he muttered when he realized that he had dismounted and was heading toward the back steps that led to the upper gallery.

He should leave well enough alone and ride off into the night. *Should,* but *couldn't,* damn it. He had seen for himself that Shiloh had returned home, safe and sound, and he had noted that her limp wasn't as pronounced as it had been the past few days. There was no reason whatsoever for him to have a private word with her—away from the watchful eyes of her protective brothers.

Hawk moved silently across the gallery when Shiloh disappeared from view. He halted when he saw her pacing the palatial room with its massive oak furniture, frilly bedspread and gold brocade canopy. Damnation, she resembled a fairy princess ensconced in her grand palace—and he wanted to tumble her onto that soft feather bed and remove her expensive satin gown and undergarments one piece at a time so he could feast his eyes, his lips and his hands on her....

Stop it! the voice of logic shouted at him. He knew he should turn and walk away before she realized he was standing outside the open door. But whatever it was that he sensed had been left unsaid between them when her brothers showed up unexpectedly this morning still needed to be said.

Too bad Hawk couldn't figure out what he should say. He simply stood there, soaking up her exquisite beauty, remembering every delicious moment of the heat and the passion he had discovered in her arms.

Hawk tapped lightly on the doorjamb. Shiloh didn't clutch her bosom or faint like a frightened damsel, he noted. She lurched around, her full skirt and petticoats swishing around her hips and ankles as she prepared to defend herself. Although she looked like a delicate lady, Hawk knew she was bold, courageous and took pride in learning to defend herself.

He couldn't help but grin when she doubled her fists and mentally braced herself for an oncoming attack. You had to admire a woman who didn't panic at the first sign of trouble.

Shiloh relaxed her stance when Hawk materialized from the shadows. "I thought you'd be long gone by now."

"I wanted to make sure you're really all right. Without your brothers hovering around, ready to answer for you."

"I'm fine, as you can plainly see," she said stiffly.

She acted about half-annoyed with him. Since he didn't know diddly-squat about what made a woman tick he was at a loss to understand why. Maybe she simply wanted to be rid of him.

Well, he could understand that, but he still needed to say something about what happened between them.

"About last night," he began awkwardly, then shifted from one booted foot to the other. "I—"

Shiloh flung up her hand to forestall him. "We are going to pretend it never happened," she burst out before he could string together some sort of appropriate comment—whatever the hell that might be.

Hawk arched an amused brow. "We are?" He watched her lurch around to pace from one end of the oversize, expensively furnished suite to the other.

"It's the only sensible thing to do." She wheeled around to pace in the opposite direction. "If you're here because you think I expect something from you, then rest assured that the blame for last night's reckless behavior lies at *my* feet."

"Really? I could have sworn it was *my* fault that things…er…progressed to…um…"

She halted abruptly and glared at him. "Stop stammering, Hawk. It's unnecessary to cast about for a polite way to say that we took a reckless tumble in the grass."

For all her bravado, Hawk noticed that her face had gone up in flames. He bit back a chuckle. Shiloh could pretend to be worldly and nonchalant, but he could tell she felt as awkward and uncertain as he did. She, however, chose to plow full steam ahead, pretending that what happened between them wasn't a monumental, life-altering incident.

He propped a shoulder against the doorjamb then folded his arms over his chest while she resumed her nervous pacing. "Right. A quick tumble. Didn't mean a thing to either of us. Is that what you're saying?"

"Exactly." She didn't glance at him, just kept wearing a rut in the imported carpet.

"So…you don't expect me to apologize for *my* lack of restraint because you think *your* lack of restraint caused us to end up where we did?"

"Precisely." *Pace, pace, pace.* "We were away from the judgmental eyes of society." *Pace, pace, pace.* "And, like a tree falling in the forest where no one hears the sound, the incident *didn't happen.*" *Pace, pace, pace.*

"Interesting logic," he said, biting back a grin. "So the moral of your story is, don't make something of nothing?"

"Couldn't have put it better myself." *Pace, pace, pace.*

Hawk couldn't stand another moment of watching her stride back and forth and not stare deeply into those beguiling green eyes to determine if she meant what she said—or if it was only stubborn pride talking. Even if last night meant no more to her than an educational initiation in passion, he wasn't leaving here until he was close enough to savor her sweet scent. He damn well planned to help himself to the goodbye kiss he had missed out on this morning.

He'd damn sure have *that,* at the very least, before he made himself scarce, he promised himself.

When Shiloh whizzed past, he hooked his arm around her trim waist and hauled her up against him. And poof! Desire slammed into him like a runaway train. Her arousing fragrance swamped him, triggering last night's exotic memories of gazing upon her while her exquisite body was illuminated by flickering campfire light.

Hawk couldn't resist. He dipped his head to devour her dewy lips just one last time. The floor shifted beneath his feet. The room swam before his eyes. He crushed her to him, yearning to memorize the feel of her lush body molded intimately to his so he could call up the tantalizing sensations when missing Shiloh got to him.

Fervent need turned him rock hard immediately and ripped the breath from his lungs. He had underestimated the powerful impact Shiloh had on him. He should have had her out of his system after last night, but apparently not. Realizing what he'd been missing had only made him want her more.

Now, he couldn't kiss her deeply enough or thoroughly enough to satisfy the ardent craving that he'd spent the whole livelong day trying to convince himself that he didn't feel.

You are such a liar, Hawk, came the mocking voice in his head. *You know damn well once will never be enough for a man who has allowed himself to become tempted and obsessed with this unattainable female.*

His senses reeled when Shiloh wrapped her arms around his neck and pushed up on tiptoe to kiss the breath out of him. Then she arched into him, as if she belonged to him and he belonged to her for that wild, mind-shattering moment.

She turned every kissing technique he'd taught her back on him with such devastating effectiveness that his knees threatened to buckle. His brain fogged over as he devoured her mouth and clung desperately to her, as if he were about to pitch off a cliff if he didn't keep a fierce hold on her.

For that immeasurable space of time, he didn't try to control the roiling passion she stirred in him. And she responded enthusiastically to the fiery need that sparked between them like lightning leaping cloud to cloud in a billowing thunderstorm.

"I have to go before it's too late," Hawk gasped when he finally mustered the willpower to break their kiss.

"Goodbye then," she said before she kissed him again—and he put all he had into their final embrace.

When he was forced to come up for air—or faint, whichever came first—Shiloh staggered backward. Her breath gushed out in huffing pants. Her creamy breasts heaved against the diving neckline of her bright yellow gown. Hawk battled the tempting urge to touch her as familiarly as he had once, to make use of that fancy bed before he rode out of her life forever.

He hauled in a steadying breath then retreated a step to put her safely out of his reach. "If you need anything—"

"I won't," she broke in, her voice as hoarse and raspy as his, her stance as unyielding and proud as his.

"Of course not. Why should you? You have your brothers to look after you." He dipped his head slightly. "Well, then, I'd best be going."

"Yes, that would be best," she murmured as he strode across her room.

Hawk walked away, refusing to look back. He told himself that he wouldn't see Shiloh again. His job didn't allow for lasting attachments to women. He and Shiloh had made a gigantic mistake together. They'd been caught up in the emotional turmoil surrounding her ordeal with the wolf pack.

It never happened, Hawk chanted silently as he

mounted the mustang then trotted off into the darkness. *It's just a mystical dream, a secret I'll carry until I'm in my grave.*

Despite his attempt to discard the forbidden memories, they converged like stampeding horses.

Pretend it never happened...? Like hell he would! He was never going to forget the taste of her, the feel of her silky skin, her alluring fragrance, because the memories burned like searing brands on his mind.

Teeth gritted, mind shutting like a steel trap, Hawk focused all thought on riding to Mills Ranch to see how many suspicious characters came and went during the night. He also wanted to know how large a population of homing pigeons came to roost in Frank Mills's belfry.

After Hawk left the room Shiloh half collapsed on the edge of her bed then dragged in several cathartic breaths. She battled like the very devil for control, but a choked sob broke the empty silence. She had tried her best to appear detached and indifferent in Hawk's presence. She hadn't wanted him to know that his refusal to pay any attention to her while he was conversing with her brothers had hurt deeply.

In addition, she had accepted full responsibility for their tryst and let him off the hook so he could concentrate on his assignment. But that didn't mean she wasn't crying on the inside, foolishly wishing for things that could never be.

Another sob burst from her lips and Shiloh flung herself facedown on her bed to vent the frustration that had hounded her for a week. She could tell herself that she didn't want Hawk in her life, but that didn't stifle all the tender feelings that roiled inside her. She could remind herself a dozen times a day that Hawk considered her an unwanted responsibility and inconvenience that hampered his investigation. But that didn't stop her from caring for him and feeling lost without him.

Damn it, see what happens when you let yourself care too much about a man? came that lecturing voice inside her head. *Brace up, Shiloh. He doesn't want you. You're better off without him. Let...him...go.*

She tried. She really did. But when she dozed off that night Hawk's taste was still on her lips and his masculine scent surrounded her like an invisible cocoon.

She'd get over him, just as surely as she'd put aside her unrequited feelings for Antoine Troudeau. It was just going to take a little longer to forget Hawk, was all, she convinced herself when she woke up alone in bed. He'd had an intense impact on her senses because they'd spent so many consecutive hours together, learning each other's characteristics and moods. They'd survived danger and they had become intimate.

Refusing to dwell on the memories, though they were never far from her mind, Shiloh closed her eyes and begged for sleep to rescue her from her bittersweet dreams.

"Come in and sit down," Noah requested as Shiloh breezed through the front door. "Gid and I want to talk to you."

Shiloh rolled her eyes impatiently. She had been home for a week and her maddening but well-meaning brothers kept insisting on these little "chats" every other day.

"Make it fast." She veered into the walnut-paneled study that sat adjacent to the dining room. "I want to grab a quick bite of lunch before I check the cattle in the south pastures to make sure we don't have a few more rustlers lurking about."

"That's the thing, Shi," Gideon spoke up. "Our cowboys are hired to handle those tasks. We prefer that you find other activities that don't involve the possibility of danger."

She arched a challenging brow. "You weren't grateful three days ago when I spotted the rustlers who were trying to make off with our cattle and I alerted our hired hands?"

Noah raked his hand through his thick brown hair and sighed audibly. "That's not the point. You aren't our resident scout who lurks in the trees, waiting to send off an alarm when you see rustlers in action. Things could go wrong."

Gideon stared her down. "Noah and I think you're on some thrill-seeking campaign that is self-destructive."

She wasn't about to tell her well-meaning brothers that she needed activity and excitement to pacify this insatiable sense of restlessness that followed her like her own shadow. She had been missing Hawk to such maddening extremes that she *did* go looking for trouble—anything to take her mind off him.

Gideon towered over her, his dark brows bunched over his narrowed gaze. "We don't want to issue ultimatums to you—"

"Then don't," she cut in. "I can take care of myself because you saw to it that I could ride expertly and handle an assortment of weapons. I wasn't in danger when I spotted the rustlers sorting off some of our cattle. Although I appreciate your concern, I don't want to be stifled and smothered."

"We aren't trying to smother you," Noah replied. "But you scared the bejeezus out of us when you turned up missing. We were desperate to locate you. Now you're thumbing your nose at danger and taking daredevil risks." He frowned pensively. "This craving for excitement is the result of your wild misadventures with that rogue Ranger, isn't it?"

They didn't know the half of it—and she wasn't about to tell them. She was desperate for distractions so she wouldn't think about Hawk the whole blessed day.

"Don't be absurd," she said with a dismissive flick of her wrist. "I'm doing my part to protect our holdings. Because I was standing watch, we were able to retrieve our stolen cattle and you hauled the two rustlers to jail. All the better that they were the same two men who were casting suspicion on us by operating from our line shack. Hawk and Fletch can identify them, too, and they're wanted for questioning about Archie Pearson's death."

Noah waved her off as he loomed over her. "We're providing you with a more acceptable brand of excitement," he insisted. "The annual spring fandango begins tomorrow. We're spending the weekend in Cerrogordo to enjoy the activities."

"You go ahead without me," Shiloh replied. "I attended enough fashionable soirees, symphony concerts and poetry readings in New Orleans to last me for at least a year."

"No," Gideon said firmly. "We *are* going. *Together.* Although you deny it, I think you developed an ill-advised attachment for that Ranger. You're hoping you might happen onto him while you're checking cattle in the pastures."

Is that what she'd been doing? Making herself available, wishing she and Hawk would cross paths? Shiloh inwardly groaned. Her brother was probably right.

Secretly she wanted to catch a glimpse of Hawk, because her foolish heart refused to let go of the forbidden memories they had made that night beneath a dome of twinkling stars.

"That is ridiculous." She felt compelled to deny it. "If anything, I acquired a taste for adventure after the drudgery of social niceties in Louisiana. I told you that I have decided to be a spinster. It suits my nature and disposition to take an active role in our ranch, instead of wasting time trying to latch onto a husband I don't want or need."

"Nevertheless, we're leaving for Cerrogordo tomorrow morning. Make time to pack," Gideon said sternly. "And try to limit your daredevil rides across the countryside, *please*. No need to come up lame before Saturday night's street dance."

Muttering at her brothers' decree that she was going to be dragged to the festivities, like it or not—and she didn't—she surged across the hall. After a quick lunch, she gathered enough supplies to tide her over until dark.

Then she headed out the front door.

Her brothers stood just inside the office, arms crossed over their chests, staring at her in disapproval. But they had enough sense to keep quiet, she was happy to say.

Outside, Shiloh mounted her favorite palomino gelding and raced off. When she noticed her brothers had their noses pressed to the office window she veered toward the gate—instead of leaping over the yard fence as she had done when she arrived an hour ago. No sense inviting another lecture, she decided. She could appease the thrill of going airborne just as easily by jumping creeks on her way south.

Hawk, where are you? Do you think of me at all? came that silly romantic voice from the region of her heart. She heard that whispering voice three times a day at the very least.

How long would it take to convince herself that she really didn't want that dark-haired, dark-eyed hulk of masculinity to be a part of her life? Two weeks? Two months?

Shiloh sincerely hoped that it wouldn't take two months to get over Hawk. She'd be stark raving crazy by then.

Chapter Thirteen

While reconnoitering the area near Drummond Ranch, Hawk saw a rider thundering downhill at breakneck speed. A wild mane of curly auburn hair flew out behind her like a banner waving in the breeze. He muttered at the daredevil female who was racing the wind. Shiloh apparently wasn't the kind of woman who knew her place and dutifully stayed in it. Of course, Hawk had figured that out early on.

"Pretty damn tough to give up something that fascinating and free-spirited, isn't it?"

Hawk twisted in the saddle to see his brother walk his Appaloosa gelding up beside the mustang. Even though Fletch excelled at sneaking up on people, it disturbed Hawk that he had been too preoccupied to notice.

Damn, his preoccupation with Shiloh was causing him to lose his focus and his edge—the two things that kept him alive and kicking while pursuing his risky occupation.

"How'd you find me so easily?" Hawk asked.

Fletch absently massaged his mending leg then

shrugged. "When I didn't see you hovering around Mills Ranch I figured you were checking up on the hellion."

"Someone needs to get that woman under control," Hawk mumbled sourly. "Not *me,* of course, because I'm on assignment, but *somebody.*"

"Don't know who would sign up for that hazardous duty." Fletch watched Shiloh's reckless flight over hill and dale. "It would take a certain kind of man to handle a woman with that much fire, sass and independence." He glanced at his brother. "The messenger who brought your missive to the Ranger encampment claimed he was on hand when Shiloh's brothers found the two of you. We heard all the details about how you fought like a grizzly to keep from being hanged and how Shiloh braved five armed, angry men to defend you." Fletch smiled in amusement. "She's exceptionally sweet on you, big brother."

Hawk snorted. "No, it was only her fierce sense of fair play rising to my defense."

Fletch let the silence stretch for a few moments then he said, "Something was bound to happen between the two of you. Sick as I was while in the cave, I could sense the attraction. My guess is that she's your woman by now," he added with brotherly candor. "I'm right, aren't I?"

"Just because our grandfather was a visionary shaman doesn't mean *you* know all and see all," Hawk said caustically.

"Look me in the eye and tell me that you and she—"

"You can shut up now," Hawk cut in sharply. "That's none of your business. And for your information, I haven't seen her, except at long distance, for a week."

Fletch chuckled. "Which has nothing to do with my prophesy, but nice try anyway, Hawk. You surely remember that I'm not easily distracted…not like *someone* I know."

Hawk expelled an agitated breath. "I think I appreciated you more when there was a state or two separating us. Are you here in an official capacity or did you just drop by to torment me for your own sadistic pleasure?"

"Both." Fletch grinned, undaunted. "I thought you might like to know that the two desperadoes that stole my horse and shot me are presently locked in jail at Cerrogordo, because the hellion spotted them stealing Drummond cattle and alerted the hired hands to apprehend them. I rode out here from town, after interrogating the captives who were very closemouthed about any involvement with the outlaw factions."

The thought of Shiloh keeping surveillance worried him. He would like to rake her over live coals for…

His runaway thoughts skidded to a halt when he reminded himself that Shiloh wasn't any of his business these days. If she wanted to become a self-appointed scout there wasn't much he could say about it. And obviously, her brothers weren't having any luck keeping her tucked away at home.

"Have you seen anything of that backstabbing bastard that I chased down here from Colorado?" Fletcher asked, his tone of voice no longer light and teasing.

Hawk nodded sharply. "I spotted an hombre who matched the description you gave me. He's come and gone from Mills Ranch several times this week. Cousin or brother, I can't say, but he seems to fit in with this bunch of ruffians that pose as ranch hands when they don't disappear for a day or two at a time. To raid, no doubt."

"I have a score to settle with Grady Mills," Fletch growled vindictively. "I'm itching to get my hands on that treacherous son of a bitch."

"It will have to wait," Hawk insisted. "I discovered the outlaw factions are keeping in touch by carrier pigeon. I've seen the birds arriving and leaving Mills Ranch, as well as the line shack that sits on the western boundary of Drummond property. As of yet, I haven't found out where else the birds roost."

"Very clever. When you figure that out you should have your mastermind pinpointed," Fletch speculated.

"I expect so," Hawk confirmed. "I've compiled detailed descriptions of every member in the four gangs, plus a description of their horses. We'll have a solid court case after we make the arrests."

"But still no conclusive link verifying a crime syndicate. Except using pigeons," Fletch finished for him.

"There is a link. Infiltrating DeVol's gang assured me of that." Hawk frowned thoughtfully. "According to the Drummond brothers, they spotted one gang camped north of Cerrogordo. Another was lurking southwest of town."

"Which might suggest that someone *in town* is passing along crucial information to target victims. Sort of like the hub surrounded by the spokes of a wheel," Fletch said, voicing Hawk's thoughts accurately. "If I'd known we were hunting carrier pigeons I would've kept my eyes trained on the sky while I was in Cerrogordo." He snapped his fingers when a thought occurred to him. "I have an idea that might change our luck in solving this case."

"What's that?" Hawk's attention shifted to the spot

where Shiloh had disappeared earlier. Damn it, he needed to keep his mind on business. Willfully, he glanced at Fletch.

"There's going to be some sort of celebration in town, beginning tomorrow," Fletch reported. "Something about the day Cerrogordo was founded. Damn place wouldn't have been established at all if those palefaces hadn't squatted on the Apacheria then demanded that the army shove us aside to appease the land-grubbing trespassers—"

Before Fletch became sidetracked by the same bitter feelings that often hounded Hawk, he waved his brother to silence. "Get back to the point, Fletch. There isn't a damn thing we can do about our people being murdered, having their property stolen and being confined to reservations. The only satisfaction we'll ever have is riding with the Rangers and hunting down every white outlaw and stuffing them in jail…or burying them in the cemetery if they resist arrest."

Fletch looked at him for a long, contemplative moment. "So that's why we do what we do? To satisfy our own need for revenge, using the white man's interpretation of law and order?"

"That's why *I* do it," Hawk said. "I can't speak for you."

"I've spent years wondering why I felt compelled to save as many innocent victims from lawlessness as possible. Not that anyone but Archie Pearson was there to help us—"

"We're getting further away from the point," Hawk interrupted impatiently. His gaze involuntarily darted south again, wondering what Shiloh was up to.

"The fandango and feast attracts folks from all over the county. I wouldn't be surprised if a few hell-raisers show up to celebrate. It might be the perfect chance to round up some of these desperadoes that we can identify as suspects."

"Unless they see the festivities as the perfect opportunity to raid unattended ranches and loot stage coaches while so many folks congregate in town."

"That's a possibility," Fletch agreed. "Already two men, DeVol and Stiles, by your description, held up a stage to San Antonio and killed the ex-soldier that was riding guard. At close range."

Hawk swore. "Sounds like my departure from the gang, with the stolen money, sent DeVol on the rampage. He might have been operating independently against the stage."

"We can alter our appearance and attend the festivities, incognito. We'll send a message to headquarters to place patrols on the stage route and scout Mills Ranch for suspicious activity."

Anticipation surged through Hawk. He felt as if he was finally making some headway with this case. The Rangers might be able to respond quickly to holdups while Hawk and Fletch singled out and shadowed desperadoes in town. The sooner they broke up these synchronized rings of outlaws the sooner he could vacate the vicinity. When he put some distance between himself and Shiloh he could function normally again. Then he wouldn't be spending his time wondering what Shiloh was doing and looking for her in the distance.

"Daydreaming, Hawk?" Fletch asked, intruding into Hawk's most private thoughts. "Why don't you avoid the mental torture and just go look her up? I'll ride over to Drummond Ranch to introduce myself." Fletch grinned scampishly. "Knowing what a grand impression you made on the Drummond brothers I'm sure they'll fall all over themselves to offer me a night's lodging before we ride into Cerrogordo tomorrow."

"I have no intention of imposing on the Drummonds' begrudging hospitality," Hawk remarked.

"Well, *I'm* going to take advantage," Fletch insisted. "I'll flash my badge and hope for one night of special treatment. That's about the only benefit a lawman has going for him. The rest of the time cutthroats are trying to blow you out of the saddle." He stared pointedly at Hawk then reined toward the ranch. *"Go...see... her...."*

Shiloh felt her pulse quicken when she spotted Hawk trotting his mustang over the grassy knoll. Blast it! It had been over a week. The sight of him still triggered a host of sensations and memories that she'd tried desperately to put behind her. It was useless, she thought defeatedly. Some men were unforgettable. Logan Hawk headed up the list.

What a crying shame that there were so many forgettable qualities about *her.* Hawk didn't seem to have trouble keeping an emotional distance from her.

"I'll escort you back to your house," Hawk volunteered when he came within speaking distance.

No *hello, I missed you* or *hello, it's nice to see you again,* Shiloh noted, disappointed. For Hawk, it was business as usual. She'd like to bean him over the head for looking and sounding so nonchalant. She'd give almost anything if she could emulate his neutral expression and bland tone of voice.

"I wasn't planning to leave my lookout post until dark," she said briskly. "That's usually when thieves come calling."

"I heard you spotted the twosome who were holed

up in your line shack and called in reinforcements. Impressive work." He stared directly at her. "Impressive but risky. You could've gotten hurt."

She shrugged him off, then directed his attention to her mending arm and ankle. "If you recall I was hurt on *your* watch, Mr. Rough-and-Ready Ranger. Seems to me that I'm faring better on my own watch."

He scowled. "Thanks for throwing that back in my face."

"Happy to do it," she said, grinning impishly.

"Well, suit yourself."

Disappointment washed over her when Hawk headed off in the direction he'd come. He was leaving. Just like that, damn him.

"Fletch and I are hoping you and your brothers won't object to offering a night's lodging before we ride into Cerrogordo. Sure you don't want to ride to the ranch with me?"

Shiloh sighed, torn. She relished his companionship, but it was sheer torture to be with him and to know that he would never want her to the same intense degree that she wanted him—despite her valiant attempts to regard him as no more than a closed chapter from her past.

"If I do decide to join you, you aren't planning to chastise me for standing watch for rustlers, are you?" she muttered as he rode off without her.

"Wouldn't dream of it."

The lie rolled easily from his tongue. It occurred to Hawk that he'd gotten exceptionally good at lying to himself about his feelings for this firebrand. He was also shamefully inconsistent about vowing to keep his distance from her and then breaking his promises. Like now. Like his decision to spend the night at her home when he'd told Fletch no.

Honestly, it was wearing him out trying to mean what he said about getting out of Shiloh's life—and staying out.

World's biggest hypocrite is what you are, he thought, exasperated.

"There's a fandango in town this weekend," Shiloh said as she eased her sleek palomino gelding up beside the mustang.

The horses sniffed each other, laid back their ears and sidestepped to put more space between them. Apparently, they weren't going to become fast friends.

"That's what Fletch told me earlier," Hawk remarked. "It might be our chance to apprehend a few of the outlaws bent on having a rip-roaring time in town."

"How is Fletch's leg?"

"Much better," Hawk replied. "He should be able to do some investigative legwork while we're in town. We plan to interrogate the two desperadoes about Archie Pearson's murder, not to mention their link to the other outlaw factions."

"You're welcome to ride into town with us tomorrow," Shiloh invited, although her tone was so bland that he couldn't tell if the prospect of his extended companionship pleased or dismayed her.

And just when had she gotten so good at hiding her emotions behind that well-disciplined mask? he wondered. There had been a time when he could read her thoughts easily enough. Now she had closed herself off the way he did....

He jerked upright and frowned at the unsettling thought that Shiloh had borrowed one of his traits. She was too lively and vibrant to bury her emotions as he did. Damn it, whatever else she might've learned from him during their brief but intense acquaintance *that* was the last thing he wanted her to emulate.

"Something troubling you, Hawk?" she asked perceptively.

Plenty, but he shrugged evasively and said, "No, just thinking how good it will be if we can wrap up this case this weekend then head to the new hotbed of trouble brewing down San Antonio way."

He glanced at her, but he couldn't tell if the prospect of having him miles away affected her in the least.

"I confiscated the pigeons from the line shack," she commented a moment later. "I don't know if they will lead you to the mastermind, but I thought it might be worth a try. Perhaps you'll want to have one of our hired hands release the birds about the time we reach town."

"Good idea," Hawk praised. "If Fletch and I have miscalculated about the possibility of the ringleader being in town we should know soon. If necessary, we can focus our efforts elsewhere."

He was silent for a moment then said, "I've thought about you a time or two this week." *Fool! Why did you have to bring that up? What possible purpose will arming her with that information serve?*

"Have you?" She glanced in his general direction then stared straight ahead. "Now that you mention it, you have crossed my mind once or twice this week." *Imbecile! Don't give your feelings away, in case he's on some sort of fishing expedition. Didn't you learn anything from your disastrous encounters with Antoine? You have to start working on* not *missing Hawk—and you had better be quick about it.* "Of course, I was curious about what progress you had made in the case."

Hawk inwardly winced. All she wanted to know was if he had rounded up gang members? His male pride took a beating.

"I found myself wondering if your injuries had healed properly," he said to cover any assumption she might have drawn about his lingering feelings for her.

"Oh, good, we're almost home," she said a little too brightly.

Which was a relief because this useless chitchat was making her insane. She felt awkward and restrained, afraid she'd expose her feelings and humiliate herself again. A week ago she had become comfortable with Hawk because she could be herself while she was with him. Now everything had changed and she didn't know how to behave around him. All these suppressed feelings of vulnerability and uncertainties were eating her alive.

"We should arrive separately," Hawk suggested. "Your brothers won't be too thrilled to see me... especially if I ride in with you."

"Of course, we wouldn't want to give them the ridiculous impression that there is something between us besides mutual interest in solving this investigation. And, of course, my gratitude to you for saving my hide a few times last week."

Gratitude? That's all she felt for him? he mused. That and a reckless night of passion that never happened because no one heard a damn tree fall in the damn forest—or some such absurdly ridiculous nonsense.

Well, for her information, just because no one else heard her soft moans of pleasure and her breathless pleas did not mean that *he* hadn't heard them, that *he* hadn't felt the wild ripples of desire shimmering from her body and echoing in his.

Come to think of it, he was outraged that she had shrugged off the kind of sexual encounter that fantasies were made of. *Didn't happen? Like hell it didn't!*

"I'll let you ride in first," Hawk said more gruffly than he intended. But he was still steamed about her fierce denial of a night that he would probably never forget.

She nodded stiffly. "I'll set two extra places at the table for supper."

"Thank you," he replied with exaggerated politeness. "Fletch and I are grateful."

He watched her canter her horse downhill—and he wanted to shake the stuffing out of her for behaving so indifferently when he was having such difficulty remaining detached. The woman was making him loco. He didn't expect her to fawn over him when he showed up unexpectedly, but hell! She didn't have to act as if forgetting him was such a simple feat.

It hadn't been easy for him, damn it. What mental mechanism did *she* have that *he* didn't that made it so annoyingly easy for her to disregard those incredible feelings he'd experienced that night when the world stood still…and time ceased to exist…and the trees crashed to the forest floor…in silence?

Hawk huffed out his breath, cursed Shiloh a few times in frustration, and then rode up to the ranch house to face Noah and Gideon's greeting scowls.

He would be as cool and remote as Shiloh when they faced each other across the table at dinner, he promised himself. He'd look right through her and see how she liked being ignored….

"Well, hell," he muttered when understanding dawned. Maybe Shiloh had distanced herself from him because he'd ignored her in his relentless attempt not to give away his feelings the night he'd arrived to interrogate her brothers. Had he hurt her feelings, while trying to protect her from her brothers' speculations?

Or did she simply not like him very much? It was killing him, not knowing why Shiloh had made love with him with such reckless abandon, and then cast him off as if their relationship counted for nothing.

What does it matter? he asked himself. Their brief tryst was over and that was best for both of them.

"I don't know why you had to invite the Hawk brothers to sleep in the house and to join us for supper," Gid grumbled to Shiloh. "We offered them beds in the bunkhouse."

"After Hawk saved my life several times, the best you can do is a cot in the bunkhouse?" Shiloh sniffed reproachfully. "If he'd saved *your* skin wouldn't you be more charitable?"

"This isn't about being charitable and hospitable," Noah said emphatically. "We have no intention of encouraging Hawk, in case he has an interest in you."

Shiloh paused from placing silverware on the table to gape at him. "Interested in me?" she repeated. "I told you that I've taken myself off the marriage mart."

"That doesn't stop a man from desiring a beautiful woman," Gideon pointed out.

She crossed her arms beneath her breasts and stared at her annoying brothers. "And you know all about temptation and desire because you occasionally frequent Paradise Social Club to appease your urges?"

Her brothers had the decency to look embarrassed.

"I suppose you're suspicious of Hawk because, being male, you know how his mind works. Right?"

"Yes." Noah grimaced when she scored a direct hit. "But the point is that we don't want you to be hurt again, which obviously you were when that Antoine person rejected you."

Shiloh went back to arranging the china and silver-ware. "Regardless, Hawk and Fletch are to be treated respectfully. Which includes your courteousness and civility at dinner."

"Fine," Gideon mumbled begrudgingly. "Just so he doesn't get the idea that we approve of him. Not that he seems the kind of man who needs anyone's approval for anything. He strikes me as the type who lives by his own code and to hell with everyone else's opinion."

Shiloh smiled thoughtfully. "I like that approach. I can't think of anyone whose opinion is so vital to me that I'd live my life according to their expectations. Being a spinster is refreshingly liberating," she gushed enthusiastically.

"God, don't start on that subject again," Noah bemoaned.

"Ah, there you are," Shiloh said when Hawk and Fletch ambled into the dining room. "And just in time. Please make yourselves comfortable while my brothers fetch some wine."

At the prompt, they strode off to pour the drinks.

"Nice place," Fletch complimented. "A palace on the prairie, you might say. Reminds me of the grand château I visited on the outskirts of Denver while working a case for the railroad. The place reeked wealth. Too bad all this prosperity has to come at the hands—ugh…"

Shiloh glanced over in time to see Hawk gouge his brother in the ribs. "You have every right to feel resentful that our prosperity comes from land that once belonged to your people. I feel the same resentment when I find myself restricted by male-dominated society."

"No one promised life would be fair," Hawk pointed out. "You make the best of the hand you're dealt and that's that."

Noah and Gid strode back into the dining room to set two glasses of wine in front of their guests.

And dinner went downhill from there.

Still, it was better than the near-hanging incident.

After the stilted conversation at dinner Shiloh returned to her room to shed her fashionable gown. Dressed in her nightgown and robe, she stepped onto the gallery to inhale a deep breath of fresh evening air.

The memory of Hawk sitting directly across from her at dinner came quickly to mind and she smiled, remembering how he had taken particular care to emulate her table manners—which, compared to the New Orleans aristocrats were sadly lacking. It was sweet, really, that Hawk had tried to improve her brothers' first impression of him. Not that Noah and Gid had been receptive, but Hawk usually didn't give a flying fig about what people thought of him.

Frowning contemplatively, Shiloh pivoted to stare down the gallery toward the guest room she had offered to Hawk. Why would he care what her brothers thought of him? Surely he wasn't trying to impress *her.* Shiloh smirked at that absurdity. She and Hawk had moved far beyond table manners on the *night that didn't exist.*

Shiloh stood there for the longest time, wondering why she'd paid such close attention to every comment and gesture Hawk had made at dinner. Lord, she hoped no one noticed her preoccupation. Her brothers were already fretting over Hawk calling on her socially— which would never happen.

Muttering at the myriad of thoughts chasing each

other around her head she wheeled toward her room. She had luggage to pack for tomorrow's trip to Cerrogordo. Plus, she was exhausted from all the activities she'd squeezed into the past few days, hoping to take her mind off Hawk.

An hour later Shiloh set her luggage beside the door. Weary, she collapsed in bed—and felt a wave of loneliness so overpowering that she nearly drowned in it.

Ah, what she wouldn't give to cuddle up in Hawk's sinewy arms and sleep contentedly for the first time in over a week.

She lay there for what must have been two hours, staring at the ceiling, counting flocks of sheep. Tired though she was, restlessness tormented her…. That same edgy restlessness had haunted her waking hours all week.

Shiloh sighed heavily as she rolled from bed to don her robe. When she stepped outside the sounds of night reminded her of the evening when she and Hawk…

Need blasted through her like a hot summer wind. Days of denying her desire for Hawk took its toll. She longed to recapture the incredible pleasure and unprecedented sensations he had introduced her to. Erotic memories spun around her, converging with such intensity that she couldn't fight back. Didn't want to fight the feelings again tonight.

Shiloh stared at the door to Hawk's room. Did she dare cast caution to the wind this one last time? There would be no other opportunities to savor the passion Hawk called from her because, when this assignment ended, she would never see him again.

Listening to the whimsical entreaty of her heart instead of her head, Shiloh moved silently toward Hawk's room. *One last night,* she mused as she eased open the door—and flinched when a cold steel blade pressed against her throat and she was slammed against an unyielding muscular body.

Chapter Fourteen

"What the hell?" Hawk retracted the knife when he realized Shiloh had sneaked into his room unexpectedly. He had seen the unidentified shadow flitting across the carpet. Instinct and training had put him on instant alert. "Damn it, woman, you can get your throat slit by sneaking up on me like that. What are you doing here—?"

To Hawk's startled amazement Shiloh grabbed him by the hair on his head and pulled his face down to kiss the breath out of him. She arched provocatively against his naked flesh and her tongue mated with his as her arms settled on his shoulders.

His body burst into flame instantaneously. He crushed her against his aching contours, wanting to be inside her more than he wanted his next breath. And he couldn't find his next breath because her adventurous hands glided down his hip to enfold his rigid flesh. She stroked him experimentally and pleasure sizzled into every fiber of his being.

He should have objected when she walked him backward until the back of his knees bumped the edge of the bed. But she was holding him powerless in her hand and his body clenched with hungry need. He did manage to croak out a feeble protest that they might be discovered together, but it didn't seem to faze her. She seemed to be on a crusade—and he was it.

When she urged him onto his back and sank down beside him, he reached up to curl his hand around her neck, drawing her sensuous lips back to his. The brush of her lips was as feathery as butterfly's wings, but her touch still burned like a brand. Every nerve and muscle in his body trembled in response to the forbidden pleasure buffeting him.

"I was craving another taste of you," she confided as she leaned closer, her breasts caressing his chest through the filmy fabric of her nightgown.

Wild pulsating need rumbled through him as she caressed his throbbing flesh from base to tip. His breath hissed out and his lungs nearly collapsed when her unbound hair drifted over his belly and her moist tongue flicked at him playfully.

"Shiloh, I don't think I can…" His voice gave out before he could tell her that he wasn't sure he could endure the exquisite torture of her intimate kiss. Icy-hot pleasure scorched him as she cupped him, then traced him lightly with her tongue and teeth.

"Don't talk. Don't think." Her warm breath misted over his aching flesh and melted his brain into mush. "I want to learn to pleasure you as completely as you pleasured me."

"I did? You already have…"

Words caught in his throat when phenomenal pleasure pummeled him. She continued to measure the rigid length of him with her lips and nibbled at him with her teeth until he groaned aloud. She aroused him by feverish degrees, dragging him to the crumbling edge and leaving him teetering on mindless oblivion.

And then she destroyed him completely when she took him into her mouth and suckled him gently. All the while, her hands drifted lightly over his thighs and belly, weaving an erotic spell that defied anything he had ever experienced. A silvery drop of need betrayed him as she kissed him intimately, again and again.

"I can't endure another moment of—" He gasped then moaned in unholy torment when she flicked at him with her tongue.

"No?" There was a teasing challenge in her voice. "I think you can endure anything, Hawk… I am trying to pleasure you, not torture you. Am I succeeding?"

"All too well. This is the kind of pleasure that can torment a man to death," he said hoarsely as he tried to pull her lush body over his. "Come here. I need you."

"Not as much as I want you to. Not yet. I want to know every inch of you before this night is out," she whispered.

And to that dedicated end Shiloh made a deliberate study of him-tasting him—exploring the various textures of his muscular body, savoring the ragged moans of surrender she summoned from him. She reveled in the feel of his hair-roughened flesh beneath her questing hands and lips. She felt empowered while she caressed his hard flesh and felt him tremble.

Perhaps she wasn't a skilled seductress, but she had tried to be imaginative in the way she kissed and caressed him. She felt his big body shudder repeatedly, heard his breath break, over and over again. Satisfaction poured through her. Although she knew she could never claim Hawk's wild heart, she had learned to exert control over his masculine body, as he had enslaved her to the reckless passions he ignited in her.

"Enough—" His voice broke on a shattered breath.

She wasn't sure she would ever get enough of him. He inspired feelings and sensations she was helpless to control. When he raised his head, his dark eyes glowing in the scant moonlight, Shiloh drew the nightgown over her head and cast it aside. She could feel his intense gaze on her as he lifted up his hands to trace the beaded peaks of her breasts.

His touch sent a burst of need burning into her very core. She straddled his hips, setting herself exactly upon him. She could feel him hard and throbbing inside her while they were locked together in an intimate embrace that felt all too perfect, all too right.

She moved upon him, pushing him deeper inside her then withdrawing with deliberate slowness. His quiet growl urged her to accelerate the rhythmic pace.

"I want to hear you beg for me as I begged for you," she murmured.

"Anything you want," he said raggedly. "Just make this maddening ache go away." His hand tangled in her hair, holding her still as he thrust into her. "You're killing me…please…"

Hawk melted into a puddle of fiery need when Shiloh leaned forward to brush her lips over his mouth, letting him taste his desire for her. He felt her feminine body encasing him like a velvet glove, caressing him with each sensual stroke, holding him deep within her silky softness.

He had never known that such mind-boggling pleasure existed. Had never known passion could be so intense that it bordered on maddening torment. But with Shiloh, he explored new heights and depths of desire.

He wanted her to the point of reckless frenzy. It took every ounce of self-control not to drive into her in his frantic need to ease the ache that riveted him.

With one fluid movement, he rolled sideways so that she was beneath him. He thrust into her again. His body trembled in his effort to restrain himself. He felt compelled to return the pleasure she offered him. He wanted her with him every step of the way when they spiraled from one dizzying pinnacle of ecstasy to another. He wanted her to feel as wild and helpless and desperate as he felt at this moment.

Hawk touched her everywhere at once, cherishing her, worshipping her. When she whispered his name frantically, he buried himself as deep as he could go. He lifted her to him, drawing her knees over his arms. He drove into her, feeling her burning around him like hot rain, melting body and soul into one throbbing essence. He muffled her wild cries of splendor as she shimmered around him. Pleasure intensified like a meteor blazing a fiery path across the heavens.

When she dug her nails into his back and gasped hoarsely, heart-stopping ecstasy cascaded over him. Her pulsating fulfillment riveted him and he clutched her close, holding on for dear life as breathless passion stole the last shreds of his composure. He shuddered in helpless release as he plunged into a vortex of pleasure that defied description.

Powerless, exhausted, Hawk slumped above her. Hearing her panted breaths against his shoulder filled him with an immeasurable contentment and satisfaction. Eventually, he eased down beside her to cuddle her close. But to his frustration, she withdrew to retrieve her nightgown.

Hawk watched her turn back to him to press a parting kiss to his lips. "Tonight didn't happen, either, right?" he asked.

Her quiet laughter settled over him, making him yearn to pull her back down on top of him and hold her close for as long as he could. "That's right. I wasn't here," she insisted.

"A figment of my imagination?" He tugged at her curly auburn hair to bring her lips back to his. He kissed her thoroughly, just in case this was the last time they were together—on *a night that didn't exist.*

"Goodbye, Hawk," she murmured before she turned and walked out into the darkness.

Not *good night,* he noted as he inhaled her alluring scent on the pillow. Just *goodbye.* He frowned, disconcerted, wondering if, at this moment, she were silently telling that fool, Antoine, to eat his heart out because he could have been the one she turned to for passion instead of Hawk.

That thought didn't set well with Hawk. It didn't matter how many times he told himself that he and Shiloh had no future. It still outraged him to think he might be her consolation prize, the substitute for the man she really wanted.

Damn it, for a man whose motto was: No strings attached, no complications to tie you down, he was feeling used. Not that he wanted Shiloh to fall in love with him, of course. And he certainly didn't want to fall in love with her because they didn't fit in each other's worlds. But still…

"But nothing," Hawk muttered at himself. "Just go to sleep and quit trying to figure out what you want. It doesn't matter what you want, anyway. This assignment is as personal as it is professional and business always comes first."

Hawk pounded his pillow in frustration a couple of times and squirmed to find a comfortable position. He didn't have time to dwell on the riptide of confusing emotion caused by his secretive encounter with Shiloh. He needed rest so he'd be mentally alert when he arrived in town tomorrow.

A faint smile pursed his lips when a vision of Shiloh rose in his mind's eye. This was still the most amazing *nonexistent* sexual encounter that he'd ever experienced. Maybe he should be offended that she refused to acknowledge what was between them. But what she did to him left him feeling too damn good to complain overly long.

Do you see what this woman is doing to you? that sensible voice in his head said. *She has you so confused that you don't know how you should feel, what you should think.*

Hawk expelled a frustrated sigh, squirmed into another position on the bed and dozed off…eventually.

Shiloh awoke the next morning with a contented smile on her lips. She had slept well for the first time in over a week. She knew it had everything to do with the wondrous night she had spent in Hawk's arms. Not to mention the satisfaction she had derived from practicing her newfound skills of seduction on him. He had confided that she had pleased him and that had done wonders for her self-esteem.

Rising, Shiloh bathed then took particular care in dressing for her trip into town. For Hawk's benefit mostly, she acknowledged. Shiloh had been the one to establish the ground rules for their short-term affair and to declare there were no strings attached. She insisted that she had no expectations when it came to a commitment, but the truth was that she had begun to spec- ulate what it might be like with Hawk in her future. She was beginning to wish…

"That's a good way to get your heart broken again," Shiloh said to her reflection in the mirror.

The only man she wanted in her life didn't intend to settle down. She had to stick with her original vow to re- main unmarried. She could be satisfied with her individ- uality and her independence on the family ranch. Yet…

Shiloh muttered at herself as she scooped up her car- petbags. She descended the steps to find her brothers eat- ing breakfast. She glanced back at the staircase, surprised that Hawk and Fletch weren't in the dining room already.

"Change of plans. They decided to leave early this morning," Noah replied in response to her unspoken question. "Hawk said that he and Fletch needed to run a few errands."

Disappointment washed over Shiloh, even though she made an effort to appear indifferent to the change of plans. Her brothers were carefully gauging her reaction to the news. She could tell by the tone of Noah's voice that he was glad to have Hawk up and gone. A pity she didn't share his feelings.

Shiloh's appetite headed south after discovering Hawk had been in an all-fired rush to leave—which suggested that his interest in her had never been any- thing more than physical.

She had made it easy for him by insisting their trysts hadn't happened. Shiloh was beginning to wonder if she had outsmarted herself.

It certainly looked that way.

That evening, Shiloh exited the hotel in Cerrogordo, bookended by her brothers. She surveyed the tables and booths that sat in the center of the street. Two blocks of Main Street had been cordoned off for the townwide bazaar, feast and street dance.

She smiled in amusement as she watched several children competing in a sack race. Other youngsters bobbed for apples. At the east end of town, several men lined up to compete in horse races.

Her gaze shifted to the two well-dressed men that ambled down the boardwalk. There was something familiar about the way they moved, but…Shiloh nearly choked on her breath when she recognized the sophisticated versions of Hawk and Fletch.

"Good God!" Noah bleated in amazement. "You also cleaned up better than expected. I almost didn't recognize you two."

He could say that again, thought Shiloh. Her wide-eyed gaze flooded over Hawk's fashionable three-piece suit and Bowler hat. He had clipped his long hair in a style similar to what her brothers wore. He no longer resembled the wild renegade in buckskins that she first encountered—or the rough-edged Ranger she'd come to know. He looked stylish and confident…and her heart twisted in her chest, knowing this fascinating man wouldn't be a part of her future.

"You look lovely this evening," Hawk told Shiloh very formally as he tipped his hat to her.

"Thank you, kind sir. You look quite dashing." She cast Fletch an approving glance. "And so do you."

Fletch took her hand politely and bowed over it. "Thank you, Miss Drummond. It is a pleasure to see you again."

There was an enigmatic smile playing on his lips and it made her wonder if he might have seen her coming or going from Hawk's room last night. Knowing his background and profession, she suspected Fletch missed nothing that was going on around him. In that, he was his older brother's equal.

"I was hoping I might have the pleasure of dancing with you later this evening," Fletch added belatedly.

"Of course, I shall look forward to it."

"Shall we take a stroll along the boardwalks while the last-minute arrangements are being made?" Hawk suggested as he tucked Shiloh's hand in the crook of his arm. He leaned closer to add, "I'm hoping you can introduce me to people who have acquired sudden wealth or are living above their means. My guess is that someone is making a killing by feeding information to the gangs, pinpointing the best times to strike vulnerable targets."

Shiloh shouldn't have been disappointed that Hawk's request to escort her down the street had more to do with business than pleasure. But she was. Resigned to serving a practical purpose, Shiloh pasted on a smile and strode down the boardwalk. She nodded a greeting to several acquaintances who stared curiously at Hawk and Fletch.

"Here is one of Cerrogordo's most influential citizens," she declared, pausing directly beside the blond-haired, hazel-eyed man who was supervising the last-minute details of arranging food that had been carted from his hotel restaurant.

"Logan and Fletcher Hawk, this is our illustrious mayor," Gideon introduced.

Hawk sized up the thin, wiry gentleman who paused from spouting orders to nod a quick greeting. He noticed the mayor didn't lower himself to carting crates and chairs for the festivities. He allowed others to do his dirty work.

"How do you do," Reggie said, nodding a disinterested greeting before gesturing this way and that to keep his employees scurrying to meet his demands.

As they continued on their way, Gideon murmured, "Reggie Clark might meet with difficulty during the next election because of his connection to Lucille Warren."

When Hawk and Fletch frowned, bemused, Noah explained, "She operates the Paradise Social Club."

"Paradise is a favorite haunt for men," Shiloh put in, staring deliberately at her brothers, who quickly glanced the other way. "Unfortunately for social club enthusiasts, the women have banded together to apply pressure on the mayor and town council. They want to pass an ordinance that outlaws houses of ill repute within the city limits."

Hawk chuckled. "A town divided? That's what civilization does for a place."

"Yes, it does," Noah replied. "But rumor has it that Mayor Clark is a silent partner. He keeps postponing discussions about closing down Paradise and the other establishments in the red-light district."

Shiloh directed Hawk's attention to the robust, red-haired man who was barking orders at several young employees who were scurrying around another booth placed in front of the gunsmith shop. "That is Hiram Evans. He has built up his merchant business rather quickly. Almost *too* quickly, come to think of it."

"She's right," Gideon spoke up. "I haven't given Hiram's means of financial backing much thought, but he's doubled the size of his store by leasing the empty building next door." He glanced curiously at Noah. "Do you recall when Hiram began his expansion? Wasn't it about the same time as the road agents infiltrated the area?"

"It was a couple of months after Shiloh left for New Orleans," Noah recalled. "Hiram claimed that he'd inherited from a long-lost uncle. Whatever the case, his immediate success has gone to his head."

"How so?" Hawk asked as he scrutinized the burly businessman whose intense gray eyes kept darting this way and that, keeping track of everything around him.

Hiram's gaze landed on Hawk and Fletch then dismissed them quickly in favor of settling on Shiloh. Hawk saw lust flicker in Hiram's gaze and he disliked the man immediately. After the introductions were made, Hiram spent more time sidling up to Shiloh than making small talk with the new acquaintances.

"I wouldn't say that Hiram flaunts his newfound wealth, but he hired the best carpenters he could find in Houston to build an ostentatious home," Gideon reported as they ambled down the boardwalk.

"If we're listing men in position to know all and see all and profit from it, we can't exclude William Proctor." Noah inclined his head toward the new bank. "Will is backing several new businesses in town, too. No one knows exactly where his money comes from, other than his local patrons."

Hawk appraised the tall, lean man whose dark goatee made his face look as long as a horse's. Leaning against the brick bank building, Will Proctor was decked out in an expensive black suit that looked as if it had been tailored to fit his rail-thin frame.

Having recently purchased elegant garments to alter his appearance—so gang members who arrived in town to enjoy the fandango wouldn't immediately notice him—Hawk knew Proctor's garments came with a high price tag.

There was also an air of superiority in the way Proctor held himself. He stared over the milling crowd, looking down his patrician nose at the locals. Proctor reminded Hawk of the holier-than-thou soldiers who patrolled the Apache reservation.

Hawk cut Fletch a glance, wondering if his brother was making the same comparison.

"Put a uniform on that haughty gent and he could pass for a patrol guard at Bosque," Fletch muttered sourly.

"I was thinking the same thing myself."

Hawk's bitter reflections trailed off when Shiloh patted his arm comfortingly. "If the banker is involved in this theft ring I'm sure you will see to it that he pays penance," she murmured. "Avenging your friend will be your inspiration."

"You're right," he agreed. "Archie Pearson *will* be avenged." Hawk glanced back at his brother. "I neglected to tell you that I found Archie's pearl-handled dagger in the saddlebag of one of the men who's locked in jail."

The news put a scowl on Fletch's face. "Wish I'd known that when I interrogated those two bastards. I had more than one ax to grind with them and didn't even know it."

Hawk's thoughts trailed off when he heard Shiloh gasp and felt her go rigid beside him. He followed her wide-eyed gaze then muttered sourly when he saw the auburn-haired dandy decked out in frilly, expensive finery strut down the boardwalk. He twirled his black lacquered cane, making the bejeweled rings that encircled four of his fingers flash in the sunlight.

"Shiloh! *Chérie amour,* there you are! I have been looking all over town for you."

Chapter Fifteen

Hawk gnashed his teeth when the highfalutin aristocrat with the heavy French accent sauntered up to
Shiloh. His vivid blue eyes focused solely on her; he
grasped her hand and pressed several zealous kisses to
her wrist. "My arrival was perfectly timed, *oui?* What
a quaint little festival you have here on the outpost of
civilization."

Hawk pulled Shiloh's hand from Antoine's grasp
before he slobbered all over her. Possessive jealousy
pelted him like hailstones. Never mind that Antoine
What's-His-Name looked to be the perfect match for
Shiloh's striking beauty. This man had betrayed her,
left her with a broken heart and soured her on all men
everywhere. For that, Hawk wanted to strangle him.

"What are you doing here?" Hawk demanded while
Shiloh stood there, speechless, staring wide-eyed at
Antoine.

He kept waiting for Shiloh to lambaste this dandified Romeo with that sassy mouth of hers. He knew
he'd enjoy watching her cut the man down to size, especially since *he* wouldn't be on the receiving end of

her sharp tongue for a change. He frowned, wondering why Shiloh wasn't letting this two-timing scoundrel have it with both barrels blazing.

Oozing charm, Antoine displayed a wide smile. "I have come to my senses, *monsieur.*" He struck a sophisticated pose then dropped into an exaggerated bow in front of Hawk. "If you are one of her brothers I wish to formally ask for her hand."

"You can't have her hand or anything else," Hawk snarled in his most ominous voice.

Antoine had the good sense to take a cautious step backward. Damn good thing, too, because Hawk was looking for any excuse to pound this pretentious opportunist flat and mail him back to Louisiana.

"Hawk is not my brother." Shiloh gestured toward Noah and Gideon. "Not that it matters because I speak for myself. It is one of the advantages of living way out here in the *outpost of civilization.*"

Obviously Antoine didn't realize he was being mocked because he smiled broadly and cranked up the charm another notch. Of course, there was a great deal of money at stake and Frenchy wouldn't say anything that might hurt his chances of talking himself back into Shiloh's good graces.

"Ah, *mon amie,* you have every right to be annoyed with me. I understand, and I humbly beg your forgiveness. I realized my mistake in the nick of time and have come to correct it."

"Did you? I doubt it," Hawk said and snorted derisively. "Now go away."

Antoine regarded Hawk fleetingly then focused his charismatic smile on Shiloh. Hawk really wanted to go for his throat. When he took an instinctive step forward, Fletch clamped hold of his shoulder to restrain him.

"Easy, big brother," Fletch said confidentially. "This isn't the time to call attention to yourself. The whole point of dressing in these fancy trappings is to blend in with the crowd so the outlaws don't spot us before we spot them. Shiloh can handle herself with this dandy if she is so inclined. As she said earlier, it is *her* choice…now isn't it?"

"Damn, I really hate it when you're right," Hawk muttered as he forced himself to relax his stance.

"*Chérie?* Grant me a stroll around town with you on my arm, *s'il vous plaît.*" Antoine pleaded in such a sugarcoated tone that Hawk developed an instant toothache.

Everything inside Hawk rebelled when Shiloh allowed Antoine to draw her to his side. Hawk had to make himself let her go—and it wasn't easy, believe you him.

When Antoine patted Shiloh's arm in pretended affection, she offered him a blinding smile. She was actually glad that Antoine had shown up. He needed to be taught a lesson and she knew she would feel much better if she could string him along and see how *he* liked it.

Besides, Hawk no longer needed her as a prop. She and her brothers had armed him with information about prospective suspects. Hawk was undoubtedly anxious to monitor the activity of his suspects. He didn't need her for that.

He didn't need her for *anything*.

"Are you sure about this?" Gideon asked as he glanced back and forth between Shiloh and her fawning companion.

"Just say the word," Noah encouraged, staring icily at Antoine, who was so focused on Shiloh that he seemed unaware of the murderous glowers directed at him.

Shiloh studied Hawk's stony stare that promised Antoine all sorts of pain and torment. It was comforting to know that he'd come running if she couldn't handle Antoine's pretentious attempt to win her over again.

"Come along, Antoine." She led him away from the scowling men. "I'll show you around our fair city. It isn't the bustling port that New Orleans is, but it does have its own irresistible charm."

"Like you, *chérie,*" he cooed as he brushed his beringed forefinger over her cheek.

There had been a time not so long ago that this man's caressing touch had filled her with warmth and giddy pleasure. Now he left her with cool indifference.

She was immune to his practiced charm, thank goodness.

Shiloh listened to Antoine yammer about how he'd realized what he'd lost when she left New Orleans and how he'd hopped a stage to make the long journey across Texas so he could reconcile with her.

Shiloh intended to deal with this smooth-talking Don Juan in her own way, while Hawk focused on his assignment.

Having her revenge on Antoine was just the distraction needed to take her mind off Hawk. She hoped.

"Pay attention," Fletch muttered while Hawk stood on the edge of the dance area, watching the Frenchman twirl Shiloh around to the beat of the music provided by the local band.

Jealousy was eating Hawk alive, damn it. He'd never had to deal with these kinds of feelings before and they didn't sit well with him.

"Why did *he* have to show up here?" Hawk scowled aloud.

"Because he obviously got paid off or threatened by the other heiress's father and decided to reconcile with Shiloh," Fletch speculated. "A meal ticket is still a meal ticket."

Hawk presumed Shiloh's willingness to wander off with that charlatan indicated she still had tender feelings for him. Hawk wanted to shake her until her teeth rattled. It must be true that love turned a person deaf, blind and stupid because Shiloh should have sent Frenchy packing immediately.

He knew she could do better than a tumbleweed Ranger who had nothing to offer her, but she still deserved a hell of a lot better than Antoine. He'd say and do whatever necessary to marry Drummond money.

"Snap out of it." Fletch gouged Hawk in the ribs with his elbow. "Take a gander at the banker. He is standing in the shadows of the alley. He has attracted interesting company. Do those men look familiar?"

Hawk forcefully shoved aside his frustrated musings and surveyed the two shabbily dressed ruffians. Since he didn't recognize them, he tapped Noah on the shoulder then gestured toward the men standing just outside the circle of light cast by the lamppost.

"Are those the men you spotted at the camp north of town while you were searching for Shiloh?"

Noah and Gideon nodded simultaneously. "I remember the Mexican with the red band on his sombrero," Noah replied.

"The bowlegged white man was there, too," Gideon said.

Hawk glanced back at Fletch. "Why don't you drift in that direction? See if you can pick up on their conversation."

When Fletch walked off Hawk forced himself to ignore Shiloh and her flamboyant dance partner so he could scan the men in the milling crowd. Now that darkness had descended more partygoers had shown up to enjoy the festivities—and the kegs of beer that flowed freely.

Hawk's attention riveted on the mayor who was standing outside Paradise Social Club with a buxom female. Her blond hair was pinned on her head in a fashionable coiffure and her formfitting red silk dress advertised her wares—to the extreme.

"Lucille Warren, I presume," Hawk said to Gideon.

Gideon smiled wryly. "Yes, and Reggie Clark doesn't try to hide the fact that he's been carrying on with the madam. Of course, Reggie's wife has retaliated by spreading word that *she* is having an affair with Hiram Evans, now that he's acquired the money to be considered one of the town's elite."

"So, Mrs. Clark is sleeping with the upstart merchant to spite her husband who's carrying on with Lucille, who's trying to remain in good standing with the mayor so he'll continue to side with her when the townsfolk exert more pressure to close the door to Paradise Social Club," Hawk summed up.

Gideon snickered. "You have the gist of it. But I can't say how the banker fits in and why he's chatting with those ruffians. I've seen William Proctor at the social club several times, but he favors the brunette named Rachel."

"Of course, he isn't the only one who favors Rachel," Noah inserted.

Hawk studied the brothers Drummond, wondering if they called on Rachel occasionally and how their sister reacted to it. Not favorably, he guessed.

Hawk glanced skyward when he heard the flutter and coo of birds. He'd asked George Porter to release the pigeons at dusk and he wondered if they might alight in the second-story windows of the bank or the gabled peak atop the merchant shop. Unfortunately, the birds weren't pigeons. They roosted in the trees rather than the tops of buildings.

His attention shifted to the bulky silhouette of the man swaggering toward Paradise Social Club. When the newcomer passed directly beneath the streetlamp, where Lucille and Mayor Clark stood watching the couples move gracefully around the dance area, Hawk came to attention.

"Morton DeVol," Hawk muttered.

"Is that the leader of the outlaw faction you infiltrated?" Noah questioned.

Hawk nodded sharply. "DeVol is headed for the bordello. I wonder if the men speaking to the banker will show up to parley with him."

"Perfect place for a rendezvous," Noah said. "No one's place of business will draw suspicion as bandit headquarters."

"Exactly what I was thinking," Hawk murmured.

"I'll go with you, Hawk," Noah volunteered. "Gid, you stay here and wait for Fletch."

"I'd like nothing better than to incarcerate Morton DeVol and his cutthroat sidekick, Everett Stiles," Hawk said as he and Noah wove around the townsfolk who clogged the boardwalk.

"Why's that?" Noah questioned, from one step behind him.

"I had to stand aside and watch those two bastards rough up a woman during a stage holdup soon after I infiltrated the gang. She was like your sister. Bold, defiant and unwilling to give up her valuables until physically forced into it."

Noah grimaced. "Standing aside must have been hard."

"Damn hard," Hawk agreed. "It was just as bad as watching soldiers violate Apache women at the reservation and being held at gunpoint and physically restrained while it happened."

Noah scowled. "Hell and damnation."

"It was indeed." Hawk veered around a cluster of men that reeked of sweat and liquor then he quickened his step to reach the brothel.

"I'm sorry for trying to string you up when we found you and Shi together in camp," Noah murmured. "The prospect of Shi being mistreated made Gid and me a little crazy."

"Apology accepted."

Hawk didn't mention that he *deserved* to be strung up for what he'd allowed to happen that night—and last night. But he didn't have time to deal with indignant and outraged brothers while he was hot on Morton DeVol's trail.

His thoughts scattered when he heard the flutter of wings and glanced up to see a pigeon duck into the dormer window on the third story of the bordello. His accusing glare swung to the mayor who was rubbing himself against Lucille's well-advertised cleavage.

No wonder Mayor Reggie Clark resisted the movement to shut down the men's social club in Cerrogordo. Clark might well be operating a criminal ring from the top story of the bordello, while appeasing his sexual appetite with the madam.

Damn clever ruse, Hawk thought. The leaders from the four outlaw factions could come and go from the social club to swap information without inviting the slightest suspicion.

Clark, a noted businessman in town, was privy to information about stage schedules and strongboxes transporting money. Not to mention keeping up with whichever prosperous ranchers had livestock ripe for the picking. While hiding in plain sight, Reggie could coordinate the activities of his rings of thieves—and no one was the wiser.

Of course, Hawk couldn't be too quick to rule out William Proctor and Hiram Evans because they had acquired wealth and prosperity recently. He needed more facts and evidence and he didn't want to get hasty and spook the ringleader into going to ground. Without the ringleader in jail, this scheme might crop up again after the Rangers rode away.

Hawk watched Reggie stroll into the social club a moment after DeVol. Hawk and Noah stepped into the elaborately decorated parlor where scantily clad women and their male customers shared drinks from the private bar. A portrait of a nude woman, draped seductively over a fainting couch, hung on the wall behind the bar.

Hawk and Noah lingered in the shadowed corner while Reggie and Lucille climbed the staircase. As if on cue, Morton DeVol—who apparently did bathe and shave on occasion, and had for this rendezvous—escorted a giggling harlot upstairs.

"You must be new in town, sugar," came the sultry female voice beside Hawk. "Is this a friend of yours, Noah?"

Hawk glanced down at the woman who batted her big brown eyes at him then turned her flirtatious smile on Noah.

"He's a long-lost cousin," Noah said inventively.

Hawk couldn't let it pass so he leaned over to Noah

and said confidentially, "If your sister discovers you're a regular here she'll skin you alive for your double standards. You know that, don't you?"

Noah grimaced. "That's one conversation I'd just as soon not have."

"Well, boys, which one of you wants the first turn?" the slender blonde asked as she hooked her arms around Noah's and Hawk's elbows to urge them toward the steps.

"Noah does," Hawk spoke up as the harlot propelled them upstairs. "I'll stand guard by the door and wait my turn."

He and Noah exchanged significant glances on the way up the steps. Hawk was silently requesting time to scout out the second and third story without drawing unnecessary attention.

Besides, the thought of tumbling around in bed with a woman who wasn't Shiloh felt like a betrayal. Even if she was outside right this moment, falling for that smooth-talking Frenchman all over again, damn her.

The thought made him scowl sourly. He was anxious to ferret out the mastermind and capture the outlaw gangs so he could ride to San Antonio—where he wouldn't have to watch Shiloh reconcile with her first love.

The prospect of Shiloh ending up in Antoine's bed turned him inside out and backward. Forcing aside the tortuous thought, Hawk headed for the staircase that led to the third story.

A burning sensation that felt an awful lot like being sliced by a sharp knife stabbed into Shiloh's heart when she saw Hawk walk into the brothel. The emotional blow caused her to sway unsteadily on her feet. Although Antoine was twirling her in rhythm with a fast-tempoed song, she teetered sideways, colliding with him.

Her secret wish that she would come to mean something special to Hawk died a quick death when he disappeared inside the brothel. Her spirits plunged to rock bottom.

"Are you all right, *chère?*" Antoine cooed as he tightened his grasp on her waist to make sure she didn't wilt at his feet. "Are you feeing faint?"

"Yes, as a matter of fact," Shiloh said shakily.

She had felt betrayed and humiliated when Antoine dismissed her in favor of Aimee Garland, the young heiress in New Orleans. But watching Hawk enter the bordello to appease his needs—after she had sneaked into his room the previous night—made her feel one hundred times worse! Damn him, he might as well have come right out and said she hadn't been woman enough to satisfy him and that she meant nothing to him.

Anger, mortification and conflicting emotions ate her alive while she braced herself against the supporting beam outside the bakery. She inhaled several steadying breaths while Antoine sauntered off to fetch her a glass of punch. She had maintained that her trysts with Hawk hadn't happened. She'd claimed there were no ties to bind them together. She had said all those things for *his* benefit, damn it. She hadn't really meant them. She'd just been trying to put up a bold front and protect her foolish heart.

What she secretly wanted was for Hawk to fall in love with her because he wanted *her*—for who she was on the inside and what she meant to *him*—not because she made demands on him after they became intimate.

It was killing her to know exactly what he was going to do after he escorted one of the harlots upstairs. She knew how it felt to be caressed and kissed by him, knew how it felt to lose touch with reality while they were one living breathing essence, soaring in ecstasy.

The image of another woman taking her place in the circle of his sinewy arms cut to the quick—and even deeper. Curse him to hell and back for singling out a harlot to appease his needs! Shiloh had obviously left him unfulfilled and he sought out someone who knew how to please a man expertly.

Damnation! Hawk had the power to betray her, hurt her deeply because she had fallen in love with him. She'd tried so hard not to, tried hard to deny her feelings for him.

All the while that she'd been spouting off about becoming a free-spirited spinster, she had secretly longed for Hawk to confide that he did have special feelings for her.

Her tormented thoughts scattered when an offensive-smelling ruffian sideswiped her as he staggered past. Shiloh hurriedly anchored herself to the supporting beam of the covered boardwalk before she cartwheeled off balance and landed in an unceremonious heap in the street.

"Well, lookie who we got here." The deep voice beside her carried a drunken slur. "Ain't Morty gonna be pleased to see what I found."

Alarm pulsated through Shiloh when she glanced into the whiskered face and bloodshot eyes of Everett Stiles—one of the men who had fired down at her from atop the cliff and had opened fire during two other narrow escapes from the rugged canyons. And damn it, here was Stiles again!

"C'mon, darlin'," Everett Stiles jeered as he snaked his arm around her waist then jerked her into the alley. "You know too much and we can't have that."

Shiloh upraised her knee, landing a disabling blow that caused Stiles to double over in pain. Unfortunately, before she could dart to safety, another assailant materialized from the shadows to pounce on her.

"Hold still, bitch," Morton DeVol growled against her neck. "If you start screamin' bloody murder I'll have a knife stuck through yer ribs before you can draw yer next breath." To emphasize his point, he slit the fabric near her waist, leaving a gaping hole that exposed her petticoat.

Shiloh knew she wouldn't stand a chance of survival if she went peaceably. But she did take five unresisting steps alongside DeVol, allowing him to think she was compliant.

When his guard was down, she burst into action. She half turned to shove the heel of her hand into his jaw. DeVol's teeth snapped together and he recoiled instinctively. She sent up a shriek for help, hoping to be heard over the loud music and dozens of conversations going on in the street.

When Everett Stiles dashed toward her, she kicked him squarely in the groin then lurched toward the boardwalk. She didn't get far before she heard DeVol's ferocious snarl behind her. When the butt of his pistol slammed into the back of her skull stars exploded before her eyes. Her knees folded up beneath her. She tried to shout for help, but DeVol covered her face with his smelly handkerchief and hooked his arm around her.

Shiloh knew Hawk wouldn't be coming to her rescue. He was at Paradise Social Club, dallying with a harlot. She was never going to forgive him for that, either....

That was her last thought before blinding pain turned the world turned pitch-black and she slumped lifelessly on the ground.

Chapter Sixteen

Hawk was on his way upstairs to the attic when he heard one of the doors creak open behind him. He muttered under his breath when Noah hurried to catch up with him.

"I gave Rachel enough cash to guarantee she'd stay in her room for a half hour before she drums up more business downstairs," Noah explained.

"I can handle this alone," Hawk insisted.

"I'm sure you can, but I owe you for saving Shiloh from disaster two weeks ago."

"If I told you that I'm the reason she landed in disaster will you go away?" Hawk bartered.

"No." Noah jerked up his chin, much the same way his sister did. "You're stuck with me. Get used to the idea."

Hawk decided there and then that defiance and muleheadedness were Drummond family traits.

His thoughts trailed off when he reached the locked door at the head of the steps. He could hear the coo and flutter of pigeons in the attic, but he didn't want to risk making the kind of racket necessary to break down the door. He was satisfied knowing he'd located the central roost for the pigeons the gangs used to communicate with each other.

"The mayor has quite an operation set up here," Hawk murmured. "Reggie Clark gathers information then pays regular visits to the bordello and sends out instructions to the outlaw factions by carrier pigeon. All the better that isolated line shacks like yours make good roosts and divert suspicion. No wonder the Rangers have been one step behind in trying to figure out how these banditos operate."

When Hawk wheeled around to descend the steps Noah blinked, startled. "You aren't going in?"

"It will hold. I need to tail Morton DeVol and Reggie Clark to see where…"

His voice dried up when he reached the second level to see the harlot DeVol accompanied upstairs standing in the open doorway to her room. An uneasy sensation pelted Hawk. He wondered if DeVol had recognized him and then alerted Mayor Clark. He swore under his breath when Lucille Warner strode toward them—to provide a timely diversion, no doubt.

"Did you two get lost?" Lucille stared pointedly at the third flight of steps. "My business associate has declared that area off-limits. I will have to ask you to leave."

Hawk didn't bother making excuses; he simply strode past Lucille and headed downstairs. He cursed a blue streak when he failed to locate Morton DeVol or Reggie Clark.

Another fretful sensation trickled down Hawk's spine when he walked outside. The scene before him seemed innocent enough. People were chitchatting with their neighbors. Several clusters of men hovered around the beer kegs, swapping tall tales and laughing boisterously. Couples were still dancing but something didn't feel right. The fact that Morton and Reggie had disappeared so quickly made Hawk twitchy.

"What's that two-timing French Don Juan up to now?" Noah muttered from behind him.

Hawk snapped his head around to see the ostentatiously dressed Antoine weaving in and out of the crowd, craning his neck while carrying two cups of punch. Hawk's gaze narrowed warily, wondering where Antoine had stashed Shiloh. Probably in some shadowy corner so he could ply her with spiked punch before stealing a few kisses and groping at her.

Hawk scowled at the offensive thought. He didn't need to be hounded by overprotectiveness and jealousy when he'd had DeVol and Clark in his sights— and suddenly lost them in the crowd.

Another jolt of unease bombarded him when Fletch and Gideon circled the dance area then made a beeline toward him.

"Shiloh has gone missing," Gideon blurted out without preamble. "That bungling Frenchman left her alone while he went to fetch a drink after Shiloh said she felt faint. Antoine propped her up against a supporting beam by the bakery. When he returned Shiloh was gone."

Hawk let loose a string of oaths as a wave of panic buffeted him. "This is not a good time for Shiloh to turn up missing. DeVol is in town and Stiles is probably lurking about. If either of them recognizes her…"

He didn't want to consider that prospect because he knew Shiloh's chance of survival was nonexistent. Morton DeVol had a history of disposing of witnesses and abusing women. Shiloh was too spirited and rebellious to deal with a vicious man like DeVol. He was a bully who wouldn't appreciate or tolerate her spunk. Sassing him was the worst thing she could do.

Hawk's troubled thoughts scattered in a dozen different directions when he heard a rumble and saw a plume of dust rising from behind the marshal's office.

"Four masked men tied their lariats to the bars on the backside of the jail cell and yanked out the window!" an eyewitness yelled at the top of his lungs.

Swearing profusely, Hawk took off at a dead run. He only made it fifty yards before an explosion shook the nearby buildings. A cloud of dust belched from the shattered windows of the bank and three masked men raced into the alley, toting bags of stolen money.

"Fletch! Find out where the banker is," Hawk shouted. "If Will Proctor is in on this scheme to bleed his investors dry I want him apprehended."

Fletch took off as fast as his mending leg would carry him.

Hawk raced around the corner of the marshal's office to see six riders thundering off into the darkness. He wanted to bound onto his horse and give chase, but his concern for Shiloh took precedence.

"What can we do to help?" Noah asked from behind him.

Hawk wheeled to face the Drummond brothers. "Check the hotel to see if Shiloh is in her room lying down."

Gideon shot off like a cannonball.

"Noah, ride south of town to alert the Rangers. They are setting up camp nearby."

"And tell them what? That hell's broken loose?"

"Tell Captain Tipton to send a patrol to Mills Ranch to round up every man on-site for questioning," Hawk instructed. "Send a second patrol to guard the stage that should be arriving in an hour. Things are happening too fast around here. Trouble is erupting with too much precision to be a coincidence. This has all the markings of a multiple strike."

"I'm on my way." Noah bolted off to fetch his horse.

Hawk stood there, battling the uncharacteristic sense of panic and impending doom that tried to incapacitate him. He could respond quickly and effectively to these multiple threats if he knew Shiloh was unharmed. But his concern for her kept clogging up his thought processes.

And when this was over Hawk vowed to strangle Antoine for doing such a sorry job of keeping track of her.

When he saw Gideon striding toward him, his face set in a grim line, he felt his heart twist painfully in his chest.

"She's not at the hotel," Gideon reported. "No one saw her enter or leave the lobby. But I overheard one man say he heard a woman's scream coming from the alley beside the bakery. When he went to investigate he found nothing but this." He held up Shiloh's shoe.

Salty curses exploded from Hawk's lips. He'd never felt so helpless and frustrated in his life. If Shiloh was the sacrifice he had to make to avenge Archie Pearson's senseless death and resolve this case, the whole damn lot of desperadoes could go free. He just wanted Shiloh back, wanted to know she was safe… Even if the first place she ran for comfort was straight into that pretentious Frenchman's arms.

"Now what do we do?" Gideon asked, looking as indecisive and nonplussed as Hawk felt.

"Go find Fletch and tell him that I'm going to track

the men responsible for the jailbreak and see where they hole up."

"In the dark?" Gideon hooted incredulously.

"It shouldn't be too hard." Hawk lurched around and headed for the blacksmith's barn where he had stabled Dorado. "They are headed northwest."

"Toward Mills Ranch," Gideon speculated.

"Or *your* ranch," Hawk added grimly. "If DeVol and Stiles abducted your sister, they'll see this as the perfect chance to get Shiloh to give them the combination to your ranch safe. Plus, they'll have a hostage if the Ranger battalion gets them cornered."

"Hell and damnation!" Gideon's Adam's apple bobbed as he swallowed hard. "Do you think the outlaws captured her?"

"There's a strong chance of it," Hawk said bleakly.

Gideon pivoted, then took off at a dead run to locate Fletcher.

Hawk zigzagged through the crowd to retrieve his mustang. The sense of urgency to locate Shiloh was making him frantic. Something about the precision of the strikes on the bank and jail left Hawk wondering if the incidents were part of a smoke screen. He knew he was missing something, sensed there was more going on, but he couldn't figure out what because concern for Shiloh's safety was eating him alive.

While Hawk raced off on horseback, toting a torch to illuminate the hoofprints, fear coiled in the pit of his belly. He'd accepted the possibility of his own death long ago, but the prospect of Shiloh perishing shook him to the core. Damn it, if Shiloh turned out to be a casualty of this assignment, he was going to hunt down every cursed renegade and make him pay the supreme sacrifice, even if it took years.

The image of luminous green eyes, surrounded by thick lashes and a full head of rich, lustrous auburn hair sprang instantly to mind and tore at his heart. Hawk gritted his teeth and urged Dorado into his fastest pace.

This is your fault, he reminded himself as he thundered off into the darkness. He'd led those vindictive outlaws straight to Shiloh that fateful day at the river. If she'd never met him then she wouldn't be in serious trouble now.

Your fault, the scolding voice of his conscience nagged. *All your fault!*

Fletch shouldered his way through the crowd that jammed the street, dragging the outraged banker by the nape of his expensive jacket.

"I demand that you release me at once!" William Proctor snapped. "You can expect to hear from my lawyer!"

"Good," Fletch said, unconcerned. "I have a few questions I want to ask him about you."

Beside him, Gideon gestured for the curious onlookers to step aside so they could enter the jail. The older, heavyset city marshal stood inside the office door, scowling as he stared through the gaping hole in the back wall.

Fletch flashed his badge. "I request that you detain Proctor for questioning until I come back."

"This is preposterous!" William ranted. He wagged his forefinger in the marshal's wrinkled face. "And don't think I won't spread the word that you're incompetent, marshal. You won't hold this job for more than another week, if I have anything to say about it!"

"Which you don't," Fletch said as he quick-marched the dandified banker toward the one remaining cell that hadn't been destroyed by the jailbreak. He gave Proctor a firm nudge then slammed the barred door behind him.

"Glad to know we have Rangers nearby," the marshal said as he hiked his breeches over his rounded belly. "I'll gather a posse if you need reinforcements."

Fletcher shook his head. "I prefer that you keep a lid on this town, in case another outbreak occurs."

"Done," the marshal agreed.

Fletch exited the office to find Gideon awaiting him. "How long has Hawk been gone?"

"Ten minutes. Fifteen at the most…" Gideon's voice trailed off when a rider, waving his hat over his head, demanded his attention.

Fletch frowned warily as he watched George Porter—the crusty old cowboy who had delivered Hawk's message to Ranger camp the previous week—skid his horse to a halt. The man's face was a mite peaked and he was noticeably out of breath.

"What's wrong, George?" Gideon demanded of his employee.

"I ran into Logan Hawk on my way to town," he explained. "I told him that, while me and some of the men were watching over the herds, in case of rustling, a whole slew of riders barged in to take over your ranch house."

He paused while Fletch and Gideon swore succinctly.

"I spotted Shiloh, jackknifed over one of the men's shoulder, being carried into the house. When I gave Hawk the news he said to come find you then alert the Rangers."

"Have you seen Noah?" Gideon asked worriedly.

"No. Hawk told me Noah went to contact the Rangers and I could intercept them and divert them to Drummond Ranch."

A sense of urgency clambered through Fletch as he raced toward the blacksmith's barn to retrieve his Appaloosa. Gideon was hot on his heels.

The prospect of Hawk trying to hold off the bandit brigade single-handedly until reinforcements arrived made Fletch twitchy. He remembered the incident George had related to the Rangers about Hawk defying the odds to protect Shiloh from harm before he realized the men who tried to lynch him were her brothers. Hawk was bold and daring to a fault, Fletch recalled. Always had been.

Fletch had lost the rest of his family and he could no longer contact his clan at Bosque Redondo. Damn it, he didn't want to lose his brother, too.

The grim prospect prompted him to ride hell-bent-for-leather to reach Drummond Ranch to intercept Hawk before he got himself killed trying to save Shiloh…whose chance of survival was decreasing by the minute.

Shiloh awoke to the sound of muffled voices wafting toward her. She was careful not to move or make a sound that might alert her posted guards that she had regained consciousness. She opened one eye cautiously, shocked to discover that she had been toted to her own home. A dozen scruffy-looking characters lounged in *her* parlor, helping themselves to *her* brothers' supply of cigars and whiskey. A thick fog of smoke clouded the room and bottles clanked against glasses repeatedly.

She cursed inwardly when she spotted Frank Mills sprawled on the tufted blue sofa. He was puffing on a cheroot and talking with Morton DeVol and Everett Stiles. Nauseous and light-headed though she was, because of the blow to her skull, she racked her brain, trying to figure out how she could cause a distraction or foil whatever scheme these bandits had hatched.

Her discreet gaze circled the room again, expecting to see Reggie Clark, Hiram Evans or William Proctor in attendance. Either the suspected mastermind had yet to arrive or he refused to expose his identity to the other outlaws who had congregated at Drummond Ranch. According to Hawk, only gang leaders like DeVol—and most likely Frank Mills—could identify the mysterious mastermind.

Shiloh held herself perfectly still when Frank Mills levered his bulky body off the couch then lumbered over to stare down at her.

"Want me to wake her up?" Morton DeVol offered with a fiendish chuckle. "I've got some plans for this chit anyhow. Might as well get at 'em after she shows us where her brothers stash their money."

To her dismay, DeVol clamped his grimy hand around her forearm to give her a jostling shake. She held out as long as she could before she had to respond. She moaned groggily—for effect—then opened one eye as she lolled her head back.

"Get up," DeVol demanded sharply. "You're causing a delay and I'm short on patience."

She massaged the back of her head and blinked owlishly, giving the impression that she was trying to get her bearings. Then she stared into DeVol's hard, angular face and graced him with the most bewildered expression she could manufacture.

"Where am I?" she bleated as she glanced frantically around the room. "And who are you?"

Her attempt to convince him that the hard blow he'd delivered to her head had caused temporary amnesia must have worked because he gaped at her quizzically.

"Where are you?" he echoed, dumbfounded. "You oughta know the answer to that."

"Damn it, pay attention, Shiloh," Frank Mills barked as he bent at the waist to get right in her face.

"Shiloh?" she repeated with feigned confusion. "Is that my name?" She rubbed her temples and squeezed her eyes shut. "My head hurts so bad that I can't think straight." She looked up at Frank. "I don't know you…do I?"

"Hell, she's gone loco," DeVol muttered. "I saw this happen to one of our compatriots two years back. A horse kicked him in the head. He didn't know diddly-squat for almost two weeks. Never was right in the head after that, either."

Frank Millis stroked his scraggly goatee and eyed her suspiciously. "Or maybe she *wants* us to think she can't remember anything. That would be convenient, wouldn't it?"

"What's the holdup, Frank?"

Shiloh peered up at the thick-chested man with a ruddy complexion who strode up behind Frank. She'd never seen this hombre before and she didn't know which gang he rode with.

"I think this little witch is playing possum." Frank gnawed on his cigar as he crossed his arms over his barrel-shaped chest. He squinted skeptically at her. "Maybe she needs some convincing that we ain't got time for her wily games."

DeVol leered at her. "It'd be my pleasure to remind the bitch who she is and what purpose she serves."

Frank held DeVol at bay when he tried to swoop

down and grab her by the hair to yank her to her feet. "Back off, Morty. You'll get sidetracked," Frank said candidly. "After we have no more use for her then you can take your pleasure."

He glanced over his shoulder at the unidentified man who was two inches taller, but every bit as bulky. "Grady, you do the honors. Take her into the kitchen and see if she remembers who she is after you hold her head in a bucket of water until she sprouts gills and fins."

Grady? So, this was the backstabbing traitor that Fletcher had tracked all the way from Colorado. She wished she could turn the tables on the big, bushy-haired brute and hand him over to Fletch.

Shiloh yelped in pain when Grady Mills jerked her off the couch and nearly dislocated her shoulder in the process. She cursed silently, knowing her formal gown and thick petticoats would hamper her escape attempt. She'd have to be resourceful.

Her breath whooshed out in an indignant gasp when Grady clamped his hand over her breasts and squeezed painfully the moment they entered the kitchen. Shiloh retaliated by doubling her fist to sock him squarely in the crotch. Grady gasped for breath. His eyes rolled back in his head. He wilted to his knees, grabbing protectively at his privates, in case she decided to clobber him again—which she did for good measure. It was then she realized she was one shoe short of a pair.

While Grady was trying to catch his breath to send off a shout of alarm Shiloh grabbed the first makeshift weapon within reach—a wooden rolling pin. She swung it in an arc, gathering momentum so that it cracked solidly against Grady's bushy head. A dull groan wobbled from his lips as he pitched forward onto the floor and lay there unmoving.

Shiloh glanced apprehensively toward the dining room door, and then sent up a prayer of gratitude that the cook and housekeeper had gone into town for the festivities and hadn't stumbled headlong into this calamity. She didn't know what had become of the cowboys that had remained behind. She hoped they were in the pastures, standing watch over the cattle so they wouldn't have to encounter this cluster of ruthless desperadoes that had set up camp in her house.

Shiloh battled like crazy to think past her raging headache. She needed to figure out the best means of escape. When she heard a howl in the distance, she jerked to attention. Suddenly shouts erupted from the parlor and dining room. Shiloh couldn't see what was happening, but she smelled smoke. Before she could dart out the back door, hoping to elude the posted guards, rapid-fire gunshots rang out.

Armed with an arsenal of weapons—the rolling pin, two butcher knives and the six-shooter she'd confiscated from Grady—Shiloh darted outside. She didn't know how many weapons it would take to get her past the guards, but she felt more secure knowing she was armed to the teeth.

Clinging to the shadows of the house, she shuffled sideways, constantly on the lookout for trouble. Whatever was going on was obviously taking place on the front lawn, she decided. She could see flickering light and shifting shadows at the corner of the house. The smell of smoke grew stronger.

Maybe Hawk and her brothers had discovered she was missing and had come looking for her. She wondered if this might be some sort of diversion tactic that had the outlaws buzzing around like a nest of bees.

Shiloh plastered herself against the outer wall when

she heard the thud of running footsteps on the lawn, and then saw a shadowed silhouette dart around the side of the house. She waited until the guard was within striking distance then leaped forward to whack him upside the head with the rolling pin.

The bandit staggered on his feet, moaned, then landed spread-eagle in the grass. Shiloh picked up his discarded pistol. She had to make a run for the barn to fetch a horse, but she couldn't do that with her skirts billowing around her. Hurriedly she shed her restrictive petticoats, fashioned her gown into makeshift breeches, and then stuffed her weapons into the folds of the fabric.

She had taken only one step toward freedom when she heard the deadly click of a trigger directly behind her.

"If you try to make a run for it, you'll be dead," came the unexpected voice from the shadows to her left.

Instant death or captivity and *inevitable* death? Not much of a choice, she decided.

Although Shiloh intended to surprise her two adversaries by whirling around to fire off shots of her own, an unseen blow slammed into her tender head. Her senses reeled. Pain exploded in her skull. Shiloh collapsed atop the hombre she had leveled with her rolling pin.

And then the world went out of focus....

Chapter Seventeen

Hawk stood in the grove of trees that circled the Drummonds' spacious front lawn. The three separate bonfires he'd started lit up the darkness. The flickering light dimly illuminated the stick soldiers Hawk had made from the hats and shirts he'd confiscated from the bunkhouse. Plus, he'd thrown cartridges on the fires, giving the impression that the Ranger battalion had arrived to lay siege to the house.

Hawk was so concerned about Shiloh that he could barely make himself stand still. He didn't want to give those bastards the chance to abuse or dispose of Shiloh. As long as the outlaws thought they were under attack Shiloh would remain tied up somewhere in the house.

Glancing impatiently in the direction that led to Cerrogordo, Hawk tossed a few more cartridges on the fires. His brother and the Ranger unit should be here soon.

But not soon enough, damn it. Hawk was going crazy, wondering how much abuse Shiloh had suffered before he arrived to set up a distraction.

He lurched around and his shoulders sagged in relief when he heard the clatter of hooves. A minute later Fletch and Gideon bounded from their horses.

"Hope you aren't planning to burn the house down around those bastards," Gideon said as he listened to the bandits return the gunfire coming from the phantom army Hawk had raised for the standoff.

"With Shiloh inside? Not a chance." Hawk glared at his brother. "It took you long enough to get here, damn it!"

"Just because my last name is Hawk doesn't mean I can fly," Fletch said. "Glad to see you haven't done anything rash yet. Like storm the house by yourself."

The thud of more hooves heralded the arrival of more reinforcements. Hawk blew out another gusty sigh of relief when the Rangers dismounted in the grove of trees behind him.

Captain Tipton strode quickly toward Hawk. He surveyed the billowing fires, noted the stick soldiers propped against the trees and then stared at the shadowy silhouettes of outlaws firing from the windows. "How many are there?"

"According to Drummond's hired hand, about two dozen," Hawk reported. "After DeVol abducted Shiloh from the town festival he must have decided to rob Drummond Ranch. I can't figure out if these outlaws are trying to make us think this is their headquarters or if this was an impromptu stop on the way to Mills Ranch." He smiled grimly. "Whatever the case, we're outnumbered, as usual."

"That's nothing new," Tipton said with a resigned shrug. "Have you come up with a plan of attack?"

Hawk nodded sharply. "Yeah, you cover me and provide firepower while I sneak in to retrieve Shiloh."

"Lousy plan," Fletch spoke up. "I'll go with you to

cover your back. Two dozen to *two* odds are so much better."

Hawk exchanged significant glances with his brother. Although they had been separated for the past few years the bond between them was as strong as ever. He was humbled that Fletch volunteered to risk his life when the chances of returning alive didn't bear mentioning.

"Thanks, Fletch," Hawk said deceptively—so his brother wouldn't suspect what was coming next. "We'll circle to the back of the house." When Fletch pivoted away, Hawk conked him on the head and watched him wilt to the ground, unconscious.

The Rangers and the Drummond brothers gaped at him in stupefied astonishment.

"When Fletch comes to, tell him I'm sorry about that. But he hasn't fully recovered from the last gunshot wound so I decided he shouldn't go with me."

"Hawk?" Noah stepped forward to latch onto his arm before he strode off. "My sister is in there. I'm coming with you."

"Me, too," Gideon chimed in.

"Thanks for the offer, but you two need to be waiting to console Shiloh when this ordeal is over."

Before someone else decided to argue with his plan or invited himself along on what could very well be a suicide mission, Hawk sprinted into the thicket of trees. Serenaded by the gunfire the Rangers provided as a cover, Hawk circled the house. He spotted two guards posted at the base of the steps that led to the second-story balcony.

Hawk snatched up a fallen tree limb, then tossed it into a nearby shrub. The guards wheeled around to fire at the possible threat. Hawk aimed and fired at the guards' knees. The ongoing gunfire on the front lawn overrode their pained howls.

He took aim at their shooting hands before they could lambaste him with bullets. Their pistols tumbled from their fists, leaving them vulnerable and bleeding. Hawk pounced on the guards, clubbing them over the head with the butt of his weapon. After he gagged the wounded outlaws with their own bandanas, he tied them to the banister for safekeeping.

On the lookout for more guards, Hawk bounded up the steps. If he was lucky, he could locate and extricate Shiloh while the core group of outlaws waged battle with the Rangers. If not... He didn't finish the pessimistic thought. All that mattered was removing Shiloh from harm's way.

Hawk went perfectly still when he peeked into the window of an upstairs bedroom—Gideon's or Noah's, he guessed—to see Shiloh bound, gagged and tied to the bedposts. He gnashed his teeth when he saw Morton DeVol hovering beside her.

Everything inside Hawk rebelled when Morton slid his grimy hand beneath the hem of Shiloh's skirt and grinned wickedly. She bucked and squirmed to avoid his touch, but he snickered at her helpless outrage and offended dignity.

"It's what you deserve for trying to turn Grady into a eunuch earlier," Morton sneered as he tossed aside his holsters then reached for the placket of his breeches. "About time you learned that your place is *beneath* a man, bitch."

Although Hawk itched to storm into the room, he made himself wait until Morton straddled Shiloh's hips and focused his concentration completely on her. Hawk couldn't risk firing off a shot inside the house, for fear of bringing a host of bandits upstairs.

While Shiloh thrashed and squirmed, trying to toss Morton sideways, Hawk exploded into the room like a discharging pistol. He broadsided Morton, sending him rolling off the far side of the bed to sprawl on the floor. Morton made a desperate grab for his discarded holsters then yanked his pistol free. Hawk snatched up the butcher knife from the end table and hurled it just as Morton drew down on him.

"Damn redskin bastard," Morton muttered. He stared at the dagger imbedded in his chest then at Hawk. "Go to hell...."

"You first," Hawk replied as he watched the ruthless outlaw slump motionlessly on the floor.

Hurriedly, Hawk untied Shiloh's wrists from the bedposts and tugged her with him toward the balcony door. She kept yammering unintelligibly at him as she tried to unfasten her gag one-handed. But Hawk was anxious to get her away from the house before another threat materialized in their path.

"Here's your missing shoe," he said hurriedly. "And whatever you're trying to say can wait until we're down the steps and dashing toward the protection of the trees."

"Hawk," she burst out when she finally worked the knotted gag loose. "There's something you need to know first—"

"No, he doesn't."

A muddled frown furrowed Hawk's brow when the unexpected voice wafted across the balcony. He glanced over his shoulder to see Lucille Warren holding a six-shooter with both hands. She was poised to shoot and the expression on her painted face indicated that she meant business.

He was so shocked to see the buxom madam emerge

from the shadowed doorway of Shiloh's room that it took him a moment to react—which made him a moment too slow on the draw when Lucille fired the pistol. He barely had time to sidestep in front of Shiloh to protect her from the oncoming bullet.

"No!"

Shiloh's furious howl competed with the sound of blood roaring in Hawk's ears. A painful sensation burned a hole in his chest.

"Get out of here," Hawk demanded as he groped clumsily for his pistol and sank helplessly to his knees.

Although he felt his strength draining rapidly, he managed to retrieve his peacemaker. Unfortunately, Lucille ducked in the doorway before he could get off a shot. Gasping for breath, Hawk clutched at his chest wound. The world spun crazily as he wilted to the floor of the balcony.

"Damn you, Hawk!"

Shiloh was crying over him, Hawk noted, wondering why her voice sounded as if it was warbling toward him from a long, winding tunnel. The fact that Shiloh tried to hoist him to his feet and his sluggish body refused to respond indicated that he'd been hit as badly as he thought he'd been.

Hawk groaned as darkness crept in on his peripheral vision and breathing became nearly impossible. He tried to focus on Shiloh's lovely face above him, tried to respond to the tugging sensation on his left arm.... Tried and failed.

Suddenly Shiloh's face disappeared into the looming darkness and Hawk sank into silent oblivion.

Shiloh swore inventively as she dragged Hawk's unconscious body toward the gallery steps. Her eyes were so clouded with tears that she could barely see where she was going. But fear for his life kept pulsating through her, providing her with the needed strength to get Hawk to safety.

Shiloh muttered another salty oath when Lucille poked her head around the doorway, preparing to blast away again. The need for revenge roiled through Shiloh. She snatched up Hawk's pistol to fire off a shot that tore through the poofy coiffure atop Lucille's head. Several tendrils tumbled over her shoulder. Horrified, the older woman screeched a curse then ducked out of sight again.

Taking advantage of Lucille's retreat, Shiloh pulled Hawk down the steps, grimacing at each bump she unintentionally inflicted on him. Although her strength was starting to give out, she gritted her teeth, marshaled her resolve and pulled him down a few more steps.

"Shiloh!"

She sagged in relief when Fletch's voice erupted from somewhere behind her. She glanced back to see him dashing forward. She vaguely noticed the two guards Hawk had incapacitated on his way to rescue her. But she only gave them a passing glance as Fletch draped Hawk over his shoulder.

"Damn it, I knew he'd do something daring and reckless." Fletch scowled as he limped toward the cover of the trees. "That's why he knocked me out so I couldn't come with him. If I'd been here with him this might not have happened."

Shiloh looked back to make sure they hadn't been spotted by the bandits. When she saw Lucille scamper out the kitchen door, headed for the barn, everything inside Shiloh cried out for vindication. She knew who was behind the outlaw factions that were operating in the area. This cunning madam was *not* going to get away scot-free.

Clutching the hem of her hampering skirts Shiloh took off after Lucille Warren. If Hawk didn't survive the serious wound he had suffered, trying to spare her, Shiloh damn well intended for Lucille to stand trial for murder.

Justice would prevail, she vowed resolutely. Now she knew how Hawk and Fletch felt in their ongoing crusade to hunt down the Indian agent's killer. That same relentless desire for vengeance put wings on her feet and blood in her eyes.

"Shiloh? Where the hell are you going?" Fletch called out to her from the canopy of the trees.

Shiloh didn't waste time explaining. She raced after Lucille, determined to stop her before she retrieved her horse and thundered to town to gather up her share of the loot. The sneaky madam was not going to find another locale to set up her clever operation, not if Shiloh could help it!

Although Lucille had a head start and was running for her life, Shiloh barreled into the barn to grab the nearest horse. She could hear Lucille's mount thundering off into the darkness and she gave chase immediately.

Since she was more familiar with the area, she took a shortcut to reach the path that led to the main road. She clamped her knees against the horse's flanks and curled over its neck as it leaped the shallow creek then raced southeast at breakneck speed.

When she sighted Lucille coming around the bend, she gouged her mount, demanding its swiftest pace. While racing side by side, Lucille reached for her pistol. Shiloh swung her arm in a wide arc, knocking the weapon from Lucille's hand before she could blow her out of the saddle. While the madam swore viciously, Shiloh grabbed a handful of her blond hair and gave her a forceful yank.

Lucille screeched like a banshee when Shiloh jerked her off the horse. The outraged madam cartwheeled across the ground and landed with a thud and a groan.

Before Lucille could gather her wits and gain her feet, Shiloh bounded from her horse and straddled the downed madam. She deflected Lucille's vicious attempt to scratch out her eyes and yank her hair out by the roots. When she managed to pin Lucille's wrists to the ground, Lucille shrieked in fury.

"You troublesome bitch!" she spat hatefully. "I won't let you spoil what I've worked so hard to arrange. I set up distractions everywhere. I even had two men waylay Proctor during the bank holdup. I can clear out tonight and no one but you will know I'm involved."

"You aren't going anywhere, but I'll say one thing for you," Shiloh said between panting breaths, "you did turn a mob of ruthless men into trained pawns and no one was the wiser."

Lucille relaxed momentarily, but Shiloh wasn't foolish enough to let her guard down.

"It seemed fitting to me that since men use women for their selfish purposes constantly that *I* should be the one to turn the tables on them all," Lucille declared smugly. "From haughty gentleman like Will Proctor to ill-mannered ruffians, I controlled them all. I even used the dim-witted mayor to protect my interests in Paradise so those snooty, holier-than-thou women couldn't run me out of business."

Shiloh wasn't surprised to learn Mayor Reggie

Clark had been a convenient gambit used to facilitate Lucille's elaborate scheme. "You knew Reggie would eventually knuckle under the pressure of closing down the social club. Is that why you hatched the scheme of setting up various factions to rob and raid simultaneously so you could raise money fast?"

Lucille nodded abruptly. "I needed a nest egg in place so I can move farther west to establish another business. There's always another lawless town somewhere that needs a brothel."

"The carrier pigeons were an impressive touch," Shiloh praised, hoping for a complete confession. "You kept your identity secret and still contacted your gang leaders."

Lucille smiled shrewdly, her blue eyes dancing with devilish delight. "It's a little trick I picked up from my mother during the war. She used pigeons to pass information about the location of federal troops to the confederate army." Her expression turned bitter. "Until my stepfather, worthless, abusive, self-serving bastard that he was, turned her in for the reward on her head. Like I said, you should never trust a man because he will betray you if it benefits him."

It was little wonder Lucille had no respect for men, not with a double-crossing stepfather who served as a prime example of treachery and probably sexual abuse.

"Let me go," Lucille pleaded with Shiloh. "You're an independent-minded woman yourself. But you don't understand what it's like for someone like me, who doesn't have your wealthy family's connections. Some of us have to scratch and claw to get by the best way we know how."

Shiloh didn't argue with that, but she didn't loosen her grasp on Lucille, either.

"If you let me go I'll gather my belongings and hightail it out of town. No one else has to know of my involvement. Frank Mills and Morton DeVol are the only ones who know I've coordinated the raids and strikes. Everyone at your house presumes I'm involved with Frank and his cousin Grady. Frank won't give up my name because he knows I'll give up his name after he hired a gunman to shoot the sheepherders."

Shiloh stared grimly at Lucille. "Innocent victims have been hurt and robbed so you could feather your nest. I'm not going to release you, Lucille, especially after you shot the man I love!" Her voice steadily rose to an angry shout.

"That rugged half-breed who came to rescue you?" Lucille snorted derisively. "You can do much better than that, especially with your wealth and social connections. If I've learned nothing else, it's that a woman should align herself with a man who can provide her with certain advantages that make life easier. Love? Bah! It's an illusion!"

Lucille began fighting in earnest again, flinging herself sideways and kicking Shiloh in the back with her knees and feet. Shiloh held her position, hoping the riders she heard approaching were on the side of law and order, not outlaws scurrying away from the battle with the Rangers.

"Shiloh? What the devil is going on?"

She was greatly relieved to hear Noah's voice. But she didn't dare shift her attention from Lucille, who was struggling desperately to escape.

A moment later Noah and Gideon brought their horses to a skidding halt then dismounted to shackle Lucille's arms and haul her to her feet.

Puzzled, Gideon glanced from the madam to Shiloh. "Am I missing something here? Fletch said you flew off without explanation and that we had better chase you down before you got yourself in more trouble... Why are you wrestling with Lucille?"

"Lucille, what the devil are you doing out here on this road in the middle of the night?" Noah asked suspiciously.

"She's trying to sneak off during all the excitement," Shiloh answered for Lucille. "She's the one who shot Hawk...."

Her voice trailed off when she saw her brothers wince. Their grim expressions didn't bode well for Hawk. Emptiness expanded inside her chest when faced with the tormenting prospect that Hawk's unselfish deed of shielding her from a bullet might have cost him his life.

Lucille had been aiming at *him,* but her shot had been off the mark. Curse it, he wouldn't have been hit if he had stayed where he was.

The aftershocks of her harrowing evening were beginning to catch up with Shiloh. Feeling weak and shaky, she swayed on her feet. A headache throbbed painfully against her tender skull. "Is Hawk all right?" she murmured.

"We put him in bed after we subdued the outlaws by storming every entrance simultaneously," Gideon explained.

"Our home looks like a battle zone with upturned furniture and shattered windows. But the outlaws are in custody. Or dead," Noah added without much sympathy.

When Lucille tried to hurl herself from Gideon's grasp in a last-ditch escape attempt, Noah removed his

cravat and used it to bind Lucille's wrists together. He
ignored her begging and pleading as he tossed her onto
the back of her horse then secured her feet to the stir-
rups.

"Did someone ride into town to fetch the doctor?"
Shiloh asked as she dragged herself onto her horse.

Gideon grabbed the reins to Lucille's mount to lead
her back to the ranch. "One of the Rangers raced off
to get Doc Brown," he assured her.

"Fletch is using his practical knowledge of treating
wounds and trying to make Hawk as comfortable as
possible until a qualified physician arrives," Noah reported.

Shiloh sincerely hoped Fletch could keep Hawk
alive until Doc Brown showed up. If not…

The bleak thought stole the breath from her lungs.
It was only after she had watched Hawk fall victim to
a bullet that she had faced the dispiriting prospect of
losing him forever. She had been crushed when she er-
roneously assumed he had entered the brothel to lie in
the arms of another woman. But she had experienced
an incredible feeling of relief when she realized Hawk
hadn't betrayed her. He had simply been chasing down
a lead.

Because of him, she had regained her faith in men.
She could be herself around him and he made her happier than she had ever been. Not to mention the indescribable pleasure she'd experienced during those
stolen moments when he'd taught her the meaning of
passion. They had become as close as two people could
get…and she might never know those feelings of intimacy and ecstasy again.

The thought of losing him, so soon after she had acknowledged how much he meant to her, tormented her

to no end. She hadn't had the chance to explore her tender feelings for him. Damn it, why was life so unfair and fate so cruel?

Desperate to see Hawk, and praying nonstop that he was still alive, Shiloh nudged her mount into a swift pace. She left her brothers to deal with the wily madam, who had masterfully organized a mob of unruly outlaws and used information she'd collected from patrons to launch raids and robberies.

After Shiloh's heartbreaking infatuation with Antoine Troudeau, she could understand why Lucille felt the obsessive need to control men. She'd had her fill of being at their mercy. Given Lucille's tragic past, and her stepfather's traitorous act against her mother, it was small wonder that Lucille was bitter and cynical.

But that didn't excuse Lucille from holding Shiloh at gunpoint while Morton DeVol knocked her unconscious a second time, then tied her to the bedpost. Plus, Lucille had committed the unpardonable sin of shooting the man Shiloh had come to love with all her heart and soul.

Shiloh inwardly grimaced when the memory of Hawk buckling at the knees and grabbing at his chest hit her like a runaway locomotive. *I can't lose him,* Shiloh mused as she raced home at breakneck speed. Even if Hawk didn't return her affection, she wanted him to survive. Even if he rode off with the Rangers and never passed this way again, she could accept that. As long as he *lived.*

Shiloh's footsteps faltered when she reached the upstairs landing. Fear clogged her chest, making it difficult to draw breath. What if she had arrived too late? What if Hawk...?

Get hold of yourself! She dragged in a steadying

breath. And then another. This was not the time to fall apart. If Hawk had survived, he didn't need to see her wailing and whimpering. She needed to be as strong and supportive as he had been each time he rescued her from disaster.

Shiloh squared her shoulders and gathered her resolve. Hawk wouldn't see her fall apart. She would maintain her composure, she vowed fiercely. If he were conscious, she'd tell him that she loved him desperately and he was the only man she was going to love—ever.

The light spearing through the open doorway indicated that Fletch had placed Hawk in the guest room where he'd spent the previous night. *Previous night?* Sweet mercy, had it been only yesterday evening that she had sneaked into Hawk's room to practice her skills of seduction?

Since then she had run through the entire gamut of emotions and had endured one hair-raising incident after another. Ending with the very real prospect that she had arrived too late to tell Hawk what was in her heart.

Holding her breath, afraid of what she might find when she entered the room, Shiloh strode down the hall. She halted at the threshold and swallowed hard. Her heart ceased beating for several seconds when she peeked inside to see Hawk sprawled lifelessly in bed. His bare chest was wrapped in bloody bandages. His face was pasty white and his breathing was erratic.

Her anxious gaze leaped to Fletch whose expression was so bleak that Shiloh's spirits hit rock bottom in two seconds flat. She swayed on her feet and had to thrust out a hand to anchor herself to the doorjamb.

"He doesn't look good." Fletch clutched Hawk's unresponsive hand in his own and held on tight. "He lost a hell of a lot of blood before I could get him situated up here…." His voice quaked as he added, "I did the best I could." His tortured gaze locked with hers. "I'm not sure my best will be good enough. No matter how bad things got I always had my big brother to count on. Damn it, I can't stand the thought of losing him, too!"

Chapter Eighteen

Shiloh couldn't remember being so mentally, physically and emotionally exhausted in her life. She had remained by Hawk's side for five days, spoon-feeding him when he roused momentarily, and then watching him drift off to sleep for hours on end.

The local physician, Gordon Brown, had removed the bullet lodged in Hawk's chest and had ordered constant sedation to keep him quiet. Although life at the ranch had returned to normal, Shiloh seemed to be floating on the same surreal plane where Hawk existed.

"Any improvement?" Fletch asked as he entered the room.

Shiloh shook her head as she clutched Hawk's limp hand. She willed him to rouse so she could offer him a sip of water, but he didn't respond. "Any news from town?"

Fletch sank down on the opposite side of the bed. "The Rangers are transporting the prisoners to Austin to stand trial. Archie Pearson's murderers, the two men you saw rustling your cattle, will finally receive their long-overdue punishment."

"And Lucille?" Shiloh asked, wondering if the madam had used her feminine wiles to ensure her release.

"She's with the prisoners," Fletch reported. "Lucille refused to reveal where she stashed her share of the money from the robberies and rustled livestock sales." He smiled dryly. "I suppose she plans to have the stolen money waiting for her after she's served her time and makes a new start. Being a woman, she might get a reduced sentence. Unless Hawk—"

"Hawk is going to fully recover," she interrupted, refusing to entertain the prospect that she might lose him.

"I sure hope so," Fletch murmured. "I thought he'd come around by now. How much laudanum did Doc Brown prescribe?"

"Plenty. He said too much thrashing might rip loose the stitches. But I've been ordered to reduce the sedatives gradually. Hopefully Hawk will remain awake for more than a few minutes at a time from now on."

Then perhaps she'd have the chance to tell him how she felt about him. If she didn't do it soon she might lose her nerve.

"Has anyone sighted Grady Mills in the area?" Shiloh asked as she laid a cool compress on Hawk's feverish brow.

Fletch's jaw clenched. "No, the son of a bitch was nowhere to be found when the rest of the outlaws were taken into custody."

"He must have cleared out when the Rangers showed up," she speculated.

"That weasel could be anywhere by now, but at least a warrant has been issued for his arrest. I won't be content until I've run him to ground," Fletch muttered.

"He'll turn up somewhere. Eventually. He'll pay for what he did."

Shiloh intended to ask Fletch what happened in Colorado that sent him chasing after Grady Mills, but Hawk moaned, demanding her absolute attention. When his lashes fluttered up Shiloh smiled into his dazed, midnight-colored eyes.

"Welcome back, Hawk. Do you feel like eating some broth?"

"Water," he wheezed.

Fletch picked up the glass then glanced at Shiloh. "Why don't you fetch him some food," he suggested. "He definitely needs the nourishment."

Shiloh didn't want to leave the room, for fear she'd miss the chance to speak to Hawk. But Fletch wanted privacy with his brother so she granted his wish.

But not before she pressed a feathery kiss to Hawk's forehead. "I'll be right back," she promised before she turned around and walked away.

With Fletch's help, Hawk levered himself against the pillow. The simple task required so much energy that he nearly wore himself out shifting into another position on the bed. It had been a while since a bullet had slowed him down and forced him to recuperate. He didn't like inactivity one damn bit.

"Hit the high points and catch me up on what's happened since Lucille blasted this hole in my chest," Hawk rasped.

"Ah, yes, that happened shortly after you clubbed me over the head." Fletch stared reproachfully at him. "And thank you so much for that. Hell of a way to treat your own brother."

"I didn't want you to end up like me," Hawk insisted. "You've been shot once this month. You reached your quota."

Fletch offered the boiled-down version of the battle against the outlaws and Shiloh's capture of the mastermind, who orchestrated the rash of raids and robberies.

"As for William Proctor, the uppity banker, it turns out that he *has* been embezzling from local citizens," Fletch went on to say. "But Hiram Evans really did inherit from a long-lost uncle so his mercantile expansion is legitimate."

"What about the mayor?" Hawk asked curiously.

Fletch snickered. "His wife tossed him out and refused to take him back until the brothel shuts its doors. Word in town is that the mayor is living in Lucille's vacated room."

"Glad to hear that justice has been served. Archie Pearson's death, along with several others, has finally been avenged," Hawk murmured in satisfaction.

"Yes. I just wish I could track down Grady Mills and see that he pays penance for his crimes. He must have sneaked off before the battle heated up." Fletch frowned disconsolately. "Sounds just like that slippery son of a bitch."

"What do you plan to do until the Ranger unit returns from delivering the prisoners to Austin?"

Fletch shrugged a broad shoulder. "I thought I might hang around to make sure you get back on your feet." He cast Hawk a sideways glance. "Or maybe the two of us could trail Grady."

Hawk thought it over and decided that riding with his brother appealed to him. Now that Grady was wanted by the state of Texas, the Rangers would be carrying a warrant for his arrest. Since it wasn't unusual for Rangers to work in pairs, Hawk and Fletch could dog Grady's footsteps.

The thought of leaving Drummond Ranch provoked mixed feelings. Spending a few more days with Shiloh underfoot held tremendous appeal. Conversely, spending a few more days with Shiloh would prolong his torment of wishing for things better left alone.

Besides, last he heard, the confounded woman was still clinging to her independence and denying that they had become intimate. Didn't that imply that she wanted to get on with her life—without *him* in it?

As if Fletch had read Hawk's mind he grinned and said, "She's a pretty amazing woman. It's going to be hard for you to leave her behind, I suspect."

Hawk simply nodded. Leaving Shiloh behind would be difficult, if not impossible. So would forgetting her, forgetting the way she made him feel inside. But he had to be sensible and realistic. All he knew was his job and men like him didn't fit into society or claim women like Shiloh.

A mismatched pair if ever there was one, he mused.

When weariness overcame him, Hawk closed his eyes, ready for another nap. Then he heard the swish of skirts and caught the tantalizing fragrance that had followed him into—and out of—his dreams for the past few days.

"Oh no, you don't," Shiloh chided as she eased down beside him. "You're not going to drift off until you eat and that's that."

She proceeded to press one spoonful of chicken broth after another to his lips. He swallowed dutifully.

"You do understand that I'm never going to forgive you for making sure Lucille shot you instead of me, don't you?" she said as she fed him.

"Mmm," was all he managed to say before she shoved another mouthful of broth at him.

"It was heroic, but unnecessary," she insisted.

"Better me than you," he said before she practically crammed the spoon down his throat in her crusade to give him nourishment.

She harrumphed at that. Fletch cast him a wry grin, apparently enjoying the fact that Hawk was on the receiving end of her spirited lecture.

"If you weren't weak and wounded I'd pound you over the head for taking that bullet," she added sharply. "It's as if you consider my life more valuable than yours and we both know that's preposterous since *you* are the most competent frontiersman and lawman that I've ever met."

"I'm not sure an extensive dressing-down is good for our patient's morale, considering his present condition," Fletch spoke up, his lips twitching.

Hawk grinned when Shiloh shifted on the edge of the bed to grant Fletch the full benefit of her annoyed stare.

"Now I would like for *you* to leave the room while I have a private word with your brother," she requested—told Fletch to get lost was nearer the mark.

"Okay, but you have to promise not to do him bodily harm while I'm gone," Fletch negotiated, grinning.

She hitched her thumb over her shoulder, impatiently urging him to make himself scarce.

Hawk yawned broadly, finding it nearly impossible to keep his eyes open. His strength was ebbing with alarming speed. "You better be quick about saying whatever it is you intend to say," he mumbled, his lashes falling to half-mast. "I've depleted most of my energy already."

He sighed contentedly when he felt her sensuous lips drift over his. Her unforgettable scent consumed his senses.

Damn, he was starting to feel better already....

Until she said, "You need to know that I've fallen in love with you, Hawk. I tried very hard not to. I don't expect anything from you in return. But I want you to know the truth before you pack up and leave for good."

He tried to rally after her shocking confession, but he was too far gone.... And so was she, he realized when he heard the door close behind her.

Talk about mixed feelings, he thought sluggishly. Any man would be proud and honored to become the recipient of Shiloh's love and respect. But Hawk knew it really wasn't love that she felt for him. *It couldn't be.*

First off, she was on the rebound from Antoine. Secondly, she felt guilty because *he* had taken a bullet to spare her. Plus, she was immensely grateful for the times he'd provided assistance and support while they'd stumbled into one calamity after another during their misadventures in the wilderness.

No, it wasn't love. It was *gratitude* she felt for him.

In addition, her brothers would never approve of a match between them. Not that Shiloh wanted marriage, he reminded himself. She'd declared herself a spinster. Furthermore, she had denied their passionate trysts had occurred. She also maintained that he had no obligation whatsoever toward her.

Which was rather insulting when you thought about it.

"Damn it, the woman is still making me crazy," he mumbled before exhaustion got the better of him— again.

* * *

Three days later Hawk mustered the strength to ambulate down the upstairs hall—with Fletch's assistance. He hadn't seen Shiloh since the day she'd blurted out her confession. After that, she'd left him in Fletch's care.

At least when he was awake, Hawk amended. According to Fletch, she checked on him regularly during the night.

Hawk pricked his ears when he heard voices wafting up the steps. He muttered, realizing that Antoine Troudeau was monopolizing Shiloh's time. According to reports from Fletch, Antoine had invited himself to stay at the ranch and was following at Shiloh's heels like a devoted pup.

"Doesn't Frenchy have anything better to do with his time?" Hawk grumbled resentfully.

"No, he's on a mission. He claims he feels responsible for Shiloh's capture and he's trying to make amends by remaining at her beck and call. He's asked her to marry him every day since he arrived," Fletch reported as he moved patiently alongside Hawk who progressed slowly down the hall.

The news soured Hawk's mood in the space of a heartbeat. If Shiloh supposedly loved him—and he had no doubt that she had confused guilt and gratitude for love—why hadn't she sent Antoine packing? He frowned, perplexed. He was pretty certain Shiloh had never completely gotten over that debonair Don Juan. Obviously, she was having trouble sorting out what she felt for whom.

Hawk pivoted to walk gingerly in the direction he'd come. "If I asked you to do something for me, would you do it?"

"Sure. Anything," Fletch said magnanimously.

"Kill that Frenchman before Shiloh gives in and agrees to marry him. He's nowhere near good enough for her."

"I'll do *almost* anything for you," Fletch amended wryly. "Sorry, Hawk. If I went around shooting people for their stupidity or their pretentious charm, I'd reduce the country's population by half. *You* can shoot Frenchy because it's a personal conflict. You're in love with that green-eyed hellion, after all."

Hawk stopped short. "I am not!" he protested loudly.

Fletch flashed him a pitying glance as he veered toward Hawk's bedroom. "Oh sorry. My mistake. I wasn't aware that you were still in denial. I have to say that I've never seen a man try as hard *not* to love someone as you have." He brightened. "But maybe that's a good thing because we can ride away together before it dawns on you that you really don't want to leave her behind. Ever."

"It wouldn't work out." Hawk sank down on the edge of the bed to catch his breath after fifteen minutes of walking the hall. "Where the hell would we live? In a wickiup in Sundance Canyon?"

Fletch shrugged nonchalantly. "Sure, wherever you want. This is *your* whimsical fantasy, not *mine.*"

Hawk swore. He needed to leave this place before he started thinking that maybe he could convince Shiloh to boot out Antoine for good so they could make a life together.

We are never going to have a life together, Hawk told himself earnestly. *All I know is the nomadic existence I have with the Rangers. Before I forget that, I need to leave here. The sooner the better.*

"Saddle my horse, first thing in the morning," Hawk

requested. "It's time to ride. The cave in Sundance Canyon is a good place for me to finish recuperating."

Fletch stared at him for a long moment, then finally nodded. "I'll see you at sunrise."

When Fletch exited, Hawk half collapsed on the bed. Damn good thing he'd come to his senses before he started thinking he fit in around here. Besides, Shiloh didn't need him to protect her from that pretentious Frenchman. She was intelligent, strong-minded and independent. If he hung around here, she would remain entangled up in her misguided affection for him. He needed to clear out so she could focus on assessing her true feelings for Antoine.

Her brothers would be here to guide and protect her, he assured himself. He'd been the place she'd come for comfort and protection each time disaster struck. But her bad luck was behind her now.

On that sensible thought Hawk fell asleep. He knew the time had come to bid Shiloh goodbye. Once and for all.

Shiloh sighed in satisfaction when Hawk's lips drifted over hers in a featherlight kiss. She assumed she was dreaming again—as she did every night. But this fantasy was more vivid than usual.

"Shiloh... I came to say goodbye. I'm leaving tomorrow."

Her lashes fluttered up to see Hawk's dark silhouette poised above her. Aching emptiness consumed her as she reached up to trace the rugged features of his face, committing him to memory by sight, by sound, by touch, by heart.

She'd known the day would come when he was well enough to resume his duties with the Rangers. Even knowing that, she still wasn't prepared to deal with the feelings of loss and loneliness that twisted in her chest.

Did he understand that he would take her heart with him when he left? Didn't he realize that she'd tried to be noble, strong, and relentless in holding her emotions in check so he wouldn't feel guilty when he walked out of her life?

Damn it, this was killing her and she couldn't let him know it. But even if she had too much pride to beg him to stay, she was going to take advantage of his midnight visit. She was going to weave her love around him without voicing the words that made him uncomfortable. But all the same, he would *feel* loved and cherished when he left, she vowed.

"I wanted to thank you and to let you know—" he began.

Shiloh silenced him by kissing him with all the affection she had bottled up inside her. She looped her arms around his neck and pulled him close, ever mindful of his mending wound. She craved the feel of his muscular contours beneath her lips and fingertips. She savored the addictive taste of him, wishing the kiss could go on forever.

She was well pleased when she heard him moan softly and felt his answering response. *One more night,* she mused as she caressed him and he caressed her right back. *One more memory to store up to counter all the lonely years to come.*

"Damn it, this isn't why I came in here," Hawk mumbled before he kissed the breath out of her. "But the hell of it is that I can't stop wanting you, despite my good intentions."

"I don't want you to stop wanting me," she whispered as she eased sideways, inviting him to stretch out beside her.

Shiloh came to her knees to rid him of his breeches so she could touch him to her heart's content. Each ragged moan and gasping breath that she drew from him encouraged her to continue her seduction. She knew that any other woman could pleasure him, but she longed to burn the memory of *her* touch, of *her* kiss on his flesh for all eternity. She wished she were unforgettable to Hawk because he was unforgettable to her.

"You've gotten much too good at seduction," he rasped, then trembled beneath her intimate touch.

"Have I? I'm immensely pleased to hear you say that… Do you like this, too…?"

When her moist lips drifted down his belly to skim over his rigid flesh, Hawk stifled another tormented groan. She had discovered how and where he liked to be touched and she left him at the mercy of his ardent desire for her. He hadn't planned to leave at dawn with her unique scent clinging to him and the taste of passion on his lips, but here he was, melting into her feather bed, craving her touch like a starving man yearning for a sumptuous feast.

Shiloh was his Waterloo. There was no denying it. He could say that what he felt for her was purely physical. He could claim that his feelings of jealousy and possessiveness stemmed from the fact that he had become her first lover—which made her unique to him. He could even insist that these feelings of protectiveness were born from all the unnerving moments when he had rescued her from disaster.

But he knew he had only been making up excuses to protect his heart. Shiloh was the only woman who had triggered such a myriad of emotions inside him. Emotions that refused to be restrained when he was with her. No matter how hard he tried, he couldn't talk himself out of the forbidden feelings she incited in him.

His thoughts evaporated when she stroked him again and again. She brought him so close to the perilous edge of self-control that he felt as if he was hanging on by a fraying thread. Sweet mercy, what the woman did to him!

"Stop!" he gasped as his masculine body arched shamelessly toward her bold kisses and caresses.

His lashes fluttered up when he felt her shift on the bed to settle over his thighs. He saw her smile down at him, her exquisite face illuminated by the moonlight that streamed through the windows. His overworked heart flipped upside down in his chest. He was never going to forget how Shiloh made him feel, how she looked when they were in the throes of fervent passion. Her smile was playful yet seductive, teasing yet so full of erotic promise.

And he was going to go up in flames if she didn't appease the maddening ache that she had left thrumming through his ultrasensitive body!

"Do you need me, Hawk?" she murmured as she wrapped her hand around his throbbing shaft.

"Do you have to ask?" he croaked, his voice giving out, right alongside his willpower.

"Say it again," she insisted. "I need to hear it."

"I need you like crazy," he admitted as she guided him intimately to her.

And then she sank down on him, taking him into her body and holding him intimately. He swore the top of his head exploded when she moved provocatively against him, setting an arousing pace that built into an intense crescendo.

Hawk let go with his mind, body and soul. He savored each incredible sensation that converged separately, then recoiled to tumble over him like a tidal wave of immeasurable passion.

Despite the twinge in his chest Hawk clutched Shiloh desperately to him. Shudder after helpless shudder pummeled him, sending his thoughts swirling like an undertow dragging him into oblivion. He held on to her for the longest time, knowing he'd never experience such amazing contentment ever again.

Exhausted, Hawk dozed off, cuddling Shiloh against him. He awoke several hours later, knowing he should return to his room before daylight. But he was too satisfied where he lay. His body refused to move from the warm circle of her arms.

Ah, when had he become so helplessly entangled in the silken web that Shiloh had spun around him? Why had he allowed himself to care so much…?

The sound of the door swinging open brought Hawk upright in bed. Despite the sharp pain of moving too quickly, he reflexively reached for the pistol he kept under his pillow. Then he realized that he'd left his weapon in his room. The best he could do to protect Shiloh was to angle sideways so that his chest became her shield of armor.

"What the devil is going on here?" came the shocked voice from the shadows. "You scoundrel! How dare you!"

Behind him, Shiloh cursed and tried to shove him away before he tried to take another bullet on her behalf. Hawk stayed right where he was and glowered poison darts at the intruder.

"Glad you showed up," Hawk snapped. "I have a few things to say to you and now is as good a time as any."

Chapter Nineteen

Shiloh wasn't sure who irritated her more—Hawk for trying to be her human shield or Antoine for sneaking into her room before daylight so her brothers might find them in a compromising situation. She took one look at Antoine's bare chest—which was nowhere near as muscular and appealing as Hawk's—and his bare feet and half-buttoned breeches then frowned suspiciously. She suspected that Aimee Garland, the heiress from New Orleans, had fallen prey to a similar scheme that Antoine concocted for his financial benefit.

"That is my fiancée!" Antoine growled in outrage. "You have spoiled her honor and I shall defend it. I intend to marry her, even if you have ravished her!"

"Drop the theatrics, Antoine," Shiloh muttered as she clutched the sheet to her bare bosom and peered around Hawk's broad shoulders. "I know exactly what you hoped to gain by sneaking in here. But your devious plot isn't going to work any better with me than it did with Aimee. Obviously her father paid you off and you came here trying to run the same scam on me."

When Hawk gaped at her, surprised, she cast him a withering glance. "Oh, for crying out loud, surely you didn't think that I don't know what he's up to. And surely you didn't think that I intended to do anything except string him along to repay him for stringing me along in New Orleans?"

The expression on his rugged face indicated that he *did* think she still had feelings for this conniving Casanova.

Shiloh sighed audibly. "Men! Sometimes your gender can be incredibly obtuse!"

"String me along?" Antoine parroted with all the feigned indignation he could muster. *"Chère,* I *love* you and I came here to compensate for the mistake I made in New Orleans."

"You made a mistake all right," Hawk growled. "You hurt her feelings and you're after her money. I'm not letting you near her."

"And *you* are not after her money?" Antoine scoffed disdainfully. "I'm not so gullible as to believe that. I know how the game is played, *monsieur.*"

Hawk's arm shot toward the door and his dark eyes snapped with fury. "Get out!"

Antoine elevated his aristocratic chin and struck a dignified pose. "No." He turned his suave smile on Shiloh. "We will do well together, *chère.* This rapscallion cannot escort you through society as well as I can. I was *born* into it."

"And you can *die* in it. Right now, if you don't make yourself scarce," Hawk said threateningly.

Shiloh patted Hawk's rigid shoulder, silently requesting that he stand down because she had her own way of dealing with Antoine. "As it turns out, I'm not all that impressed with living in proper society and attending its pretentious parties," she informed Antoine. "I'm staying here to help run the ranch. If we marry this is where we'll live on my money."

"Here?" Antoine hooted, owl-eyed.

"Wide-open spaces suit me best," she enthused. "I'm not interested in the glittering lights, constant gossip and mandatory social schedules of New Orleans."

Antoine's face fell like a rockslide.

Hawk beamed in devilish delight. "What? Not what you expected, Frenchy? Well, you'll get used to living out here on hell's fringe. You probably won't even be attacked by roving bands of outlaws and hungry packs of wolves, as Shiloh and I were a few weeks ago. And there is always the annual town fandango when you get bored and restless."

The color drained from Antoine's refined features. Shiloh might have felt sorry for this misplaced opportunist if she didn't revel in seeing him receive his just desserts.

Her thoughts scattered when she heard footsteps in the hall, and then saw her brothers burst from the darkness. "Oh, damn," she muttered in frustration.

"What in the *hell* is going on?" Noah roared in outrage.

Gideon turned his thunderous glare on Antoine, noting his state of undress. "And just what are *you* doing in here, you French swine? Trying to accomplish the same thing that Hawk beat you to?"

"Damn you, Hawk," Noah growled. "We should have lynched you while we had the chance!"

Shiloh scooted sideways to face her indignant brothers. "You are not stringing up Hawk. He's still recovering from the gunshot wound."

"Then he won't suffer too much more since he's been about half-dead for a week." Gideon smirked unsympathetically.

"He must not have been as near death as he wanted us to believe, considering what he's obviously been doing in here," Noah muttered reproachfully. "This is a fine way to repay our generosity and hospitality!"

Shiloh made slashing gestures with her arm, demanding to have the floor. This was *her* bedroom, after all, and she intended to speak her piece.

"What is going on between Hawk and me is none of your concern," she told her brothers bluntly. "I'm a spinster and I intend to live my life by my own rules."

Noah crossed his arms over his bare chest and glowered at Hawk. "Which, I suppose is fine with you because your tumbleweed lifestyle doesn't coincide with marriage. How very convenient for you," he added snidely.

"Leave him alone," Shiloh snapped. "Just because I'm in love with him doesn't mean that he has to love me back or propose marriage." She stared pointedly at her brothers. "How many wives would you two have if you proposed to every woman you seduced, including the ones at Paradise Social Club?"

Noah and Gideon shifted awkwardly and refused to make eye contact with her.

"This is different," Noah mumbled lamely.

"Your double standards don't apply to me," Shiloh announced with a dismissive flick of her wrist. "I have decided to adopt the male attitude of doing whatever I can get away with, especially when it comes to affairs."

All four men gaped at her in stunned disbelief. Shiloh suppressed a giggle. She thoroughly enjoyed spouting off that outrageous comment—for shock value.

"You cannot be serious!" Gideon tweeted.

"That just goes to show you how little you know about me," she countered, delighting in getting their goat.

"Whoa, back up a minute." Hawk half turned to stare directly at Shiloh. "You really do love *me,* not *him?*" he bleated, looking bewildered and confused.

"How could you love *him* and not *me?*" Antoine asked, looking as bewildered and confused as Hawk.

"Doesn't matter. Neither one of you scoundrels measure up," Noah decreed. "If Shiloh won't let me shoot or hang the both of you, then leave this house. *Now!*"

"But *monsieur,*" Antoine purred pleadingly. "I've had no breakfast and I'm short of funds."

Noah hitched his thumb toward the door. "You have thirty minutes to clear out. Then I'm coming after you with a shotgun. I might not be the experienced sharpshooter Hawk is, but I *will* bring you down, guaranteed."

Grumbling, Antoine spun on his heels and left.

Noah turned his steely-eyed stare on Hawk. "And now for you and your responsibility to Shiloh."

"He isn't going to give up his way of life for me and he's just been reunited with his brother," Shiloh said in Hawk's stead. "Hawk is leaving in a few hours. That's all I have left with him. Now go away and leave him be."

Hawk glanced over to see tears shining in her eyes. "You honestly love me?" he said incredulously. "How could you? I've done nothing to deserve your affection. I have nothing to offer you that you don't have already, Shi."

"You should listen to him," Noah encouraged her. "For once he's making perfect sense."

Hawk was damn tired of all the interruptions. He made a stabbing gesture toward the door. "Leave," he ordered curtly.

"No," Noah and Gideon said stubbornly in unison.

"Yes," Hawk demanded brusquely. "This is probably the last thing you want to hear, and I've tried not to say it or acknowledge it to her or to myself, but I'm in love with her."

"You're right," Gideon muttered. "I did not want to hear that."

"You love me?" Shiloh squealed, her wide eyes glistening with unshed tears. "Truly?"

Hawk stared into her bewitching face as dawn spread its golden rays across the horizon and seemed to shine directly on her. His previous attempts to stem the tide of tender emotion and cling fiercely to common sense abandoned Hawk. He was tired of fighting the truth of his feelings and scrambling to invent reasons why he shouldn't fall in love with her. Although he felt awkward about baring his heart in front of Shiloh's overprotective brothers, he needed to speak from the depths of his soul before the suppressed emotions exploded inside him.

"Of course, I love you," he blurted out awkwardly. "What man wouldn't?"

"Antoine, for one," she pointed out, then muffled a sniff.

"Well, he doesn't count because he's an idiot," Hawk countered. "You're smart and beautiful and brave. I admire your courage and your undaunted spirit. But how *I* feel about you doesn't change anything. You're determined to be a spinster and you would have denied tonight happened, too, if we wouldn't have had unwanted witnesses barge in here."

Shiloh jerked up her chin. "The only reason I kept insisting that I wanted to be a spinster is because I knew you planned to ride off without looking back. Furthermore, *you* are the idiot around here if you can't figure out that I only said what you wanted to hear in order to let you off the hook. I didn't want you to feel obliged or trapped because I didn't think you held any true affection for me."

Hawk stared blankly at her, and then he glanced at her brothers, who looked as puzzled as he was. "Am I supposed to be able to follow that twisted logic? How is a man supposed to know how a woman's mind works?"

Noah and Gideon shrugged helplessly, then peered, befuddled, at Shiloh.

"See there?" Hawk said. "Your own brothers can't figure you out and they have lived with you two decades. So why am I expected to understand how you think when they don't?"

"You can sort all that out later," Noah said suddenly.

Hawk frowned, bemused by the wry smiles that appeared on Noah's and Gideon's faces.

"The two of you will have a lifetime to learn how to deal with each other," Gideon decreed, then glanced at his brother, who nodded in silent agreement. "We've decided that a marriage between the two of you is the only solution to this situation."

"No!" Shiloh objected, and found herself ignored.

"Besides, Gideon and I are tired of trying to control Shi," Noah added. "She's too rambunctious and high-strung."

"But—" Shiloh tried to interject another comment but Gideon beat her to the punch.

"She's *your* problem now, Hawk. Since a third of this ranch is hers, then you need to stay here and help oversee the place." He stared speculatively at Hawk. "Considering how well behaved your mustang is, we are placing you in charge of training our herd of horses for contract sales to the nearby forts and stage coach company."

Hawk's jaw nearly dropped off its hinges. The brothers Drummond were accepting him as part of their family? Despite his mixed heritage? He couldn't quite believe it. *Why?*

"What changed your minds?" He had to ask.

"We've seen the way you look at each other when you think no one is watching," Noah said wryly. "They are telling glances, believe me."

"Obviously she loves you and you've proved yourself caring and possessive of her, as well as capable of protecting her from harm when the need arises." Gideon glanced surreptitiously back and forth between them. "And considering what happened last night, marriage is the next sensible step."

"You are not going to pressure him into marrying me," Shiloh protested. "If he wants to leave, then that's what he'll do. Nothing you say will stop him if he wants to go."

Hawk motioned Noah and Gideon out of the room. Thankfully, they exited without objection. He half twisted to stare at Shiloh, who was all bristling pride and undaunted spirit. He asked himself how he thought he'd ever be able to leave her behind, knowing that he was crazy in love with her and always would be.

"I can't go," Hawk confided as he limned the delicate features of her face with his forefinger. "I tried not to need you too much so it wouldn't be so painful when I left. But I don't think I could leave you without losing a vital part of myself. Even when I did my damnedest not to let my feelings show, you got to me. Probably always will."

"I get to you?" She smiled, extremely pleased with that confession.

He nodded his tousled head, then pricked his ears when he heard the hoot of an owl in the distance. Hawk pressed a quick kiss to her lips, snatched up his discarded breeches, and then said, "I'll be right back, sweetheart."

Hawk walked onto the terrace to see his brother sitting astride his Appaloosa, holding Dorado's reins. Fletch glanced past him when Shiloh, dressed in her robe, appeared from the shadows. Her auburn hair flamed in the glowing rays of sunrise and her emerald-green eyes sparkled like morning dew on the spring grass.

Hawk swore he'd never seen such a spectacular sight in his whole life. And admittedly, he had seen some pretty amazing sights. But nothing compared to her.

Nothing ever could.

A knowing smile quirked Fletch's lips as his focus shifted back and forth between Hawk and Shiloh. "I didn't think you were going to make it out of here with your heart intact." His grin widened wickedly. "I never thought I'd see the day that Logan Hawk turned into a homing pigeon. But it looks good on you, big brother. So I guess I'm going to have to chase the sunrise alone."

"'Fraid so, Fletch." Hawk slipped his arm around Shiloh's waist and held her possessively against him. "I don't know how to leave her behind. This is where I want to be. With her."

Fletch arched a curious brow. "Noah and Gideon approve of this mismatch?"

Hawk grinned into Shiloh's upturned face that glowed with so much love that his heart filled with happiness. "They put me in charge of breaking and training horses. I'm also in charge of keeping Shiloh under control."

Fletch barked a laugh as he leaned over to tether Hawk's black mustang to the tree. "Well, good luck with that last part, big brother. Honestly, I don't see anyone exerting much control over this hellion. She has too much spirit."

Shiloh laid her head against Hawk's shoulder and smiled good-naturedly at Fletch. "You're always welcome here so don't be a stranger. Come back soon, Fletch."

He tipped his hat and smiled gratefully. "Thank you, firebrand. I must admit that the accommodations here are a damn sight better than the cave in Sundance Canyon."

Hawk watched his brother ride away. He felt a little guilty that he hadn't joined the crusade to track down Grady Mills. But he was too much in love—for the first time, the only time in his life—to walk away from Shiloh. He was tired of chasing the sunrise. He preferred to embrace his secret dream.

"Last chance to get rid of me," Hawk whispered as he brushed a feathery kiss to Shiloh's forehead.

"It would have broken my heart if you had left," she confided as she led him back to the bedroom.

A sense of peace and belonging settled over Hawk as Shiloh pivoted in front of him to kiss him hungrily, desperately.

"I love you with all my heart and soul," he told her earnestly.

"Forever?"

"And then some. Marry me?"

She grinned impishly as she leaned back in the circle of his arms. "I thought you'd never ask."

"Is that a yes or a no?"

"Definitely *yes*. Anytime. Anywhere." Shiloh peered into his ruggedly handsome face, feeling her love for him expand to fill every part of her being. "When the love of my life dropped out of the sky, it got my attention…and what do I need to do to keep *your* attention?"

"Just love me back," he whispered before he wrapped Shiloh in his arms and left no doubt as to his unfaltering devotion to her. Only her.

And she offered him the same solemn promise. She made absolutely certain that he knew that her love and devotion to him would last far beyond eternity.

Sure enough, it did.

* * * * *

Silhouette

SPECIAL EDITION™

Welcome to Danbury Way—
where nothing is as it seems...

Megan Schumacher has managed to
maintain a low profile on Danbury Way
by keeping the huge success of her
graphics business a secret. But when a
new client turns out to be a neighbor's
sexy ex-husband, rumors of their
developing romance quickly start to swirl.

THE RELUCTANT
CINDERELLA

by CHRISTINE RIMMER

Available July 2006

_Don't miss the first book from the
Talk of the Neighborhood miniseries._

The Marian priestesses were destroyed long ago,
but their daughters live on. The time has come
for the heiresses to learn of their legacy, to unite
the pieces of a powerful mosaic and bring light to
a secret their ancestors died to protect.

The Madonna Key

Follow their quests each month.

HOTEL MARCHAND

**Four sisters.
A family legacy.
And someone is out to destroy it.**

**A captivating new limited
continuity, launching June 2006**

The most beautiful hotel in New Orleans,
and someone is out to destroy it. But mystery,
danger and some surprising family revelations
and discoveries won't stop the Marchand sisters
from protecting their birthright…
and finding love along the way.

SPECIAL PRICE!

This riveting new saga begins with

In the Dark

by national bestselling author

JUDITH ARNOLD

The party at Hotel Marchand is in full swing when the lights suddenly go out. What does head of security Mac Jensen do first? He's torn between two jobs—protecting the guests at the hotel and keeping the woman he loves safe.

A woman to protect. A hotel to secure. And no idea who's determined to harm them.

On Sale June 2006

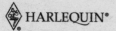

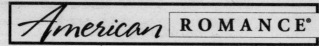

IS PROUD TO PRESENT A GUEST APPEARANCE BY

QUILL
BOOK
AWARD
WINNING
AUTHOR

NEW YORK TIMES bestselling author

DEBBIE MACOMBER

The Wyoming Kid

The story of an ex-rodeo cowboy, a schoolteacher
and their journey to the altar.

"Best-selling Macomber, with more than
100 romances and women's fiction titles
to her credit, sure has a way of pleasing readers."
—*Booklist* on *Between Friends*

The Wyoming Kid
is available from
Harlequin American Romance
in July 2006.